CAST TWO SHADOWS

CAST
TWO SHADOWS

The American Revolution
in the South

Ann Rinaldi

GULLIVER BOOKS
HARCOURT, INC.
San Diego   New York   London

Gulliver Books is a registered trademark of
Harcourt, Inc.

Library of Congress Cataloging-in-Publication Data
Rinaldi, Ann.
Cast two shadows: The American Revolution in the South/Ann Rinaldi.
p.   cm.—(Great episodes)
"Gulliver Books."
Summary: In South Carolina in 1780, fourteen-year-old Caroline sees the
Revolutionary War take a terrible toll among her family and friends and comes
to understand the true nature of war.
1. South Carolina—History—Revolution, 1775–1783—Juvenile fiction.
[1. South Carolina—History—Revolution, 1775–1783—Fiction.
2. United States—History—Revolution,
1775–1783—Fiction.]   I. Title.   II. Series.
PZ7.R459C95   1998
[Fic]—dc21   98-4770
ISBN 0-15-200881-0

ISBN 0-15-200882-9 (pb)

Text set in Fairfield Medium
Designed by Trina Stahl

C E G I J H F D
A C E G H F D B (pb)

Printed in the United States of America

To Patrick Ronald,
my fifth grandson

It is a wonderful seasoning of all enjoyments
to think of those we love.
(Jean-Baptiste Poquelin Molière)

Prologue

MAY 31, 1780

IT WAS ALONG toward eleven in the morning when they hanged Kit Gales. As pretty a morning as I'd seen that spring, sky like a baby's eyes, the sun a warm blessing on the High Hills of Santee, the river a sparkling jewel in the distance. And the red coats of Lord Cornwallis and his men a blight on the dunes.

We'd sat our horses on the sandy hills, me and Kit and Sam Dinkins, and watched the army come.

We could see them long before they spotted us, a red and brown snake of a line coming along the river's edge on the way to Camden: Lord Cornwallis and his redcoats, strung out behind him across the dun-colored sandy plains like a long mare's tail. So many men, wagons, flags whipping in the breeze, horses whinnying and saddles creaking, men shouting. The gorgets around the officers' necks gleamed like gold. Their sword hilts shone. And they had negras on horses driving cattle ahead of them.

"Wonder where they got the cattle?" I murmured.

"Stole 'em, I reckon," Kit said. "Like they'll be stealin' everything else when they get to Camden." Kit's freckled face was worked up into a scowl. I saw him take out his long pistol and hold it, worry it in his hands. Sam saw it, too, but said nothing.

We'd been riding for hours, the three of us, as we often did of a morning. I'd grown up with Kit and Sam. I'd run with them in the woods and fields. We'd roamed on the land around the Santee and Wateree Rivers. The sandy plateaus and forests of evergreens are perfect for riding. On a morning like that one the pine trees would sing for you. But they weren't singing now.

They were smoking. Never had I seen anything like it. Puffs of smoke were blowing out of the branches at intervals, like signals. We sat our horses and stared. "Are they on fire?" I asked.

"It's because the cold set in last night for a spell," Sam said, "and now the air is warm." Sam knew everything about trees, rivers, creatures, and guns. He was positively taken with guns. But I never thought anything of it. All young men hereabouts were.

"It's a sign," Kit said.

"Of what?" I asked.

He looked at me. I waited for that crooked smile of his. Kit was my age, fourteen, but that morning his face was set in the ways of a man. His mouth was a grim slash, and I saw his eyes as old. It frightened me. He'd wanted to go off to the war when Charleston fell earlier in the month, but his father and brother were both gone, and his mother would not let him go.

2

Two days before, his brother Charles had been killed at Waxhaws, north of us, by Banastre Tarleton and his cavalry. Charles had been with Colonel Abraham Buford of the Continental army. They had tried to surrender. One hundred and thirteen of Buford's men were killed, run through with bayonets, one hundred and fifty wounded. Kit's brother had been stabbed twice while alive, three times after he was dead. They were now calling Tarleton "Bloody Ban."

I saw on that bright, sun-kissed morning that Kit was going to war. That bright God-given morning, he was already there. "A sign," he said again. "The pine trees are cryin'. That smoke is their tears."

"Crying?"

"Because of them." He indicated with his head to the army in the distance. "Because of what they represent. Because they're here. Where we live. Invaders. C'mon, Sam." He nudged his horse forward, down the sandy slope.

"Kit? Where are you going?" I felt the panic fill me. When I opened my mouth, I felt the words snatched from me by the breeze and carried out over the dunes. "Sam?"

Had they planned this? How could they? We'd heard Cornwallis and his army were coming north from Charleston. We hadn't known, when we started out that day, that they would be as far north as the High Hills of Santee.

"Comin'," Sam said, and he, too, nudged his horse down the slope.

Kit turned, took off his hat, and grinned at me, and

3

he was a boy, my age again. His reddish hair shone in the sun. "You stay here, Caroline. No matter what happens, you hear?"

I nodded. I could not speak.

"And if anythin' happens, you run right home. Fast as that prize horse of your brother's can take you. Promise!"

I promised. And I sat Fearnaught and watched them ride down the sandy hills, through the brush and pine trees to the river, yelling and whooping. And firing their pistols.

Dear God, firing their pistols! The shots echoed off the water of the river, across the sand dunes where we'd ridden together, growing up. And the pine trees smoked. The pine trees gave off their sign.

IT ALL happened so fast. One moment the army was snaking along in the sun, flags flapping in the brisk wind, officers sitting their horses so proudly, and in the next it was chaos.

Sam and Kit went hurling down the sandy slopes like avenging angels, firing their pistols. There were shouts, barking orders, whinnying horses, returning shots, confusion. I covered my eyes with my hands. When I did look, Sam and Kit were on the ground, their saddles empty, their horses prancing around in confusion, wondering what to do now, soldiers reaching for the bridles, missing them, and their horses dashing off in the direction of home.

And Sam and Kit were taken in hand. Prisoners. "No!" I wanted to scream, "No." But I didn't. I just sat

4

there on Fearnaught and watched in horrified fascination as the officers and Cornwallis crowded around my friends, held a brief consultation, and then hauled Sam, hands tied in rope, to the back of a wagon.

Then someone pointed to a tree. More rope was gotten from somewhere and they were half pulling, half dragging Kit to the tree.

It was the first tree up from the river. Not very big, but it had good branches. And it wasn't smoking.

Another horse was procured. Some soldiers forced Kit onto it. His hands were tied behind his back. Other soldiers were throwing a rope around the lowest branch of the tree.

They are going to hang my friend.

Panic seized me. I looked around. For what? Someone, oh, someone. They were going to hang my friend! Could they do that, here in broad daylight, in the place where we'd always ridden? Our place! Not theirs! Could they do that here and now? With no trial? No court of law?

They were doing it. And it came to me then. They could do whatever they wanted. This was why they were here, wasn't it? To show us they could do whatever they wanted?

Briefly, I considered racing into the fray on Fearnaught. But what would that do? Knock some of them down. Maybe they'd shoot me. They had guns, I didn't. I wished I had a pistol!

I considered racing for help. But what would that do? Home was a good hour's ride. Kit would be dead when I got back.

I was only a girl on a fine horse, alone and watching helplessly while they hanged my friend.

Kit was under the tree, the noose around his neck. He was sitting so straight. His hat was off, on the ground, the sun brought out the red glints in his hair. I could almost see the freckles on his face. What was he thinking? What?

I heard a shot, fired into the air. The horse bolted.

Kit swung.

"No, no, no!" I wailed it. I hid my face in Fear-naught's mane. She whinnied and I quieted her, lest they hear us. I put my hands on her neck. Oh, it was so warm, and I was so cold. But I couldn't keep my face in her mane forever. I had to look up sooner or later, didn't I? To tell myself that it was true?

I looked. Kit's lifeless body was swinging in the morning breeze. Just moments before, we'd sat here to-gether, the three of us on a childhood jaunt, watching the army, like the children we were, speculating about them and where they'd gotten the cattle.

Now Kit was dead. It was a blasphemy in the morn-ing, a blight upon the land. How could the river still sparkle in the background? The birds still sing? The sun still shine? Didn't something have to stop? In honor of this abundance of life taken so senselessly?

Nothing stopped. The pine trees we knew so well smoked around me. The army went back to its business.

I leaned over Fearnaught's neck and retched up my breakfast in the sand. I retched and retched until I thought my stomach would come up through my mouth and my brains would lurch out of my head. And my heart would stop altogether.

Then, finished and shivering, I wiped my mouth with my sleeve. I needed water, fresh springwater. Where was that spring? How far back?

I turned Fearnaught's head in the direction of home. I took one last look down the slope. The army had done its dirty business; now the soldiers were in line again. Someone gave out an order, and they commenced to march.

I pressed my knees into Fearnaught's sides. Her ears were flattened back. She knew something was wrong. I walked her carefully through the smoking pine trees, away from the river. I would take the back way home.

Chapter One

JUNE 30, 1780

"GIVE ME SOME of that bacon, Caroline. You don't have to take it all for yourself."

I shoved the plate across the faded cloth of the table at my sister. It was a far cry from Mama's table downstairs, with its damask cloth and good china plate. I know Mama was thinking such, too. What had we come to, living like this? We'd been confined to one chamber upstairs, the three of us, since June first. Since Cornwallis came and threw my daddy in jail.

As would be expected, we were ready to kill each other by now. The only respite had been when Georgia Ann left for her nightly suppers with Lord Rawdon, the British colonel who had taken Cornwallis's place. Cornwallis had left on the tenth, and almost immediately when Rawdon took over, he'd requested her presence at supper. I don't know what she found to talk about with that fool man, but just having her out of the room of an evening was a blessing in itself.

"Only had one piece of bacon, Georgia Ann. Don't feel like eating anyway. You're the one stuffing yourself." I longed to go outside. I couldn't eat since Kit was hanged. And I missed my daddy. He'd done his best to comfort me that day when I'd come home, exhausted and crying, when Kit was hanged. I'd cried myself to sleep that night. And woke the next morning to hear pounding on our door, the shuffling of feet, and Daddy being hauled to prison. In his nightshirt. They hadn't let Mama see him, though the jail was in town. They did let her send clothing.

"You ought to try to eat more, Caroline," Mama said.

"Can't, Mama." But I sipped some coffee and nibbled some bread to keep her happy.

"These pancakes are common," Georgia Ann said. "Made with only milk and brandy. I'll wager Rawdon is eating rich pancakes, with half a pint of sack and cream in them."

"Don't complain." Mama sipped her coffee. "We have food. Who knows what your father is eating this morning? And don't quarrel. Remember, we may not be at our own table, but we must uphold our dignity. Your father would want that."

"I'm sure all he wants right now is a good wash and shave." Georgia Ann brushed her dark curls off her face and stuffed her mouth with some of the common pancakes. "That jail is so overcrowded. Rawdon told me last night that he's rounded up a hundred and sixty more Patriots hereabouts who refuse to take up arms against England and threw them in our jail, too, so that rebel Sumter won't get any recruits."

"Has he seen your father?" Mama asked.

"He said he's being decently cared for, Mama. He promised me."

"His promises mean nothing," I put in.

"You hush, you! What do you know of Lord Rawdon? He's a gentleman!" Georgia Ann's face went mean, saying it.

"A gentleman, is he? Then why won't he let us visit Daddy in jail?"

"We are at war," she said quietly. "When you are older you will understand such things."

"I think I understand, Georgia Ann." My voice was venom. "I understood the moment I saw my friend Kit hanged. You didn't see it, but I did. And I see it every time I close my eyes at night."

"Mama, she's getting morbid again," Georgia Ann said. "Make her stop."

But I went on. "And what about the way they let his body hang on that tree for three weeks? With a placard pinned to it, forbidding his burial? And what did they do to Samuel Wyly at Waxhaws? Asked him to give up his shoe buckles, and when he bent to do so, struck his head with a sword. After that, they tore apart his body and set it up on a pike by the road!"

"That was the result of Tarleton's orders," my sister said, "not Rawdon's. And Rawdon didn't hang your friend, either. Cornwallis did that."

"Oh yes, Cornwallis," I flung back. "A peer of the realm. Isn't that what you called him? Descended from knights and kings."

"Mama!" Georgia Ann appealed. "She's mouthing

off like a rebel. And you know we can't have that or everything will be ruined!"

"Your sister isn't a rebel," Mama assured her, "are you, Caroline?"

"I'm not anything," I said. "I just don't believe in Rawdon's promises."

"You are a Loyalist," Mama insisted. "Like the rest of us."

"Why can't I be a rebel like Daddy?"

"One doesn't just become a rebel, Caroline. Your father did after much soul-searching and prayer. He is a community leader. And a man. Men are the lawgivers because they have the better share of reason bestowed upon them by the Almighty."

Flapdoodle, I thought. But I didn't say it. *Does that go for Rawdon and Cornwallis, too?*

"But we women have the advantage, because we have it in our power to subdue the men without violence. We have more power in our tears than in our arguments. Remember that."

"Tears won't get Daddy out of jail," I said. "But I'm sure Georgia Ann is already thinking of other ways to subdue Rawdon."

My sister reached to slap me, but I dodged her. "Mama, I'm going to kill her if she doesn't hush!" She started to cry.

"Now, now, girls, please! We mustn't fight amongst ourselves. We must survive. Georgia, darling, did you tell Rawdon last evening that we are loyal to our king? And your brother is off fighting with the Loyalists?"

Georgia Ann shrugged. "Yes. He said that American

Loyalist troops are rude countrymen, bumbling about with rusty muskets, who don't know a thing about soldiering," she recited.

"Oh dear." Tears came to Mama's eyes.

"Don't worry, Mama," Georgia Ann soothed. "Rawdon's invited me to sup with him again tonight. He said his sentiments about American Loyalists do not carry over to our women. He said we are fair nymphs."

"What's a nymph?" I asked.

"Don't walk out with him alone," Mama cautioned.

"I won't." Georgia Ann helped herself to more common pancakes.

"Will somebody please tell me what a nymph is?" I persisted.

My sister tossed her head at me. "I told you she should be sent to Charleston to school, Mama. Her classical education is being sadly neglected. And look at her, in that ordinary brown calico. Can't she wear something better? Can't she comb her hair? She looks a disgrace."

I knew how I looked. And I didn't care. I hadn't cared about anything since they'd hanged Kit. There didn't seem to be any sense in it. "At least I'm not still in my nightgown." Hers was brocaded, with a blue silk drape in back. "And you *do* walk out with Rawdon alone. I saw you last night in the orchard."

"Georgia Ann, you mustn't," Mama wailed.

"Mama, he is most cultured. His family lived in Ireland for a century and received titles for their services, so the English kings could rule there."

"You were taken with the fact that Cornwallis is an

earl," Mama reminded her, "and he put your father in prison, slaughtered our hogs and chickens, depleted our warehouses of every store we had, to say nothing of leaving with ten of our negras, including Doreen. And I trained her up for cooking for ten years! And look there"—she pointed out the window to the slope of lawn beyond her garden, where white tents bloomed like rosebushes. "They have taken down the fences for their firewood. And where are they relieving themselves? In my Cherokee roses."

Good for you, Mama, I thought. *Tell her.*

"Don't fret about the negras, Mama," Georgia Ann answered. "They went with Cornwallis of their own choosing. He promised them freedom. Rawdon told me."

"He *promised* them freedom." Mama was not stupid. She'd met with Cornwallis before he left. "He told me that he is selling them to plantations in the West Indies. And when I asked him to at least allow us the use of one more room in this commodious house, do you know what he said? 'Reflection convinces me, madam, that enemies should not be allowed any conveniences.' Enemies! I told him my son has made the choice for the king. Do you know what he said to that? He said, 'But this is a rebel household. You should have made a better choice in husbands.' "

"Don't upset yourself so, Mama." Georgia Ann picked up the china pot and poured more coffee. "Like I said, men do what they must in war. I am negotiating tonight with Rawdon to have Daddy released from prison. I know what I'm doing. Don't worry."

"You are *what*?" Mama asked.

"We will sup again tonight. He told me he needs horses for the cavalry. I saw him looking in the stable yesterday. He's much taken with Fearnaught."

I jumped right on my sister then and almost tore her eyes out of her head. "Fearnaught is Johnny's prize! The best blooded horse in all of the Parish of St. Mark's! What right do you have to promise her to Rawdon? You know Johnny's going to race her after the war!"

Mama had to pull me away from her. "Girls, girls! Oh dear, I wish your father were here! Caroline, behave yourself this instant. Look, you've upset your sister's hair."

Pulled off her gauze and lace cap with the artificial flower on it is what I did. And undid one of the hair rolls on the side of her head. *Good*. "She deserves it," I said. "Doesn't have the sense God gave a goose. She's got no right to give away Fearnaught. You know what she means to Johnny, Mama."

Fearnaught! I felt a stab of fear. She was Johnny's favorite. He had turned down many offers of money for her. She was held in esteem only with Grey Goose, and he'd taken Grey Goose with him to war. No British officer would put his spurs into Fearnaught's flanks if I could help it. She was from the Red Doe stock along the Cooper River. Horses from that line were priceless.

"It could get Daddy out of jail," Georgia Ann said. She was white-faced and crying, straightening her cap on her head. "We need to strike some bargain with him to get Daddy out of jail."

"Not Fearnaught," I said. "Never Fearnaught. Anyway, they don't keep their word, these British. Remember what they did with our negras."

Before she had a chance to reply, there was a knock on our chamber door. "I'll get it," Mama said. It was Jade, the one remaining negra on the place who could cook, though what I knew about dancing was more than what she knew about cooking. And I hate to dance.

"He doan like the pancakes, Miz Sarah. He doan like anythin' I cooks, an' I been workin' my fingers to the bone fer him fer a for'night now. He say fer supper he wants she-crab soup. He say if'n I doan get him somebody on the place who kin make it, he gonna sell me off to the West Indies. Kin he do that, Miz Sarah?"

Mama made her come in and sit down. Jade was crying. Then Mama fetched quill, paper, and ink and penned a note. "Take this down to Colonel Rawdon," she told Jade.

The woman shook her head. "No, ma'am, please. Doan ask me. He's madder than a flop-eared hound caged up in coon season. Please, Miz Sarah."

Mama held the note out to Georgia Ann.

She, too, shook her head. "I can't let him see me in such disarray," she said. And she crossed the room to her dressing table, where she had all her pots of creams and salves and lotions.

"I'll take it down, Mama," I said.

She looked at me. And I saw her blue eyes grow a shade darker. "You said you'd never speak to one of them after they hanged your friend. For a month I couldn't get you below stairs when Rawdon invited you to supper."

"Twice he invited me. Only to be polite. He invited you, too, Mama. You wouldn't go."

"I am different. My husband is in jail."

"My daddy is in jail," I said, "and my friend is dead. But I'll do this now." I took the note from her.

"Perhaps you should read it first, Caroline. You may change your mind."

So I read it. And felt the blood drain from my face. "You sure you mean this, Mama?"

"I do not say or write what I do not mean, Caroline. You should know that by now."

"What?" Georgia Ann turned from her dressing table. "What are you telling him, Mama?"

"Since you do not wish to deliver the note, you must wait to find out," Mama told her, then sat down and poured herself another cup of coffee. I watched her for a moment. Always I'd thought her spoiled, willful, and conceited. But since Daddy had been put in jail, she seemed to be showing strengths I never knew she had.

I folded the note up and went to the door. There I paused. "Suppose she doesn't want to come?" I asked Mama.

"She'll come," she answered.

In a shot Georgia Ann was out of her chair. "Not Miz Melindy. You're not going to bring her into the house. She hasn't set foot in this house in years."

"Two years," Mama said.

"Mama!"

"She makes good she-crab soup. She makes good everything. Maybe it'll becalm the colonel. Take his mind off Fearnaught. Soothe his spirit so he'll be inclined to let your father out of jail."

"Rawdon will make Caroline fetch her." Georgia Ann stood over Mama now. "You're going to let him send Caroline down to that cabin? After all these years? You want to put her through that?"

"I don't mind, if Caroline doesn't," Mama said.

"I don't," I said. Then I looked at my sister. "I've been through worse," I reminded her. "It'll be nice to take a walk outside again. I haven't been outside in ages."

"Good." Mama smiled. "Now go back to fixing your hair, Georgia Ann. Jade? Go about your business. You won't have to cook anymore, just keep the house. Is the colonel still putting his boots on my brocaded settee?"

"Yes, ma'am. But I cleans it. An' I cleans his boots."

She left. I followed her out of the room.

"You could at least make her change out of that dreadful brown calico," I heard Georgia Ann pleading. "How can we uphold the family honor if she looks a disgrace?"

Mama made some reply. It sounded like "Don't worry about Caroline upholding the family honor, worry about yourself," but I couldn't be sure of it. There was an awful buzzing sound in my ears. I sat down on the steps and covered my face with my hands.

I was to deliver Mama's note to Rawdon. He would be wearing the bright red coat of the British army, the same coats they'd worn the day Kit was hanged. I had sworn I would never speak to one of them. *Can I keep myself from saying dreadful things to Rawdon now? I must.*

Then, if he allowed, I was to go down to the quarters and see Miz Melindy. *Suppose she won't talk to me? Suppose she throws me off her porch?*

"Miz Caroline?"

I looked up. Jade was standing a few steps below me, crumpling her apron in her hands and looking up. "Yes?"

"I fergots to tell yer mama. A woman stopped by the door of the kitchen this mornin'."

"What woman?"

"Doan know, Miz Caroline. She look jus' terrible. Say the Indians brung her up the creek. Say she lookin' fer that Cornwallis."

"Did you send her to Rawdon?"

"She say she come to the house, but the soldiers chase her. She look awful poorly, Miz Caroline. I give her some vittles an' she left. But she say she be back. Say she gotta see that Cornwallis feller or she jus' die."

I wondered if it had been Mrs. Wyly, begging for her husband's body. But why would Indians bring her on the creek? She lived right in town. "Thank you, Jade. You did good," I said. "We won't ponder the matter now. We have worries of our own."

Chapter Two

JUNE 30, 1780

THE LAST TIME I had spoken to Miz Melindy was when her sister Cate tried to burn our house down. That was nigh onto two years ago now. I was twelve then, and Georgia Ann was fifteen. It was Georgia Ann's fault. Cate was feebleminded and always doing crazy things. Had herself a pet hog that would follow her all over the place. Miz Melindy kept a right good eye on her, though. Cate was her younger sister by ten years.

I sat there on the stairway mulling it over. I could hear Colonel Rawdon and his aides at breakfast in our dining room. If I craned my neck, like I saw an ostrich do in one of those fancy schoolbooks of my sister's, I could see Rawdon. Or at least his polished black boots and his bright red coat. I decided it was not worth the effort. I knew what he'd look like. Same as the rest of them. Civilized as a parson, but crazy as a hooty owl once you got to know him.

After Kit's body had hung from that tree for three weeks in the heat, some of his friends went at night and cut it down. They climbed that tree after digging a hole under him, slashed the rope, and let his body fall into the hole. I'd wanted to visit his makeshift grave, but Mama wouldn't even let me sneak out of the house. She promised that after this was all over, this war, or invasion, or whatever you wanted to call it, his family would disinter him and we'd attend a proper burial in our churchyard. But it didn't help any. What was it about these British that they put people's bodies on pikes or let them hang unburied? Wasn't killing enough?

I was sick from it. Something inside me did not work right anymore. I woke each morning with a pall over me. I stopped, midday, to sit and stare at nothing, trying to ponder a way to be rid of the sickness inside me. It hung there like Kit's corpse, rotting. There was no getting around it.

Rawdon was talking in that clipped accent they all had. "I'll deal with this deserter. Bring him before the assembled regiment. Have the officers leave the field. Turn him over to the enlisted men and have them hang him."

"Will they do it, sir?" Another officer spoke.

"They will. Or hang themselves."

More hanging. How could Georgia Ann sup with this man? She was taken with him, I decided, because she was taken with anybody who had pretensions. She had so many herself. It came from that French school in Charleston, where she'd gotten her Polite Education. At the time of our near house-burning she was just home from school. She'd recently had her portrait painted and was all filled up with herself. Told Daddy she required her own personal maid. So he gave her Cate. Right off Georgia Ann put that Polite Education to use. Ordered Cate around like Boney, our overseer, ordered the field hands. I don't know how Cate took it as long as she did. Then one day she spilled the King's Honey Water that Georgia Ann used to keep her complexion white.

King's Honey Water comes dear, and you can't buy it anywhere but in Charleston, a hundred and twenty miles south of us. Which is not to say we haven't got a fine town here. Camden is on the east bank of the Wateree River. My daddy made this town. It wasn't much of anything when he came up from Charleston in 1764 to establish his flour mills. He knew all about fine flour. His flour became famous and made him his fortune, and soon he owned not only grist and flour mills but an indigo works, a tobacco warehouse, a brewery, and a distillery.

Now Camden is a fine town. So many homes, a sawmill, stores, like the Pine Tree that Samuel Wyly owned before the British cut him to pieces, a Quaker meeting, which Sam's wife still goes to, a Presbyterian church, and a subscription school, although I had my own tutors. Not to mention the magazine, where all the ammunition and supplies for war were stored until Cornwallis threw Daddy in jail and took it over. Daddy built that magazine for the colony. Daddy is a man of means. He owns some ten thousand acres of land that we keep in lumber, wheat, cattle, horses, and vegetables. And now, with the war, we plant flax.

But nowhere in any establishment here can you get King's Honey Water. So Georgia Ann did what only Georgia Ann would do. She slapped Cate good.

And Cate did what only Cate would do. Tried to burn down our house.

Now a house for a bottle of Honey Water may not seem like a fair exchange, excepting if you know how bad the blood is between my family and Miz Melindy's in the quarters. First thing I expected Miz Melindy to do was put one of her burlap conjure bags tied with strands of horsehair under the back porch. In the bag would be a mix of hair and nails, worms, maybe a coon foot and some needles. Everybody knows a conjure bag can harm the person it was meant for. Even make them die a slow death. There's talk around here that Miz Melindy is a "trick negra," which means that if you get on the wrong side of her she can cast a spell and do you real harm.

But you can't prove it by me. I lived with Miz Melindy for the first two years of my life, and there is nobody kinder that I know in the Parish of St. Mark's. Though if I venture down to the quarters now to speak to her, she will chase me and pretend she never laid eyes on me before, like she didn't nurse me when I was a baby and screamed night and day because I was choleric. And nobody at the plantation house wanted to do with me.

Of course, my being choleric wasn't the only reason

they wanted no truck with me. But the other reason we don't talk about. We go out of our way not to speak of it. We walk around it, like we'd walk around one of those burlap bundles tied with strands of horsehair.

I was drawn from my thoughts by movement in the dining room. The officers were getting to their feet, putting on their swords and gloves. Two strode right through the hall below me and went out the front door.

"Tell the inhabitants of this Godforsaken town that I will give ten guineas for the head of any deserter belonging to the Volunteers of Ireland. And five guineas only if they bring him in alive," Rawdon called after his men. "By God, you can't trust the Irish, I always said. They may have deserted from Washington's army, but they'll not desert from mine."

His voice echoed in our genteel house. I trembled at the sound of it. The front door slammed behind the two officers, and the house got quiet. I stood up, drew in my breath, and told myself I was doing this for Kit and for my daddy. I don't know what such resolve meant. I wasn't a rebel. It was all male notions, this rebel or Tory business. Politics. Wasn't it? It had to do with men and commerce, meetings and high-toned talk.

I knew the lie of that even as I walked down the hall into the dining room. But I was not ready to face the lie of it head on. Not yet. I'd figure that out later. Right then I had to face the monster who had taken over our house, who, with the opening of his English mouth, could sentence a man to death.

He was lounging at the dining room table, his boots up on a velvet-tufted chair. There were breakfast leavings—cold grits, bits of roasted pork, and pancakes—on plates. He was nibbling macaroons and calf's-foot jelly that Georgia Ann had brought home from Charleston that spring. The room smelled of tobacco smoke. Rawdon was reading a newspaper.

"Sir?"

He turned, saw me, and stood up. He rapped the newspaper with his hand. "Rebel women here do have their pretensions. They tell me Ann Timothy publishes this *South Carolina Gazette*. Can it be true?"

He was tall and lean. I suppose Georgia Ann would consider him handsome. I don't know what makes a man handsome. My daddy is a fine-looking specimen of man and he is short and graying. Rawdon had a strong nose and heavy black brows. His eyes had a bruised look about them, as if he'd been up all night. *Perhaps he is worried about deserters,* I thought. *Good.*

"Yes sir," I answered him. "Ann Timothy publishes the *South Carolina Gazette*. And her mother-in-law before her published it."

"Getting ahead of themselves, aren't they? Like the colonies? Well it's a rag. It can't hold a candle to our London papers. And who might you be?"

I curtsied. "Caroline Whitaker. Your servant, sir." How I hated saying those words! "Georgia Ann is my sister."

"Ah, the recluse." He patted his mouth with a linen napkin and took my measure. And in spite of myself I did feel dowdy in the brown calico. "Well, keep on as you're going and you'll be pretty as Georgia Ann someday, I'm sure."

"Thank you, sir." I stepped forward and handed him Mama's note.

He read it and scowled. "Why wasn't I told yesterday that there is another negra on the place who is a good cook? I made inquiries. Sent my men down to the quarters to ask. Who is this woman?"

"Miz Melindy, sir. She's old now, but she can cook. Lots better than Jade."

"My sainted ninety-two-year-old aunt can cook better than Jade. Is this the trick negra?"

"She's no trick negra, sir, unless you consider the way she can make she-crab soup."

"My men heard about the quilts she makes. Heard Cornwallis managed to get one. They went down there last night. She threw slops at them. Said she didn't have quilts. And couldn't cook."

"She can," I told him.

"Then why would she say such? I even offered the king's shillings to anyone who would provide such a service for me."

"She lies, sir."

He grunted. "Everyone in this benighted colony lies. Well, go and fetch her then. Tell her either she comes up here and cooks for me or I'll ship her out."

I shook my head. "It'd carry more weight, sir, if you sent a note in your own writing."

"Can she read?"

"No sir. But she knows Miz Sarah's handwriting. And if you write a note, I'll read it to her and show her it comes from you."

He reached for pen and paper and wrote with a

26

flourish, handed the note to me, and frowned. "Why are you and your mother suddenly so interested in finding me a cook?"

"My daddy's in jail, sir. We hope you'll let him out."

He clasped his hands behind his back and began to pace. "Some things are beyond even my authority. But I shall consider it."

"Thank you, sir." I started to leave.

"Wait! There is something untoward here. If the woman wouldn't come for the king's shilling, why would she come today for nothing?"

There it was. I had hoped he wouldn't make me come to it. What to do now? Tell him? Mama had not instructed me in this. What did she wish me to do? But I knew the answer to that. Anything short of shaming us to get Daddy out of jail. "Because I am going to ask her," I said.

He looked down his nose at me. "You have special influence with this trick negra?"

"Yes sir, I do."

"Perhaps you would like to tell me about this influence."

So I told him. There was nothing else for it, was there? "She's my grandmother," I said.

Chapter Three

JUNE 30, 1780

I MUST SAY HE took it well. Didn't raise one black bushy eyebrow. Well, I suppose a man known for his valor at Bunker Hill, a man about whom Georgia Ann said, "His performance there stamped his fame for life," was not about to be undone by the fact of my having a negra grandmother.

He simply gave me a little bow. Smiled. "And your father a rebel leader hereabouts," he said. "Ah, well, it does not surprise me. Tell me, then, why are you so white?"

Might as well tell it all. "My mother was the cook, sir. Her father was white." No use in telling him her father was Old Boney, our overseer, who still ran the place. This man might take it in his head to taunt him. Old Boney got vicious when taunted. And we needed him more than ever now that Daddy and Johnny were both gone.

"You colonials, on these far-flung plantations.

Regular little kingdoms the planters have going here. There is no telling what goes on in such places, is there?"

I did not answer.

"Well then, go fetch this woman. I am entertaining your lovely sister again. The crabs are being brought this afternoon from Charleston." And then he stopped. Had a thought. Snapped his fingers. "Just you?" he asked. "Not your sister Georgia Ann? This negra with the magical cooking powers is not her grandmother, is she?"

"No sir," I said.

He seemed to sigh in relief. "Go, go, and be quick about it."

I should have said yes, I thought, as I went through the hall and out the front door. *I wonder if he'd still be supping with Georgia Ann.*

Fresh air! Oh, how I'd missed it. I hadn't been outside in so long. I didn't know what to do first. Walk through the kitchen garden and inspect the herbs and vegetables? Run across a field? No, I had to see if Fearnaught was all right. I would visit her in the stables before I went to Miz Melindy's. But I stood for a moment enjoying the early-morning air. It was like being wrapped in silk. My nostrils caught the smells of the plantation, the pungent barn smells, the fragrance of the wheat fields, the yellow jasmine. I stood and stretched, felt the sun on my face. Then I looked.

All around me on our land were soldiers. Whole regiments of them. Some were marching, some lounging, some breakfasting, some walking their horses. Some in red coats, some in green. The green were cavalry. White tents blossomed like spring trees, sunlight flashed on muskets, smoke curled up from cooking fires. Oh, what a blight on our beautiful plantation! And yes, they had trampled the boxwood and Cherokee roses.

But in the distance our cattle grazed peacefully on the hillocks. And I saw that Mr. Bone, or Old Boney, as I called him, had some hands working in the clover and wheat fields, some in the orchards, others in the asparagus beds. My eyes scanned the horse pasture. Good. Fearnaught was not there. Isom, who trained Johnny's horses, must be keeping her out of sight in the stable.

I found her in her stall, munching oats. She whinnied hello. "Oh, Fearnaught." I hugged her. "You miss me, don't you? Oh, Fearnaught, do you recollect the last time I rode you? On the High Hills of Santee? You saw, too, didn't you? And you sense things are wrong. Johnny always said you had more brains than most men he knew. Well, you don't have to worry, we're not going to let them take you. We'll keep you hidden."

"I wouldn't take that horse out, if'n I was you."

I turned, startled, but it was only Old Boney. For a moment I didn't know what to say. We never spoke. When we met he scowled at me and told me to stay out of the way. I was never in the way. So I put it down to the fact that I was a reminder to him of his indiscretion.

I was his granddaughter, by virtue of that indiscretion, which he'd committed with Miz Melindy. My mother had been their child. I was an embarrassment to him. Which was all right with me. I was used to being an embarrassment to people. My whole past, far as I could remember, was spoken about in whispers, when spoken of at all. But I didn't see why Old Boney had to take on about it so.

"They still up at the house?" His rough voice startled me. He was holding a horse's harness and looking at it.

"Yes," I said.

"How long they fixin' to stay?"

"We don't know."

"Damn scoundrels took everythin' from the warehouse: tea, sugar, coffee, salt, eighteen hogsheads of Indian cornmeal, one of rum. They took bacon, hams, butter, axes, wedges, an' even the stuff yer pa was keepin' fer people who sent it up from Charleston."

"Oh, no!"

He nodded. "Silver plate, hogsheads of indigo, tobacco, an' other stores. I don't give a tinker's damn 'bout politics, but they ain't gonna destroy this place. I worked too hard to make it what it is. I'll take up a musket myself soon if they don't stop takin' the negras. What you hear of yer pa?"

Never had I heard him make such a speech. Not even to Daddy. He spoke only when it was necessary, then in as few words as possible. "He's middling well."

For as long as I remember he had held a grudge against Daddy for something; some wedge was between them. But I could never get a purchase on what it was. I watched him take off his hat and scratch his hair. With a shock I realized it was red. How had I never noticed that before? Was that how I'd come by my reddish brown hair? But there was not time to think of it now. He was about to speak again.

"Sorry 'bout your friend. What they done, killin'

him, was wrong. But lettin' him hang like that . . ." He shook his head and uttered a profanity.

"Thank you," I answered.

"You see that gal come creepin' round here this mornin'? Come from Georgetown on the river with the Catawbas?"

"No, I heard about her," I said.

He looked down at the harness in his hands. "Scotch," he said. "From Glasgow. Come with the British army. Says her name was Agnes. Says she was lookin' fer her lover."

"And who might that be?"

"Says no less than Lord Cornwallis hisself. Was with him in Charleston. Heard he was here in Camden. Sickly, she is, with malarial fever."

"Oh, no! Did you tell her Cornwallis has left?"

"Didn't speak with her. The soldiers chased her from the house. But I 'spect she'll be back. Can't go far, sick as she is."

"How terrible for her."

He nodded yes. "Why'd they let you out?" he asked then.

"I'm doing an errand for Mama. Rawdon gave permission."

"Well, you'd best be on your way, then. Best thing to do is stay outta their sight, mind your own business, till they're gone. And you kin tell Miz Sarah I got things in hand."

"I will," I said. "I know she depends on you, Mr. Bone." Somehow he had always held Mama in high esteem. He'd rather talk to her than Daddy any day.

More grunting. "Your errand don't have to do with the horse, does it?"

"No. I just stopped in to see her. I think we should keep her hidden. Colonel Rawdon already has his eye on her."

He nodded. "They lost hundrets of horses when their fleet ran into a storm off Cape Hatteras on their way down here in December."

"Maybe you could ask Isom to take Fearnaught somewhere. There's a cabin up in the mountains where Johnny always goes to hunt."

"Good idea." He scratched his face and glanced at me shyly. "You mean the one where that Catawba girl lives?"

There it was, out in the open. Another matter we never spoke of. Before the war, Johnny's absences were put down to the fact that he was a noted hunter and rider, familiar with the woods and paths from the Santee River to the Catawba Nation. But apparently, here in the stables and quarters, the help had always known he stayed, for weeks sometimes, with Nepoya, his Catawba woman, in the hills.

"Yes. She'll take good care of Fearnaught for Johnny."

He considered it for a moment, put his hat back on, and nodded. "I'll have Isom take her up there tonight."

We nodded, and he moved on. So did I, out into the bright sunlight and down the back path from the stables to the quarters. Here the negras were going about their business in the washhouse, the carpentry shop, the buttery. The blacksmith, old Israel, was shoeing the horse of a green-coated cavalry officer who stood by patiently waiting. The officer gave me a haughty glance. I walked by swiftly, my head down.

There was a large old pine tree a short distance from Miz Melindy's cabin. I hid behind it and watched her. She was on her porch, sewing. She was famous hereabouts for her quilts. Many a neighbor had purchased one from her, and Daddy allowed her to keep the money.

It had always been a source of puzzlement for me to see her. She was so black and I am so white that I didn't need any King's Honey Water for my complexion. This was a thorn in Georgia Ann's side, don't think I didn't know it. She was forever slobbering herself with almond paste or barley water strained through pure linen and doctored with a few drops of balm of Gilead. Still, her complexion was not as white as mine.

So, how did this happen?

Cecie, my real mother, was right pretty, I understand, with slender hands and a pert little nose. Being as Boney was her father, she was light-skinned. My daddy thought she was real pretty, too. He loved the she-crab soup she made. Said nobody could make it quite like her. I figure he must have been powerful fond of that she-crab soup and her gravy for veal cutlets that was made of white wine, butter, oysters, and sweetbreads. I understand she could whip up a good syllabub, too. Considering the fondness my daddy has for good cooking, and pretty women, it doesn't take much imagination to wonder how she got to be my mother.

Shortly afterward, Miz Melindy took me in and kept me for two years. I have no recollection of my own mama Cecie in that time. She slept in her own cabin, and I was kept out of the kitchen at the big house. But all along, my brother, Johnny, who is ten years older, and Georgia Ann would come down to the quarters and play with Cephas and Isom, Cecie's younger brothers. Sometimes Johnny and Georgia Ann even brought me up to the big house to eat with them. They'd dress me up in Georgia Ann's old dresses. Then one day some casual visitors came by and thought Mama Sarah had had another baby. And she got all shylike, because after all, what could she say? Word got out, like word does in these parts. Carried by the hooty owl or the wind.

"Y'all recollect that winter of sixty-five to sixty-six, when Miz Sarah said she had a stillborn child? Well, she didn't. Seems like we were all taken with worrying about the Stamp Act and the threat of the slave insurrection, we didn't pay mind. Miz Sarah, she had a baby girl. Was sickly, is all, and she sent it to the quarters for nursing. Y'all recollect that trick negra they've got over there? Well, she nursed it with some of her decoctions. And it's doing right fine. So just get over there, because Miz Sarah is receiving. We brought her some fancies from Charleston. Y'all know how she likes her sundries that make her so fashionable."

So they came. With West India rum or Miscovado sugar or pickled herrings from Ann Ball's shoppe on Motte's Wharf in Charleston. Or garden seeds and flowering shrubs from Martha Logan's on Meeting Street.

It was 1768. Camden had just been given its name. Before that it had been Pine Tree Hill. The new name was done by an Act of the Assembly.

Mama Sarah received them, was flattered by all the attention. It had been a matter of distress to her that she couldn't again get in the increasing way, that she was no longer considered a fruitful vine. Women in these parts marry early and have many offspring. Some have as many as sixteen. Why, they make a woman's lying-in a regular topic of conversation at socials. They have whole sets of childbed linen made of silk and lace. Mama was going to bequeath hers to Georgia Ann.

I became a part of the family.

Georgia Ann says that with my being brought to live with the family, Mama and Daddy arrived at "some kind of an understanding." And that there was giving and taking on both sides.

From then on, though, I was told to stay away from the quarters. Johnny still went to play with Isom and Cephas, and I was always running down there after him. And being chased away by Miz Melindy, scolded by Johnny, and punished by Mama Sarah. Then, one day when I was four, Johnny told me that if I didn't stop going down there Miz Melindy would be sold south.

We were in the yard, and he showed me the shadow cast by the carriage Daddy had purchased for Mama Sarah when she was carrying Georgia Ann, because Mama Sarah came home one day from Charleston saying she would just faint unless she could soon take the air in a carriage like her sister had. The carriage was edged in gilt with a crest on the side that Mama Sarah said was her family's crest from England. She's a Carlisle. The carriage cost a hundred and twenty pounds sterling. But Mama must have it, or she might miscarry. And she must have, too, one of her negras dressed in livery, blue broadcloth and brass buttons, to drive it.

The carriage cast a fine shadow in the afternoon sun.

"You see that shadow?" Johnny asked me.

I said yes.

"Well, it casts one shadow. So do I. But you cast two."

I looked. I saw only one shadow of myself and I was confused. "Where's my two?" I asked.

"You can't see it. But it's there. You cast two, because your real mama, who died, was part negra. And Miz Melindy is your grandma. And it upsets Mama to have you go down there because she loves you so much she wants you to think of her as your mama. And her mother in Charleston as your grandmother. People who cast two shadows are very special."

"Why?"

"You know how Daddy breeds horses so we get the best qualities from the sire and the dam?"

I said yes. He and Daddy were always going on trips to Charleston plantations for good horses. They'd just brought three down from a plantation on the Cooper River.

"You have the best qualities from two races."

"Two?"

"Yes. The negra race has good qualities. So do the Indians. White folks just aren't willing to admit it yet.

37

So you have special powers. But such people must be very careful and always do as they are told. Especially little girls."

I believed Johnny. I didn't especially care about being compared with horses, of course, but I knew how precious they were to him. Besides, Johnny could charm the kilt off a Scotsman. That's what Daddy always said.

Look what Johnny did just five years ago. Went with Daddy to the second session of the Provincial Congress they had in Charleston and accepted the command of a militia company they offered him, even though he'd resolved never to fight against the king. But he accepted, because to refuse would have meant he'd be arrested and held in Charleston. Then what does he do? Rides off with his militia company and arrests his fellow officers and charms the others into declaring their loyalty to George the Third.

Oh, Johnny could charm you, all right. So I didn't go down to the quarters anymore, not for eight years, not until Cate tried to set our house on fire. To get back to that fire. The house didn't burn. Cate had stuffed some old rags and paper under the brocaded settee in Mama's lady's parlor after we all went to bed and somehow lit the whole mess and run back to the quarters. What saved us was that my brother, Johnny, came in late from two weeks away in the mountain country west of us, visiting his Catawba lady friend. Johnny saw the smoke and woke us all up.

With the help of Miz Melindy, Johnny put the fire out before anything more than the brocaded settee was damaged. Nothing else was touched, not Mama's rosewood spinet, her Turkey rugs, not her pier mirror or japanned tea tables. Just the brocaded settee.

Cate was sold south. Daddy was always good to his negras, but he couldn't tolerate a feebleminded one who tried to burn the house down. I felt so bad for Miz Melindy that I broke Johnny's rule and went right down to the quarters and sought her out.

I thought of how she'd greeted me that time. "What you want, girl?" she asked, sitting there making one of her old quilts, her hands wrapped in lint because they were burnt. I told her I was sorry about Cate.

"Sorry the laziest word that ever be," she said. "Come along after all the bad done and try to wash it away. Sorry a lazy word. Come along too late."

Well, there wasn't much I could say to that, was there?

"You'd best git on up to the house where you belongs," she said. "Afore you has to tell them sorry you was here." So I went. And that was the last time I visited her.

As I stood with Rawdon's note in hand, Miz Melindy looked so old sitting there. Even from behind the tree I could see how white her hair had gotten, how wrinkled the skin around her neck looked. So old and sad, her sister sold off, her daughter dead. And so much had happened to me since. I'd had tutors, I'd been to Charleston with Mama and Daddy, to visit my grandmother there.

Grandmother Carlisle has a fine house in Charleston made of Bermuda stone. It has a secluded courtyard in back, where Grandmother Carlisle has dogwood, azalea, and wisteria. People call it the "pirate house" because it is said that in years gone by pirates met there to trade with respectable Charleston merchants. And there is a room upstairs where it is said Anne Bonney, a woman pirate, stayed. It is my room when I go there.

But before me sat my real grandmother, the one I'd neglected all my growing-up years. And now I was going to ask her to come up to the house and act as cook. For a British officer who, that very moment, was sitting in our dining room with his polished English boots propped up on the velvet-tufted chairs, eating the last of the calf's-foot jelly and macaroons that Georgia Ann brought home from Charleston last spring. And yelling because there wasn't a soul in the benighted house who knew how to make she-crab soup.

She had refused yesterday. What made me think she'd come for me today? To get my daddy out of jail? She had no use for my daddy. Likely she wouldn't come. I wouldn't if the people in that big house had sold my sister.

A pretty mess, wasn't it? I didn't mean the war. Somehow I thought the war would resolve itself. Wars always do, after the men get finished making their speeches and riding off in a flourish, dividing up the spoils and getting their pretty uniforms all soiled and torn. I meant my family. There was no resolving them. Sometimes I thought we were just a bundle of worms, all tied up in a burlap conjure sack and tied with strands of horsehair, bound to hurt anyone who didn't stay clear of us. And hidden under the back porch. Which was probably where we belonged.

Chapter Four

JUNE 30, 1780

S HE NEVER LOOKED up when I approached the rickety porch, never stopped her sewing. Some chickens clucked around my feet. And the old rooster, Scooby, rushed at me. As I recollected, he liked to peck at my legs.

I chased him away. "Hello, Miz Melindy."

She did not answer.

"Scooby's still alive, I see. How old is he now?"

"Older than God, I 'spect. An' near old as me." Still she did not look at me. But she wasn't chasing me, either.

Encouraged, I walked closer to the porch. "See you're making a new quilt, Miz Melindy."

"Umm."

"It's right pretty."

"See they finally let you outta the house. What you come fer, girl?"

"To visit. I come to see you."

She pored over her quilt frame. "I say, what you come fer? That man with the popinjay red coat send you down here to git me to come up and cook fer him? That it?"

"Miz Melindy, I'm ashamed to say it, but yes."

"Why you 'shamed?"

" 'Cause I haven't been to see you for two years."

She laughed, high pitched, more like a cackle. "Why should you come round? Didn't want you, did I?" Now she peered at me. Her eyes were bright, just like I always remembered. The eyes hadn't gotten old. "Doan want you now, either, girl. I'd throw some slops at you, only I ain't got a pot o' slops handy. And my bones be too rusty to git up and fetch some."

I said nothing.

"You sure growed."

"I'm near tall as Georgia Ann. Near smart as her, too. Only, she knows French from her fancy school in Charleston."

She sniffed. "That ain't no 'complishment. Only means she kin order people round in two languages now, 'stead of one. Hear she's still doin' it, too, even wif the popinjay in the house. Hear he be winin' and dinin' her." Again the laugh. "He knows what's good fer him, he'll hightail it outta here fast as he kin, afore Georgia Ann gits her claws in him. You come down here to git a quilt fer that popinjay? His men come fer one. I threw slops at 'em. Thinks just 'cause that Cornwallis fella got a quilt they could have one."

"Did you give Cornwallis a quilt? Or did he take it?"

"He come pokin' round down here wif his men an'

took one o' my quilts. Wifout so much as a by-yer-leave. Say he never seed sech a purty quilt. Smiled, and his face got all screwed up like he was bitten by a hornet."

"When he was in school at Eton another boy hit him in the eye during a hockey game. At least that's what Georgia Ann told me."

"Too bad that other boy didn't knock his brains out. What's this hockey?"

"It's a game they play in England. You know how our men go to cockfights and horse races? They play hockey. The way Georgia Ann explained it, they push things around with sticks."

"An' learn young how to push round peoples. Promised me freedom if'n I goes along wif him, is what he did."

"Why didn't you go then, Miz Melindy?"

"You doan trade off the devil you gots fer the devil you knows nothin' about."

"Well, you were right. Ten negras went with him. And Cornwallis told Mama they're going to be sold to the West Indies plantations. They work their negras to death there, Mama says. You know who all went, Miz Melindy? Besides Doreen, who did our cooking?"

She made a low moaning sound in her throat, then ticked off the names on her fingers. "Quaco, Squash, Kofi, Phibbi, Clinch, January, Old Abram, an' his daughter Obee, an' her baby."

"Obee will never survive there," I said. She was Georgia Ann's age. I remembered her as always sickly. And what of her baby? I didn't ask, and I saw Miz Melindy brooding the matter, so I gave the conversation another turn. "They killed my friend, Miz Melindy. They killed Kit Gales."

"I knows 'bout that," she said. "He was the little boy wif the freckles used to come on his horse fer you."

"He wasn't so little anymore. Coming on to be a man. Not only did they kill him, they left him hanging for three weeks. Wouldn't let anybody bury him properlike."

"They's evil people. Bad," she said.

"And they put my daddy in jail." She had nothing to say to that. She'd never liked Daddy.

"You heard from that almost-brother of yours?"

So, she'd remembered! Johnny called me his almost-sister. "Not since Charleston fell."

"An' my Cephas wif him," she said.

"They'll be all right, Miz Melindy. Johnny's lived with the Catawbas, remember. And learned their ways. Such ways will keep him. And he and Cephas fought the Cherokees, didn't they?"

"I think the British worse'n the Cherokees. All the Cherokees wanted was to keep land what belong to 'em. These British want land what ain't belong to 'em."

"Still, Johnny is right smart. But that don't mean they'll be home soon. So you can see why we have to get Daddy out of jail. Georgia Ann is up to the house making Rawdon all kinds of promises to keep him happy. Why, she's near to promising him Fearnaught for his very own."

That brought her around. "My Isom 'sponsible fer that horse. Master Johnny left him 'sponsible."

"I know, Miz Melindy. Which is why you must come

44

up to the house and cook for Colonel Rawdon. I must strike a bargain with him if we are to save Fearnaught. Colonel Rawdon decides to make off with the horse, there isn't a thing Isom can do!"

She nodded and sighed.

"I know you don't like coming up to the house. But Rawdon wants, real fearsomelike, somebody who can make she-crab soup."

"Where he gittin' the crabs?"

"Shipped in from Charleston."

"It be three days hard ridin' from Charleston."

"I suppose they'll get fresh ice along the route. They've been taking everything else they need in the countryside."

"Who told this popinjay I could make she-crab soup?"

"I did."

"You's gettin' right uppity. S'pose that's what comes from livin' up there an havin' fancy tutors. Where'd they get off to? Doan see 'em round anymore."

"They have family in Charleston, and they left to make sure everything is all right there. They'll be back in the fall."

"What'd they learn you?"

"He taught me to cipher, English grammar, geography, and dancing. She taught me how to candy fruits and preserve flowers, and do crewelwork." I would tell no one what else Amelia had taught me.

"An' nobody teached you that burnt hartshorn fights congestions and what special tree leaves kin be made into tea to fight fevers?"

"No," I said shamefacedly.

"You gots lots to learn, girl."

"I know." I stepped forward. "I have a note here from Colonel Rawdon." I put it in her lap. "I know you can't read, but I wanted you to see it's not Mama's handwriting."

She opened it and scanned the writing. "That mama of yours want me to come?"

"Yes. Very much. She even sent me to fetch you."

"That so?"

I thought I saw tears in her eyes. I nodded.

"What else that popinjay man like 'sides she-crab soup?"

"Everything. Spinach in cream, cakes, Tansy pudding, Georgia Ann said."

"Mebbe I fix him some coosh-coosh."

I remembered her coosh-coosh—boiled meat in salted water, stirred in with milk and molasses. "He'd like anything you make, Miz Melindy."

"Look like they need some coosh-coosh, all of 'em. Mebbe some Hoppin' John, too. Jade make 'em anythin' like that?"

"No. She tried rich pancakes. Pork, hominy grits. He left most of it on his plate at breakfast. He was eating macaroons and calf's-foot jelly."

"Cowpeas, boiled with rice and pork. Do 'em good," she said.

"Yes. And maybe some poke salad," I said.

She looked at me. "You 'members that?"

"Cut and parboiled, then fried in hot grease and seasoned with pepper and salt. Eaten with new spring onions," I told her. "Goes good with ashcake and sweet milk."

She nodded and held out her arm. "Hep me up," she said. "We show this popinjay what cookin' really be 'bout."

Chapter Five

JUNE 30, 1780

I DO NOT KNOW WHAT will be the end of it," my daddy's grandmother had written to her sister back in 1695. She came to this country at age sixteen. She married a weaver and they grubbed the land, felled trees, and operated a whipsaw together. She worked the ground like a slave, Daddy said. Her husband died, and she married again, my daddy's grandfather. He built a house, the same house on the Ashley River where my daddy grew up. There they opened a distillery and cooperage. She took in boarders. When Great-grandmother Judith wrote that letter she was telling her sister not to visit them "for the whole country is full of trouble. Smallpox lays upon the land and has been mortal to every person hereabouts, especially the Indians. There has been a lack of shipping, an earthquake, and a burning of the town. I do not know what will be the end of it."

That was the way I felt the day Miz Melindy came to our house to cook.

What would be the end of it? My friend Kit dead, Sam Dinkins and my daddy in jail, the British in our house for weeks, walking across our Persian carpets, putting their mugs of grog on Mama's good walnut tables, eating our food, relieving themselves in our Cherokee rosebushes.

I think even Great-grandmother Judith would have been hard put to know what the end of it would be.

I had to help Miz Melindy. I could see that right off. She didn't move as good as she used to. And Rawdon had demands. He sent an aide to the kitchen with a note. He must have a ragout pie after his she-crab soup. He must have a mushroom sauce with his fowl. And Quaking pudding, which required a quart of cream and twelve eggs.

Someone had to whip up the cream. Jade was absolutely no good at such things. The kitchen, which is a brick building somewhat away from the house, was in a shambles. Miz Melindy set Jade to cleaning it. Then the crabs came, packed in straw and the last of some ice, and the soup had to be made immediately, before the crabs spoiled.

"You can't do this alone," I told Miz Melindy. "I'll help you."

"We ain't alone," she reminded me. "An' it doan look like we's gonna be, either."

That was true enough. A British soldier had slipped into the kitchen and taken a chair by the door with his

49

Brown Bess musket propped up next to him. He wasn't leaving. He was going to sit and watch us. He looked like a private. He also looked hungry.

"What's he want?" I whispered to Miz Melindy.

She chuckled. "Watchin'. Makin' sure I doan put poison in the food."

I gasped and stole a sidelong glance at the young private. "How will he know?" I whispered again. "He can't see what you do while your back is turned. And he doesn't know what's an herb and what isn't."

"Gon' taste it," she mumbled. "Now you best git back to where you s'posed to be."

Miz Melindy may have been old, but she was not dull. She was right smart. I couldn't leave her alone in the kitchen. I had to stay and help. With that purpose in mind, I sought out Colonel Rawdon.

Our house, which was three stories high with a verandah on each level, sat on a fine knoll. It was surrounded by tall poplar and elm trees and handsome bushes. There was a wood fence in front on either side and a neat roundabout for carriages. A common was in front. There Rawdon had a tent set up, with the Union Jack flapping nearby and soldiers lazing about. He was sitting in a fruitwood chair that had been taken from the house. He was dictating a letter to his aide.

On the ground lay a Tory newspaper out of Charleston. "Not a Rebel in Arms in the Country," it screamed.

But Rawdon knew different. There were rebels in arms aplenty. "I hereby authorize you, Mr. Rugeley, to pay a bribe of five hundred guineas to any one of

Sumter's guerrilla officers who will convince the man to advance and fix his position behind Berkley's Creek, where there is a very spacious position. There I will be able to attack and destroy Sumter's army. I know I can depend upon you to convey my wishes in as circumspect a manner as possible."

Sumter's army! Five hundred men holed up at Clem's Branch, off the Catawba River, just below the North Carolina border. The only army for the American cause left in the South.

Johnny knew Thomas Sumter. They'd fought the Cherokees together. And now Rawdon was writing to Henry Rugeley, my uncle! Mama's brother, who lived twelve miles north of us in the fork of Flat Rock and Grannys Quarter Creek. He was a prominent Loyalist.

Did Rawdon know that Henry Rugeley was my uncle? Likely not. If he did, he'd send me there with the note. Like Mama did when Charleston fell in early May and the governor, John Rutledge, came by riding with Daniel Huger and John Gervais, his aides.

I shall never forget that day. Daddy was seeing to the supply of ammunition in the magazine, and Mama went right out on the front verandah to meet them.

"Madam, is your husband home?" Rutledge asked. "We need a place to tarry."

"Where is your seat of government?" Mama asked.

"Right here, madam, with us. We three. Wherever we find it safe to hang our hats for a few moments."

"With news of the British coming up from Charleston,

my husband is seeing to the magazine. I know I can trust you with that intelligence, since he is one of you."

Rutledge nodded. "You are in danger enough, your husband being a rebel. We shall not put you further in harm's way. Can you give us the name of a good rebel household hereabouts?"

Mama sent them twelve miles north, to Clermont, Uncle Henry's place. "He is a Tory," she told them, "but he is, first and foremost, a Southern gentleman. You will be safe there. As the wife of James Whitaker, I vouch for Henry Rugeley. He is my brother."

Rutledge and his men thanked Mama and rode on. And Uncle Henry took them in.

Then we got word, at four the next morning, that Banastre Tarleton and his dragoons were coming through in pursuit of Colonel Buford and his American force of three hundred. Tarleton was already known not to be a man of good parts. So what did Mama do? Sent me right on to Uncle Henry's to warn the governor that Tarleton was coming.

I rode Fearnaught. I took the sandy hidden paths along the Wateree and arrived at Uncle Henry's as the sun was rising. Uncle Henry woke his guests, had servants pack biscuits and ham, gave them a goodly supply of peach brandy, and sent them on their way before Tarleton arrived.

Then he sent me home. I shouldn't be there when Tarleton came, he said. In the distance, from Fearnaught's back, I saw Tarleton and his men, green-coated devils; saw Uncle Henry invite them into his house.

Later we learned that they proceeded on to Waxhaws, where they did their slaughter of the Americans and cut Samuel Wyly to pieces.

RAWDON STOPPED dictating his letter, saw me, and got to his feet. "Your servant, miss."

I curtsied. "Your servant, sir."

"May I be of assistance?"

"Miz Melindy is in the kitchen now, starting on the she-crab soup. But she's old. And she needs help."

"Then fetch another negra from the quarters."

"There isn't any, sir. So many of them left with Cornwallis. I'd like to help her."

"You belong upstairs in your chamber. I'll not have you wandering about."

"The soup needs constant stirring. To say nothing of the exertion needed to whip up the cream for the Quaking pudding. With help from me, you'll have your supper on time, sir. Without my assistance, well, it might be late."

He looked at me with that measure of arrogance that made me feel like a speck of dirt under his heel. "Very well, but you are not to wander about. And when you finish you are to repair to your chamber. Do you understand?"

I understood. The man was a fool. Especially if he thought my uncle Henry would ever convince one of Sumter's men to be a turncoat. First, I didn't think any of Sumter's men would do it. And second, Uncle Henry had too much honor to ask them. But how could I expect anybody who fought with an army that hanged

fourteen-year-old boys to have honor? I smiled and curtsied again and ran back to the kitchen.

THERE WAS a method to my madness. Miz Melindy
needed help, yes, but the longer I was out of my chamber, the more intelligence I would be able to gather
about what was going on.

The supper was a success. Although every time a
dish was completed and handed to Jade to take to the
house, the young private had to taste it first, to make
sure it wasn't poisoned.

I watched him as he tasted. Jade would hold the dish
and give him a special spoon. He looked as if he was
enjoying every moment of it.

"Why aren't you frightened that you'll be poisoned?"
I asked him.

He grinned. "The question is, why would they let
one of their own be poisoned? Why not use one of their
negras?"

"Why, then?"

"I volunteered. If I get poisoned, I get poisoned. It's
a chance. But better than the fate that awaits me otherwise."

"What is that?"

"Execution."

My eyes widened. "You're to be hanged?"

"Aye."

"For what?"

"Desertion. I ran. They caught me."

"Why did you run?"

"I was to get a two hundred."

"Two hundred what?"

"Lashes. For misconduct. So I ran. Then when they caught me, I was to be executed. Until they gave me this chance. Take the risk of being poisoned, and if I live, no execution. So, now, wherever Colonel Rawdon goes where the colonials cook for him, I eat the food first."

"How do you know we won't poison you?"

"You're good people. I can see that. Wouldn't dishonor yourselves in such a manner."

I felt touched by the words. They brought tears to my eyes.

"Do you think I could have another spoonful of that she-crab soup?" he asked. "I'm fair to starving and sick to death of the meager fare we get in the field. Last month I was on a week's confinement of bread and water for failing inspection."

I let him taste another large spoonful. "Do you know anything about conditions in the prison in town?" I asked.

He nodded. "Your father's there," he said.

"Yes."

"Why would I tell what I know?"

"For a dish of she-crab soup, a thick slice of fresh-made bread, and butter all your own. And maybe some poke salad."

His eyes fair watered. "The prison is crowded," he said. "Rawdon is bringing more and more prisoners in every day, so the rebels can't recruit them. There's a pen outside, as for cows and pigs. Men loll about on the dirt in the sun. Many are sickly."

"What are they feeding them?"

"Salt pork. Old bread. But some will be leaving soon."

"Leaving?"

He hesitated. I got up and dished him a big bowl of soup, cut a slice of bread, and spread it thickly with butter. He took it. A feast. He ate ravenously. "Talk is that many will soon be hurried on a foot march to Charleston."

"That's a hundred and twenty miles!"

He nodded and spooned soup into his mouth.

"What for?" I asked.

"To be put on prison ships in the harbor. Or shipped out, if they're important enough."

"Shipped out where?"

He shrugged. "Honduras. Bermuda."

"For what?"

"Prison."

He looked at me. In the pale blue eyes I saw my fear reflected. No, it was his fear, too. For what? *Why, he's younger than I thought,* I minded.

"If you let them know I told you I'll be hanged for sure," he said matter-of-factly. "No more chances to taste such food. There are executions every day."

"Executions?"

"Deserters from our army. Troublemakers from yours."

"I don't have an army," I told him.

"Your daddy's a rebel leader."

Miz Melindy was busy in the far end of the kitchen,

though I had no doubt that she knew what was going on. I felt the young private waiting for my answer. How could I give him one? Aren't you a rebel like your daddy? he was asking. How to explain? I took a deep breath.

"It's confusing," I said.

"Aye, tell me."

"We're English," I said. "Born and bred. We were always proud to be loyal subjects of the king. Even my daddy. He's always cherished his rights as an Englishman. He wouldn't even accept the invitation to go to the First Provincial Congress in Charleston in January of '75."

"So what happened then?"

"Your people fired on the Americans at Lexington. Daddy went to the second session of Congress in June. With my brother. My brother is fighting with the Loyalists now for the king."

He rolled his eyes. "A civil war," he said.

"Why do you say that?"

"Families taking different sides. Neighbor fighting against neighbor as we've seen in the Carolinas. Civil wars are the worst."

"At first Mama told us not to worry about Daddy. That he was just suffering a disaffection with the Crown. She said good Englishmen do that on occasion."

"Aye," he said again. "Back home, men like Fox, Pitt, and Burke all denounced, in Parliament, English domination of the colonies."

"But now I'm afraid it's too late for Daddy. Now it's treason, isn't it?"

He did not reply.

"When are they going to do this march to Charleston?"

"July," he said.

I nodded and stood up. "It's time to whip the cream for the Quaking pudding. You'll love tasting that. You'll think you're in heaven," I told him.

"I think I'm in heaven now, in your country here," he said. "This South Carolina. Little bit of heaven, I'd say, except for the way you people are killing each other. I've never seen such brutal fighting. Scalpings, burnings, lootings. Every sort of crime committed by citizen against citizen under the name of war. It's a much more savage war here than up North."

"Were you up North?"

"Bunker Hill. With Rawdon. But what beautiful country this! And worth the fight, I'd say."

I thanked him for the compliment and went to whip the cream. My arm near fell off doing it. Tendrils of hair hung dankly about my face, and I was near to exhaustion. I let the private taste the Quaking pudding. He pronounced it better than heavenly.

"Makes me think of home and Mum," he said.

But then Jade could not be found to take it to the house. The private picked up his Brown Bess and stepped outside with me. "You know the chief criticism the British higher-ups have of you people?"

I stood with Mama's good silver punch bowl in my hands. "What?"

He jerked his head in the direction of Miz Melindy.

"How can you speak liberty and keep slaves? It's a puzzlement to them."

"The two are different," I said.

"How?"

"I don't know, but if I understand the rebel cause, it's that first they must be free themselves before they can free others."

"Do they speak of freeing the negras?"

"Some do. Quakers, like Mrs. Wyly. But her husband was cut to pieces at Waxhaws. And if you want to speak about puzzlements, you can explain that to me. Or tell me how you can be in an army that treats you so vile."

He smiled. "It's more than I had at home," he said. "At home I had nothing. No work, nothing. Even the eight pence I get a day, minus the off-reckonings, is better than what I had at home."

"The off-reckonings?"

"They take out for clothing, its washing, necessaries, everything. Still, it's better than I had at home."

"Then why did you run away?"

"At first to escape the lashing," he said. "But now that I see the land, the farms, even the meanest of them in the backcountry, I'd be part of it in a minute if I could."

So he was going to run again then. Is that what he was telling me? His brown eyes met mine, begging for understanding. I smiled. I started to move down the brick path, carrying the Quaking pudding.

"Wait."

I waited.

"I like you. I'm not poisoned. And to show you my appreciation, let me give you another piece of intelligence."

I nodded.

"Rawdon has taken a fancy to that horse of yours. The one your sister speaks of. Says he's never seen such a piece of horseflesh. What Rawdon takes a fancy to, he usually gets."

I knew I must be careful. I must not tell him that Fearnaught had, this night, been taken to the hills. "Thank you," I said. And I moved down the path.

In our dining room sat Georgia Ann and Colonel Rawdon. Candles flickered in Mama's silver candleholders, and the best china plate was being used.

"Ah, the pudding," Rawdon said.

I set it down and stepped back. Georgia Ann was being a nymph, or so I supposed, wearing her good blue chintz gown and her stiff stays, which pushed her bosom up. I felt dowdy and in disrepair in comparison. Besides, even if I'd worn such stays, I didn't have anything much to push up. I curtsied and was about to leave when Rawdon stopped me.

"Just a moment. I understand you play the pianoforte."

"Yes sir."

"I would like you to play for us. A little music would go fine with this pudding and my cream and sherry."

I looked at my sister, but she was delicately spooning her pudding into her mouth. "I cannot play, sir. I am very dull," I said.

"How long do you intend to continue being dull?" he asked.

"Until my father is let out of jail."

He laughed. "I cannot wait until then. Come, give us a tune on the pianoforte. Why should I be deprived of music because of the war?"

"Why should I be deprived of my father?" I said.

He scowled. "You know the reason. He refused to sign the oath of allegiance to the king and persists in rebel activities. Now let us not belabor the point. Can you play 'Greensleeves'?"

"No sir."

" 'God Save the King'?"

"I can play 'God Save the Thirteen States.' "

"Caroline!" Georgia Ann set down her spoon in vexation.

"It's quite all right, Georgia Ann," he said. " 'God Save the King' is the same tune as 'God Save the Thirteen States.' The rebels do not have much in the way of originality. Go play 'God Save the King' for me," he directed.

"If I do, in my heart I will be playing 'God Save the Thirteen States,' " I told him.

He laughed. "Saucy little wretch. I care little for what is in your heart. I care for what reaches my ears. Go play. And play whatever else you know. Now."

"Caroline, you play 'Greensleeves.' " Georgia Ann called after me as I went across the hall to the parlor, where the pianoforte sat. "You know you can play it. And much more. You play, or I'll box your ears good, you hear?"

I played "God Save the Thirteen States." Then "Greensleeves." Then I played "Johnny Has Gone for a Soldier." It was from the French and Indian War, but I thought of my brother, Johnny, as I played it. I don't know what all else I played, but I fair lost myself doing it.

When I finished and tiptoed out into the hall, I found some British officers there, listening. They bowed to me when I passed. "Lovely, miss, just lovely," one said.

I may have been wearing only brown calico, and my apron was full of spilled whipped cream, my hair in disorder, but I felt like I was wearing blue silk as I went out into the sweet dusk.

WHEN I got back to the kitchen, the private was gone. Miz Melindy was getting out the fixings for bread dough. I helped her, and we mixed it and set it to rise for the morning.

"You watch yerself wif that young man," she said.

"He's just hungry and homesick," I told her. Then I helped neaten things up. A crescent moon hung above the trees when I walked her back to her cabin. As I returned through the quarters, the glow of cooking fires from the cabins, the soft hellos from the negras, the playing of some fiddle music almost becalmed me. Helping Miz Melindy was hard work. I'd scarce thought about Kit. I had no time to sit and stare and brood over the matter. Yet in moments like this, when the moon and fiddle music came close to becalming, there was still this thing inside me I could not get around. Kit's body, hanging there for three weeks.

I thought of Daddy. How could the men make a march to Charleston in this heat? Would Rawdon execute Daddy if we didn't treat him right? Why had I been so loud and unpleasant? It wasn't Rawdon who had hanged Kit; it was Cornwallis. Mama would call it virile boldness. I did not understand my own feelings. But I knew it all came back to the lie I had told myself, about politics being men's business, having to do with commerce, meetings, and high-toned talk.

It was not, and I knew it now. Politics first had to do with high-toned talk, meetings, and commerce. But pay it no mind, say it isn't your concern, and soon it gets down to the real business. Hanging a fourteen-year-old boy. Letting him rot on a rope for three weeks. Putting a man in prison for his beliefs. Taking an old negra woman's quilt, strutting like a peacock in a person's house, using their things, courting their sister.

And it had to do with wanting somebody's prize horse.

"It's a matter of fundamental rights." That's how Daddy had put it. I understood now. Everybody had a different fundamental right they had to protect, a different breaking point. With some it had been the fool stamps the year I was born. For others it was the tea ships, way back in '73. With others it was property, or taxes, or the port of Boston being closed.

But it all came down to politics. And choosing sides. And if you didn't, well, the time soon came when they trampled on your fundamental rights. First Kit. Then my daddy. Now Fearnaught. "Never seen such a piece of horseflesh," Rawdon had said. *Well, he isn't going to get Fearnaught.* Nobody had a right to take what you held dear. And if Fearnaught was the only thing I had to fasten my hatreds on now, and my truths, well then, fasten I would.

And if that meant I was a rebel, so be it.

A birdcall, a single piercing note, the kind Johnny learned from the Catawbas, came from some nearby bushes. I halted on the path and peered around. I was in darkness. Cicadas chirped loudly. From the barn came a horse's whinny. Campfires gleamed in the distance, and I could smell the cooking fires of the soldiers in our meadow. Someone was hiding behind those bushes over there. *Who? Could it possibly be Johnny?*

It was Isom. I walked to the bushes. "Isom, what is it? What's wrong?"

"Good to see you, Miz Caroline. Dey told me you was outta de house. I gots a note fer you. From Johnny." He held forth a folded bit of parchment.

I took it, feeling a sense of thrill. But I could not read it in the dark. "What does it say? Where did you get it? Have you seen Johnny?"

"No, Miz Caroline. I met Nepoya in de woods on my way to bring de horse. She give me de note an' take Fearnaught to a pen in de woods up where she live. An' she give me dese." He held out a bow and a quiver of arrows.

I took them. They were beautifully made. "What are they for?"

64

"She says you may have need."

"But how did she get the note from Johnny? And where is he? Oh, he is alive, isn't he, Isom?"

"Yes, Miz Caroline. He be alive. But hurt. You know how Nepoya gits about dese days."

"Yes." Nepoya flitted in and out of town like a spirit. Likely she'd been visiting with Mrs. Wyly, who'd told her the British were in our house. So she sent the arrows, as a sign of friendship. The Catawbas were devoted to the whites. Mr. Wyly had been the colonial agent for them. In '75 the Catawbas had even sent runners to Charleston to find out the meaning of the Provincial Congress. Puctree, Nepoya's brother, had been one of those runners. And when the Congress sent a thousand pounds of powder and lead for hunting to the Cherokees, to appease them at that time so they wouldn't align with the British, Puctree went along on the mission.

The British took the powder and shot and killed Puctree. Nepoya will never forgive them. She called Johnny a fool for fighting with the Loyalists. He'd told me that once. "She says before this is finished I will be a rebel," he said. And he'd laughed, saying it.

"I can't read it. It's too dark, Isom. What does it say?"

"Johnny wounded."

I felt the black night closing in, saw the candles in the house windows grow distant. "Bad?"

"He needs fetchin', Miz Caroline. Dat's what de note say. But what it doan say be more 'portant."

"What?"

"Johnny been whipped. By de British. At Charleston. De person who brung de note to Nepoya tell dis. A British officer dere want Grey Goose. Johnny won't give her. Johnny knocked him down. An' dey do dis court-martial to him an' whip him. He escaped. Wif Grey Goose an' Cephas. Dis not in de note. Lessen he git caught by British."

I nodded. My ears were ringing. I was so tired from cooking. My mouth was parched.

I trembled in weariness and anger. Nobody whipped my brother, Johnny. It seemed the final outrage. He was so strong, lean, graceful, sure. A cat, Johnny was, a regular painter cat from the mountains. So much his own person, a person to be reckoned with. He gave orders, did not take them. He rode like a knight, hunted like an Indian. Why, he'd been using a musket since he was eleven!

"He needs fetchin' home, Miz Caroline," Isom was saying. "Dat's in de note. He musta done heared dat de British is on dis place an' wants to pass hisself off as one of 'em."

"Yes. And what of Cephas?"

"He wif him, but dey both inna bad way. Cephas got de shivers an' shakes, Nepoya say."

"Where?"

"De girl say in dat place where de Catawba becomes de Wateree."

I knew the place. A little northwest of us by Fishing Creek. I clutched the note in my hand and thanked Isom. "You'd best go to the quarters. And I must go to the house."

66

"Who you think dey send, Miz Caroline? You goin' to ask dose men in de red coats to bring Johnny home?"

"Yes, Isom."

"You best tell 'em he still be fightin' fer 'em."

"Thank you, Isom, you're right."

"Git 'em both home an' fixed up good by Miz Melindy. Wif her poultices fer Johnny's wounds. An' her snakeroot tea or boiled wild gingerroot fer fever."

"Yes," I said again. He called his mother Miz Melindy.

"Den we study on what Johnny should do. Den he be strong enough to study on it."

I thanked him again. He was thinking clearer than I.

"I go fer him if'n dey lets me."

"I'll remember that, Isom." But I was already turned and thinking on what I was going to say to Mama and Georgia Ann as I walked to the house.

Chapter Six

JUNE 30–
JULY 4, 1780

W HEN I GOT back upstairs and into our
chamber, Mama and Georgia Ann were already in bed, though not sleeping. Mama was
reading. Georgia Ann was doing something to her nails.
A single candle glowed on a table on either side of the
large four-poster they shared. I slept on the trundle bed
that pulled out from under it. I sat down in a chair by
the window and took off my shoes. My feet hurt from
standing so much. I set down the bow and arrows. Georgia Ann was watching me.

"Where'd you get *those*?" She came alert.

I didn't have to answer her, did I? I took off my
brown calico. It was dirty from cooking and soot from
the fire. My hair smelled of soot, too. I wished I could
wash it. Well, maybe I'd brush it out and use some of
Georgia Ann's powder in it. I stood in my chemise before the open window, feeling the cool night air on my

body. Outside on the hills in the distance was the glow of campfires from the British encampment.

I needed to wash, so I went to the table that held the basin, picked up the pitcher, and poured some cool water into the basin. I picked up a rag and some soap, scented it was, Georgia Ann's soap, and began to wash my face and neck and arms.

"Mama, she's got a bow and arrows. And she won't say where she got them. Likely from Nepoya. Was she here?" She flung the question at me.

I didn't answer. I felt so much older than her suddenly. Had the hard work of the day rendered me that way? Or what I'd heard from the private?

"And look, she's got a note." She'd gotten up and snatched the folded parchment from the chair where I'd set it down. "Mama, it's from Johnny!"

I ran across the room and grabbed the parchment from her. "Leave it be. It's mine!"

"You were going to keep it for yourself? A note from Johnny?"

"No, but it's mine."

Mama got out of bed and put on her blue silk robe. In the light of the candles she looked pale and tired. Yet her blond hair, which was mixed with gray and spilled down her shoulders, made her look girlish and vulnerable all at the same time. "Johnny? You have a note from Johnny?" she asked.

"Yes, Mama, I was going to give it to you." I handed it over and went back to finish my washing.

Mama took the note closer to the candle on her side

of the bed and read it. "Dear God," she murmured. "Johnny is hurt. But he's alive, oh praise be!"

"He needs fetching home, Mama," I said, "and I aim to ask Rawdon."

Georgia Ann sat next to Mama and read, too, then jumped up, reached for her silk robe, went to a mirror, smoothed her hair, pinched some color into her cheeks, and was starting for the door when Mama stopped her. "No, Georgia Ann. Not tonight. Wait until morning."

"I just left him, Mama. Daddy's Madeira has made him mellow. And he's playing cards with his aides. He likes playing cards. He always wins. He'll send someone for Johnny in the morning. All's I have to do is ask."

"But you aren't dressed. It's unseemly," Mama said.

"It's more than unseemly, it's stupid," I put in. "No man likes to be bothered when he's playing cards."

"Oh, and I suppose you think *you* should ask him," my sister snapped.

For once her sass, her superiority, didn't touch me. Because I knew more than she did. My tutor's wife, Amelia, who had become my friend and taught me much, once told me that all it takes to outwit your adversary is knowledge. "That's why men don't want us women to have much learning," she'd said. "It is why they tell us the chief virtues are modesty, meekness, and affability."

I'd learned a lot from Amelia, a lot her husband, with his ciphering and geography, didn't realize she was teaching me. A lot nobody knew she was teaching me.

"I know some things," I said.

"Oh, of course you do. How to make conjure bags and coosh-coosh, likely, from spending the day with Miz Melindy. Well, all that's important right now is that Johnny's hurt, from fighting at Charleston. For the British." Georgia Ann tightened the tie of her robe and tossed her hair. "Rawdon will send men in the morning to fetch Johnny. All I have to do is ask. Johnny is, after all, a loyal subject of the king."

And with that she went out the door.

"Oh dear," Mama said. "I am afraid that Georgia Ann is losing whatever modest reserve she has had."

"Never mind that, Mama." I reached for a bit of flannel, dried my face, neck, and arms, and bade Mama sit. "There's more you should know than the letter tells."

"More?" Her hand flew to her heart.

"I didn't want to tell Georgia Ann. And you mustn't, either. I don't trust that she won't tell Rawdon. Johnny wasn't wounded fighting for the cause. He was whipped by the British at Charleston."

"Whipped?" Her eyes went wide. "They don't whip their own."

"They whip their own, Mama. Two hundred lashes sometimes. And they not only whip, they execute. Rawdon's giving orders all the time for the hanging of his own deserters."

"Who have you been talking to?" Mama asked.

"It doesn't matter. I've been keeping my eyes and ears open."

Mama drew in her breath sharply, stood up, crossed

the room, then turned to confront me. "Tell me every-thing, Caroline."

I looked into her trusting eyes, trying to decide if I should tell her everything. No. I wouldn't tell her of the impending march that would send Daddy to Charleston. Of the possibility of his being shipped out. I told her about Johnny.

She gasped. "Johnny? Turned against the British! I can scarce believe it. Why wasn't it in the note?"

"In case it was intercepted," I said. "Nepoya gave the note to Isom. Whoever gave the note to her told her what really happened to Johnny. And where he's holed up. Johnny's a fugitive, Mama."

"Oh, my boy," she said. "He believed in them so!" She walked, musing, thinking. "Is there any possibility that Rawdon will have heard about Johnny's actions in Charleston?"

"There's always that chance, Mama. But it's un-likely. Their intelligence is so bad. And they have much to plague them."

"Then if he still thinks my son is loyal he may send men to fetch Johnny."

"No, Mama. All Georgia Ann's charm won't work. He can't spare the men. I told you, I've been keeping my eyes and ears open. In the morning I'm going to ask him to let me go and fetch Johnny home."

"You? Dear child!"

"I'm not a child anymore, Mama. Not since I saw Kit hanged. Anyway, there isn't time to be a child. Raw-don let me out of the house. Trusted me to help Miz Melindy in the kitchen. He'll trust me to do this."

"But why should he allow this? Even if he doesn't know Johnny has turned on them, my husband is still the town's leading rebel."

"I've studied on it," I said. "And from what I can see, Rawdon needs intelligence about Sumter's army. I heard him dictating a letter asking Uncle Henry to bribe any of Sumter's officers to convince Sumter to fix his position behind Berkley's Creek, so he can attack them."

"My brother will never do that," Mama said.

"I know that, Mama, but Rawdon doesn't. He's desperate to attack Sumter, to pin him down, to get information on him. And if I tell him Johnny can get him intelligence on Sumter, he'll let me go fetch him, I just know it."

Silence in the room. From below stairs came the shouts of Rawdon and his men in their drinking and card playing.

"Alone?" Mama asked. "You can't go out there alone. There are rebels all over the countryside, lifting their fists in anger, doing hit-and-run raids on Loyalists. Worse than that, there are desperate men on both sides settling old scores and family feuds in the guise of attachment to either the Crown or independence. There is widespread looting, burning out. You can't take a horse and wagon and go out into such a landscape alone."

"Then I'll take someone with me," I said.

"Who?"

"I don't know, but I'll think on it. I know the backwoods and can get there fast."

I saw Mama's shoulders sag. And then she asked the one question I hadn't studied on. "Why would Johnny gather intelligence for the British after what they did to him?"

The question hung in the air, unanswered. Georgia Ann came back into the room.

"Well?" Mama asked her. "What did he say?"

"He's busy playing cards, Mama. He's winning. I couldn't distract him. He hates being distracted when he's winning." She took off her robe and got into bed.

I couldn't help feeling grimly satisfied that my sister had failed in her mission. I got into my trundle bed and snuggled under my bedclothes. "Won't it be nice to have Johnny home?" I asked.

"I'll ask Rawdon in the morning," Georgia Ann said.

Mama blew out her candle and told Georgia Ann to snuff out hers, that we had to be up early in the morning, there was much to be done.

But in the morning, Georgia Ann slept, as I knew she would. When I brought Rawdon's breakfast to table, he stared at me, his bushy eyebrows knitted together.

"Fetched home?" he asked.

"Yes sir." I set the food down and stood very straight. I looked more presentable this morning. I was wearing a blue chintz gown and a clean white lawn apron, and had a lace cap on my head. I felt like a prissy peacock, but Mama had insisted on it.

But more important, my resolve was strengthened. "A note came to us. My brother, Johnny, was wounded at Charleston and has been trying to make his way home since, with his manservant, Cephas. But Cephas

has the shivers and shakes and they need fetching."

"The whole benighted country needs fetching." He attacked the fresh perch, eggs, ham, and bread. "Tell me," he said, buttering some bread, "why I should send out men to bring home one Loyalist soldier who likely can't shoot straight and his negra slave?"

"Johnny can shoot straight, sir."

"These provincial militia units are of little use to us," he said.

"My brother gave a good account of himself in Charleston, sir. He risked my daddy's affections to stay loyal to the king. And he's been shooting a musket since he was eleven."

"The problem with these colonies," he said between bites of fresh perch, "is precisely that. In England the lower classes do not have access to firearms."

That he would consider us the lower classes stung me. "Our men have had to fight off the Indians," I said. "Johnny fought in the Cherokee War."

He grunted. "Where is he then, that he needs fetching?"

"I know the place, sir."

"Where?"

"In that place where the Catawba becomes the Wateree."

He scowled. "North of us," he said.

"A little north, sir, yes."

"If he's on his way home from Charleston, and wounded, why didn't he come here? Why go north of us?"

I had dreaded the question. I did not know why

75

myself. But I had contrived an answer. "Perhaps he's already gathering intelligence, sir. Perhaps he and Cephas are hiding from rebels."

"Cephas?"

"His manservant, sir."

I could see he did not quite believe me. "But Johnny knows the hills and swamps, the good hiding places. He knows how to live in them on next to nothing, to track, to hunt, to..." My voice trailed off.

I had his attention now. The hand with the buttered bread stopped halfway between plate and mouth. "I shall give thought to the matter. Now tell me, what is our trick negra cook planning for supper?"

"A young roasted capon in wine sauce, with mushrooms, browned potatoes, and poke salad, I think. And she's making a cake for dessert."

"Good, good. I shall dine with your lovely sister again. You may go now."

"Just one thing, sir."

"Yes, what is it?" He had picked up his newspaper and was clearly vexed that I was so bothersome.

"I know you can't spare your men to fetch my brother home. I'd be willing to take a horse and wagon and go fetch him myself."

"You?" He scowled. Then he laughed. "You think I'd let you off this place to inform every rebel what my strengths are here? Are you daft, girl? You and your family are my prisoners, may I remind you?"

"You could send someone with me, sir."

"You said it yourself. I haven't anyone to spare." He went back to his reading.

I was taking my chances pushing him, and I knew it. But I had to. "My brother could gather all the intelligence about Sumter's army that you need, sir," I said. "Mr. Rugeley won't bribe any of Sumter's officers to ask Sumter to change the position of his army."

He rattled the newspaper and set it aside. "How do you know what I asked of Mr. Rugeley?"

"I heard you dictating the letter when I came to speak to you yesterday. Mr. Rugeley has too much honor, even if he is a Loyalist."

"You presume much! Are you to tell me that you know Mr. Rugeley now, too?"

"He's my uncle, sir."

He let his breath out slowly. He closed his eyes, as if to gather strength. I fair trembled waiting until he gathered himself together. "Sweet heaven! The trick negra is your grandmother and the leading Loyalist hereabouts is your uncle! Do you have any other relatives I should know about?"

I kept a still tongue in my head.

"Do you know what you are asking of me? You know what my plans are, because you overheard me dictating a letter. And you expect me to allow you to go traipsing around the countryside with such intelligence? To relay it to the first rebel? Do I look like a buffoon to you, girl? Answer me!"

He shouted it. I trembled. "No sir. I was offering to help, is all. And I'm no rebel. I'm Loyalist. Like my mama and sister and brother."

"A true Loyalist who played 'God Save the Thirteen States' yesterday instead of 'God Save the King.'"

"That was to vex my sister, sir."

"Oh?"

"Yes sir. She's always taunting me. She's prettier than I am and so much more accomplished. I was jealous of her yesterday, sitting here all prissied up in her fancies and you fawning over her so. Forgive me, sir. But I was."

He puffed all up at that. Like a tom turkey in the barnyard. "Well, you've a way to go yet to achieve your sister's beauty, but be patient. I'm certain that someday a good British gentleman will be fawning over you. Though I hope not a soldier. I hope to God we'll all be home in Mother England by then."

"Yes sir." I curtsied. "Thank you, sir. By your leave."

"Yes. Of course. And let me give this matter some thought. It may take time. Be patient."

"Oh, I will, sir, and thank you ever so much." And I fled the room.

IT TOOK some time. That day and two more to be exact, during which we settled into a kind of truce, Rawdon and I. I kept helping Miz Melindy in the kitchen. Daily, I worked with her to deliver savory dishes to Rawdon's table.

Nightly, my sister supped with him.

I was grateful for being able to work in the kitchen, though the days were sweltering hot. I would have gone completely daft in that upstairs chamber. I did not know how Mama and Georgia Ann abided it.

Mama read her Bible a lot, fretted about Daddy, did handwork, wrote in her journal. Georgia Ann fussed with herself, spent whole afternoons preparing herself for her supper with Rawdon, and when she wasn't doing that, she was talking about how wonderful he was. His family in England was of substance. He was destined for greatness. He was so charming with her. A true gentleman.

"Then why doesn't he let you out of this chamber all day?" I had asked her one afternoon.

"I beg your pardon?" my sister said.

"You're a prisoner. No better than Daddy is in jail. Why doesn't he let you out for fresh air? You're a prisoner is why, and he dallies with you."

"Not true!" And she burst into tears. "Not true. He holds me in high esteem. He has great affection for me!"

"Then why doesn't he let me fetch home Johnny?"

But she had no answer for that. And neither did I.

Twice more I asked Rawdon to let me take a wagon and go fetch Johnny. Twice he waved me off.

I knew he was busy. He wasn't just sitting around playing cards and paying court to Georgia Ann. He was always signing papers while an aide stood by ready to take them someplace. Couriers came in from the British posts to the east and west, and twice he sent out detached patrols of cavalry. His British Legion, he called them. The riders came back wilted and as green in their faces as the color of their coats. The horses were sweating and lathered, overworked in the heat. Once I heard murmurings from his officers that quickly subsided when I came through the hall with a tray of food.

"Tarleton finds out he's using his cavalry this way, there will be hell to pay."

"If only he could find out what Sumter was getting in the way of men, money, and supplies."

My ears picked up all kinds of things. Two of Rawdon's cavalry had come down with malaria from riding through the swamps.

I was worried about Johnny. How was he faring? Was he still alive? Did Cephas know how to care for him? Would he think we hadn't received the note? That we weren't coming? The waiting was unbearable. The worry sat on my shoulders like a vulture, pecking away at my brains.

And then I heard Rawdon telling one of his officers that he'd just received a letter from Cornwallis in Charleston. "He wants offensive operations commenced against Sumter. Sumter won't even come out of hiding!" His mood was foul. I dared not even linger when I served his food.

We'd hear the drumrolls early in the afternoon. From the distance they were carried on the limpid air, like thunder. At first we didn't know what they were. But Private Brandon, who still sat tasting the food in the kitchen, told me.

"Executions," he said.

"Of British?" I asked. "Or Americans?"

He shrugged. "Could be either."

I knew those executions could not have come about without Rawdon's signature. A chill went through me then, in spite of the oppressive heat. I felt as if some gigantic evil bird were hovering over our whole plantation. Or like somebody had put a conjure bag under the back steps. I thought of Daddy. Had the march to

Charleston begun yet? I asked Brandon. No, not yet, he told me.

Then on the fourth, a train of wagons pulled onto our plantation. I was setting down breakfast on the dining room table when they arrived. Rawdon jumped up and went to the window. "Supplies," I heard him mumble. He did not seem happy about supplies. Why?

I soon knew why. The supplies came from Cornwallis in Charleston. And they were for an offensive. No sooner had Rawdon turned from the window than an officer from the supply train came into the dining room, took off his tricorn, and saluted. "Greetings from General Cornwallis, sir."

Another note. I stood in the background and watched Rawdon's face grow red, reading it. "What does he send us?"

"Rum, salt, ammunition, and regimental stores."

"He wants an offensive against Sumter." Rawdon spoke to himself. "How am I supposed to mount an offensive when the snake hides in the woods and swamps?"

The officer did not reply. I saw him eyeing the splendid breakfast, but Rawdon did not offer him anything. Did not invite him to sit down. "When do you return?" he asked.

"As soon as we can get provisioned. Some horses need shoeing," the officer said.

"Provision yourselves at the officers' mess. There's a fine blacksmith in the quarters. I'll have my answer for Cornwallis late this evening."

The man left. So did I. I crept out after him. Rawdon had forgotten I was there.

AT THE noon meal I spoke up. I had just set down the Salamagundy, a cold dish of sliced chicken, anchovies, eggs, and onion arranged on cold lettuce leaves. There would be Tansy pudding for dessert. "Will that be all, sir?"

He waved me away with his hand. But I did not move.

"If I could go and fetch Johnny, sir..." My voice was not working right. I cleared my throat and started again. "If I could go and fetch my brother, he can inform you what Sumter is up to. He may even be able to get into the camp. He knows all those men, sir. He grew up with them."

He was lifting a piece of chicken to his mouth. "What?" His scowl was fierce.

"I said, sir—"

"I heard what you said. Why didn't you tell me your brother knew Sumter's men?"

"Well, sir, I didn't say he knew all of them. I said some. He grew up with some of them."

He threw down his white linen napkin. He pushed back his chair and got to his feet. I stepped back. He was so tall and that red of his coat so, well, so red. He glared down at me.

Georgia Ann, who was taking the noon meal with him, was sitting there sipping her claret, getting all giggly and making eyes at him the whole time. I think she had already had too much claret.

"Yes, all right," he said.

I stopped dead in my tracks. "Did you say yes, sir?"

"I did." He reached for his wine, stood there sipping it. "You may leave tomorrow. Take a wagon. How long will it take for you to fetch him?"

I thought fast. "Two days to get there, two days home. But when he gets home he'll need rest, sir. And attending. His wounds will need fixing." We'd have to travel slow if Johnny was hurt.

"I'll send to town for a doctor. We'll have him on his feet in no time."

I felt panic. We couldn't let a doctor see that Johnny's wounds were not from musket balls. "All Johnny needs is Miz Melindy to tend him, sir. She knows the art of physick. Been caring for people around here for years. She once got fifty weight of tobacco for curing the ague and fever of a neighbor."

"Then she can go along with you," he said.

"Sir?"

"You heard me." He took another sip of wine. "The trick negra can go along with you. Find me someone to do the cooking and you and she can fetch your brother."

Someone to do the cooking? My mouth fell open. Was he just playing with me then? He had such a cruel streak! "I don't know who else on the place can cook, sir. There's no one."

"Doesn't your mother cook?"

"Beg pardon, sir?"

"Your mother. Georgia Ann told me she'd trained up Doreen, who left with Cornwallis."

"Yes sir. But you want my mother to cook for you?"

"And why not?"

Did he not understand? Mama was the mistress of the plantation. Mama knew how to do things, yes. She'd been trained to look well to the ways of her household, as had all proper Southern women. But she'd been trained to supervise others.

"Mama has many domestic accomplishments, sir. Her kitchen garden and her larder are proofs of her industry. But she does not labor. She oversees others."

"Well, if she wants her precious son home, she'll labor now, won't she? You want your brother home, don't you?"

I looked at him bleakly, then at my sister.

"Her son's life depends on it," he said again. "So she can just get herself to that kitchen and cook for me and for Georgia Ann. Go tell her I request it."

Georgia Ann looked startled now, too. "I don't think my mama would like that," she said.

Rawdon looked down at her, bowing slightly. "I am not in the habit," he said, "of consulting your mama, or any woman, about my plans, Georgia Ann." His voice was quiet, even gentle, but deadly.

"Well, of course not, darling. Why would I think such? When you have such a gift for command?"

Darling? I stared at my sister, but her face was placid. Was she being sarcastic? She was not. She meant every word of it. How could she have Mama cook for this despicable man and wait on him, and her, too? But apparently she could. Very easily.

It was all so confusing. All backfiring in my face. Mama cook? Miz Melindy come on the journey with me? Mama was so delicate she couldn't bear the heat of the kitchen all day. Miz Melindy was so old! The journey might kill her! But I did not say these words to Rawdon, lest he change his mind altogether and leave Johnny to die.

"Could I have a musket?" I asked him.

He scowled at me. "What?"

"If I go, I'll need a musket. There's all kinds of pernicious characters riding around out there these days. Desperate men on both sides, settling old scores and family feuds in the guise of attachment to either the Crown or independence." I echoed Mama's words.

"You don't know how to shoot a musket," Georgia Ann said.

"Yes, I do. Johnny taught me. Sir? Could I have a musket? I'll come right back with Johnny. You can trust me."

Rawdon sat back down at the table and commenced to eat. "I know you'll come back," he said, "because I have your mother here now, don't I? And your father in jail in town. No, you may not have a musket. Now go and tell your mother what I require. Or your brother will rot in the woods and swamps."

I looked at my sister. But no help was forthcoming there. Help? She needed it herself. She was smitten with the man. I curtsied and left, thinking, *But he needs Johnny, too. Oh, why does it all have to be on his terms?* I felt the sting of it, the unfairness. But I knew why. Because they were the kind of people who would hang a fourteen-year-old boy, who would cut a man to pieces instead of just shoot him, who would make an old negra woman take a journey that might kill her. Everything was on their terms now, all of it. And this was what my sister called the gift of command.

"OF COURSE I'll do it," Mama said.

I stood in our chamber and stared at her. "Do you know what it requires, Mama? Standing over the hot fire all day, bending over the skillets and tripods in the fireplace. Peeling, cutting, chopping, stirring."

"Jade will help me."

"He'll have you bringing it to his table, too. To serve him and Georgia Ann." I did not spare her. I could not. Likely this was what Rawdon planned: to humiliate Mama, the wife of the leading rebel in these parts.

"I'm stronger than you think. I look forward to getting out of this chamber. The change and the activity will do me good," Mama said. "Now you just run along and tell Miz Melindy to be ready to go. Ask Mr. Bone to give you the sturdiest wagon. I'll gather blankets, lint. Ask Melindy to bring her decoctions. We must get Johnny home safely."

"Mama."

"Go!" She was in a flurry of activity already, jumping about the room, gathering up a petticoat, ripping it into strips for lint. "Food, you'll need food. I'll go directly to the kitchen and gather some that won't spoil." Then she stopped. "I wish he'd send Isom with you. For protection. Two women alone. I don't like it. You must take a musket. I know Johnny taught you to shoot, don't deny it now. And it's a good thing."

She was babbling, then she stopped. "They've taken all our muskets. Ask him for one."

"I did, Mama. He won't give it."

"Then we'll get one from Mr. Bone."

"Boney?"

"He'll have one hidden away, if I know him. You think that man didn't hide muskets when he saw them coming? You run along to Miz Melindy now. I'll be down to the kitchen directly."

I started for the door.

"Caroline?"

"Yes, Mama."

"What does Georgia Ann say of all this?"

"She calls him darling. Says he has the gift of command."

"She's smitten with him, isn't she?"

"I'd say so, yes."

Mama compressed her lips for a moment, as that truth flooded her whole being. She'd had so many hopes for Georgia Ann. Then she spoke. "You are not my blood child, Caroline. We both know that. But at this moment, you are more my daughter than Georgia Ann could ever be."

In all the years I'd been part of the family, Mama had never referred to my real mother. Or the fact that I was not hers. Never had I felt that I truly belonged, though I was treated like a daughter. But I realized then that had been Georgia Ann's fault, not Mama's.

Always I had longed to hear such words from Mama. Tears came to my eyes when she said them. I ran across the room and hugged her, hard. She patted my back. "Go," she said.

I went.

Chapter Seven

JULY 5, 1780

I WAS LEAVING THE plantation. I hadn't been away since last Christmas, when I went to Charleston with my family. But this time I was not going in Mama's gilt-edged carriage with the crest on it to visit and feast and attend routs, assemblies, and plays, to stay in Anne Bonney's room in Grandmother Carlisle's house made of Bermuda stone.

This time I was going in a worn-down wagon pulled by two mules. This time I was going to bring Johnny home.

Things had come to life around me. Mama was not wilting away in our chamber anymore. She had worked in the kitchen with Miz Melindy all afternoon the day before, and into the evening, concocting tasty dishes to please Colonel Rawdon. Then they worked far into the night to cook for our trip. I helped, until Mama sent me off to bed.

ONLY YESTERDAY Isom and I had stood watching as Mama came down the brick walk from the house, as gay as a young girl on her way to a rout, clad in calico and apron, a crisp white cap on her head, nodding imperiously to any soldier who crossed her path. ·

Miz Melindy had been grumbling in the corner of the kitchen. " 'Tain't right, makin' that woman come fer to cook fer the popinjay. 'Tain't right." She was kneading some pie dough, slapping and punching it as if it were Rawdon himself. Her back was to the door.

At the doorstep Mama stood there, looking around the kitchen. She made no sound, said nothing, but stared at Miz Melindy's back. For a moment there was terrible silence. And I minded that these two women had not spoken for years. Since when? Since I was born? No. Likely since Miz Melindy had come to the rescue when Cate tried to burn our house down. Isom and I stared at each other, wondering what would happen.

Slowly, Miz Melindy covered the dough, wiped her hands on her apron, and turned. "Miz Sarah," she said.

Mama nodded. "Miz Melindy."

More silence. Mama stepped into the kitchen. For a moment they stared at each other. Then without further ado, Mama spoke. "We have work in great plenty before you and Caroline leave."

Miz Melindy nodded.

"You must take food. And remedies."

"I'll have Isom cut off the heads of three chickens," Miz Melindy said. "I'll set 'em to fryin'. I'll cook up a mess of pole beans an' make a double batch of biscuits.

I'll fetch up a pail of lard an' a side of bacon, an' some aigs."

Mama nodded. "Good. I've got Jade preparing lint bandages. I know I can count on you for remedies for Johnny's wounds. And Cephas's ailments, whatever they be."

"I'll get ready my poultices. An' my snakeroot tea fer fever. And a mess o' other decoctions. We's gonna git Mistuh Johnny home arright, Miz Sarah. You doan worry none 'bout that."

"I shall be eternally indebted to you if you do," Mama said.

"No need," Miz Melindy replied. "We all gots our loves an' hates on this place. An' our reasons. But we all of one mind 'bout one thing. We all love Mistuh Johnny. Doan know anybody who doan."

"But first we must make supper for Rawdon," Mama reminded her. "How can I help?"

"I was just about to clean this fish," Miz Melindy said. "Isom caught this early this mornin'. But I cain't ask you to clean fish, Miz Sarah!"

"And why not?" Mama laughed, and got to work. "But first, Isom, would you fetch Mr. Bone? Tell him I must speak to him, here in the kitchen."

"Yessum."

"Be as quiet about it as you can, Isom. No soldier must see him come in here. Miz Melindy, I hope you don't mind. But I know Mr. Bone has a musket hidden away somewhere. And Caroline must have a musket with her on this trip. It isn't safe out there."

Isom left. Of a sudden Private Brandon stepped into the kitchen to take his usual chair by the door. He looked surprised at seeing Mama, but took off his hat and gave a little bow. Then he sat down.

Miz Melindy scowled and shook her head slightly, then tended to her cooking.

"Private Brandon and I have become friends, Mama," I said. Then I turned to him. "This is my mama."

He stood up.

"She's going to be cooking for Colonel Rawdon for a while. Miz Melindy and I have to go on a mission. Colonel Rawdon is sending us. You'll love the perch. Isom just caught it. Would you like your bit of it cooked with eggs?"

"Much obliged," he said. He was shy of Mama.

Quickly I beat up some eggs and scrambled them in a pan of butter, put in some fish, and sliced some bread. "Wouldn't you like to eat outside under the tree?" I handed the plate of food to him.

He looked doubtful.

"You're doing your job," I said. "Tasting the food. Aren't you?"

He nodded, took the plate, and went out just as Old Boney came in and stood there, hat in hand, and nodded to Mama. "Mornin', Miz Sarah."

He said nothing to Miz Melindy. Did they not speak? Once they had come together to have a child, my real mother. Did no one think of that now but me? Was I the only one who minded that unspeakable things had gone on in our family? How could Mama even think of bringing Old Boney in here? As far as I knew, he and Miz Melindy never spoke. Didn't Mama know that bringing certain people together was dangerous?

But within a few moments they were all sitting around the old oaken table, drinking coffee, eating eggs and biscuits, talking, planning, plotting.

How to get Johnny home, there was the nub of it. Nothing else mattered. Outside Isom engaged the private in conversation under a tree.

Yes, Mr. Bone had a musket. He would make some cartridges tonight. It was a Brown Bess, the kind the British used. He would not say how he'd come by it. "Do you know how to load a Brown Bess, Caroline?" he asked me.

I said I did. A musket was a musket, after all.

It would be hidden in the bottom of the wagon under some blankets. So would the cartridges. He'd roll them for me. I knew how to bite off the end of the paper cartridges, pour some of the powder into the pan, close the hammer, pour the rest of the powder, the musket ball, and paper wadding into the barrel and force it in with the ramrod. Johnny had taught me all that.

That very day, on the sly, Boney would fashion a false bottom in the wagon. He would select two good mules. "No horses. The British are too hungry for horses."

We would need two good buckets of water, some rum and peach brandy for Johnny and Cephas, flints, some kindling for starting a fire. Sometimes you couldn't find kindling in the sandy paths along the river.

"She should have a written pass from Rawdon," he told Mama. "Else they'll never get through the British patrols."

"I'll ask him for the pass," Mama promised. "Now you should leave, Mr. Bone. And not arouse suspicion."

He left. Not a word or a look passed between him and Miz Melindy. *Do they have any thoughts for each other now?* I wondered. *Do they even remember that together they had a child? And if they hadn't, I wouldn't be here today? How did they first meet, he and Miz Melindy? Was he handsome once? Maybe I'll ask her on our journey. We'll have to talk about something, won't we?*

Will she tell me? What else will she tell me if I ask? There is so much behind those eyes of hers. What else does she know?

And so it was that we left on the fifth of July.

MAMA WAS up at first light on the fifth, creeping about the room dressing, getting ready to go to the kitchen and make Rawdon's breakfast. She woke me holding a candle, and I dressed by its light. Georgia Ann was still sleeping. The night before I had laid out my good boots and sturdiest petticoat and shortgown. Mama gave me her straw hat to ward off the sun. I would take along a warm shawl. Mama handed me a reticule.

"Soap and flannel for washing and drying," she said. "Some of Georgia Ann's lotion for the face. Be sure you use it in the hot sun. You don't want to ruin your complexion now, do you? Go to the kitchen and have a good breakfast. I'll be along directly."

That Mama should be worried about my complexion in the midst of all that was going on made my heart feel like struck flint. I nodded wordlessly and went downstairs and outside to the brick kitchen, where Miz Melindy was already up and about, making breakfast.

We ate in silence, lingering over breakfast. In the distance I could see the morning cooking fires of the army camped on our land. It would be hot today. The coolness of morning was giving way by the time we finished eating and checking all our supplies.

I was to drive the wagon. It was agreed upon. The names of the mules were Orphelia and Jackaroo. And they were about as mismatched a set as their names suggested.

Orphelia looked young. She had a nice sheen on her coat, and she held her head high and proud.

"She's five years old," Old Boney said. "She's done sheddin' all her first teeth. She's a fast walker. No draggin' the hindquarters. Jackaroo, now, he'll hold back till she gets tired. Then he'll pick up the slack. You'll make better time if you keep on Jackaroo so's he don't make her do all the work. Tell you what, though, they ain't mean. They won't kick or bite. You just talk nice to 'em and be firm."

Old Boney knew everything there was to know about the creatures. And before we set off he spoke to them both, giving instructions about good behavior, as a father would speak to a child.

Everything was packed: a tripod for the fire, a fry pan to put on it, wooden bowls and spoons for eating, a cast-iron pot. The musket was hidden in the false bottom of the wagon, and there, too, were the cartridges in the otter-skin shot bag. Old Boney had fashioned a canvas cover over the wagon bed and tied it securely with rope.

Miz Melindy's decoctions were secured under the canvas, as were extra blankets, rope, and a small hatchet. There were small barrels of cornmeal, some apples, even hardtack, the kind Johnny took into Indian country with him. Mama had made hoecakes and corn dodgers, and filled sacks with provisions for us and the mules. Sitting up there on the front seat of the wagon next to Miz Melindy, I was frightened and proud all at the same time. The others were all standing around looking up at me—Mama, Old Boney, Isom.

"You stay in the backcountry now, out of sight," Old Boney admonished.

"I know the hidden paths," I said.

"If you hafta use it, remember, that musket has a kick. Hurt yer shoulder."

"I know."

"Here's the written pass from Rawdon." Mama handed it to me. I put it in the pocket I wore around my waist. "And here." She handed me a good pair of leather gloves. "For your hands, so you don't get blisters holding the reins."

"But they're your best gloves," I protested. "The ones Uncle Henry gave you last Christmas."

"Take them."

I took the gloves and put them on. Then I cracked the whip, and the mules started off across the stable yard. Chickens scurried out of the way, negras stopped

95

what they were about to stare at us. Did they know? I decided yes. They knew everything. A few of them mumbled good-bye and good luck to Miz Melindy. I drove on the path that led around the house, past the gardens, right to the wooden fence in front of the house. A British soldier stood there at the gate, opened it, and let us pass through. Then I heard it close behind us.

I did not look back. If I had I would only have seen our house, tall and white, with the three-tiered verandah, set against the pink morning sky like a wedding cake. I would have seen red-coated soldiers all around, guarding it as if it were a fort.

I kept my eyes on the heads of Orphelia and Jackaroo. Their ears were like a compass, leading me to Johnny. The sun was already hot.

"WHERE YOU goin'?" Miz Melindy asked.

"Through town."

"That's dangerous."

"This trip is dangerous," I told her.

"What fer you go through town?"

"I want to drive by the prison. My daddy's there."

"You won't see him."

"Want to drive by it just the same. Seeing it is like seeing him," I told her.

"Crazy chile."

Was she going to be ornery on this trip? I minded that she hadn't had much to say all morning. Did she not want to go? She had seemed flattered to be included, rushing around and stuffing her sacks with her remedies. What was wrong now?

"When was the last time you were off the plantation?" I asked her.

"Never. Not since I come here wif yer mama an' daddy."

I had never thought of her as having a life before. "Where did you come from, then?" I asked.

"You gon' be nosy an' crazy, too?"

"Well, you never told me."

"Lotsa things I never tol' you. See no reason to now."

"Well, I *am* your granddaughter."

She grunted.

"Look, all this time, working in the kitchen with you, I wanted to say it out plain. And I was waiting for you to say it out plain. But you didn't."

"Nobody say it all these years. Plain or fancy."

"That's right, Miz Melindy. But that wasn't my fault, and you know it. I was told never to speak of it, never to come and see you. It was—" My voice failed me.

"Shameful," she said. "That the word you fishin' for?"

"I don't know what word to put on it," I said. "But I don't think the word is shameful. I think shameful is what General Cornwallis did to my friend Kit, killing him and then letting him hang there for three weeks and forbidding anybody to bury him. I think shameful is what the British did to Johnny. And how they have Daddy in prison."

We rode along in silence for a while. The wagon wheels creaked. The soft plodding of the mules' hooves lulled me, as did the warm sun on my back. She sat in silence beside me. I had the feeling she was waiting for me to go on, to say something to mend the moment between us.

"Seems like I don't have the right word to put on things anymore," I said.

"Shameful do," she said. "It do before the popinjays come in their red coats. An' it do for after they leave. They give new meanin's to words, that be their fault. We gotta keep the meanin's we have."

What was she saying? But I knew. She was saying we knew right and wrong, we knew what was important to us and what wasn't, and just because the British had come and turned our world inside out, it made no never mind. We must hold fast to what we knew.

But what did we know, then, she and I? Of a sudden it became urgent that I find out. I wasn't going to make a two-day journey with her sitting right next to me on that seat and not know how she felt about me.

"So, do you think it's shameful then, Miz Melindy? That I'm your granddaughter?"

"You is set on talkin' 'bout this now, ain't you?"

"Yes."

"Why?"

"Because I'm not going to step around it anymore, like a conjure bag."

She laughed. "Only shameful thing 'bout it be what yer daddy done."

"Didn't you do the same thing with Mr. Bone?"

"Saucy chile. Nosy and crazy and saucy."

"Didn't you?"

"I ain't talkin' 'bout what yer daddy done wif yer mama. I's talkin' 'bout what else he done."

"What?"

"An' I ain't talkin' 'bout it now."

"When, then? I know you hate my daddy. I could never figure why if he did no more with your daughter than you did with Mr. Bone. What else did he do, then? Besides sell Cate off, I mean? And when will you tell me?"

"Maybe never. Maybe tonight. Cain't right tell. Depends."

"On what?"

"On how things go wif us. We gots other things to think of now. More 'portant things."

"Like what?"

"Like there be the prison you so set on seein'. So look, girl. Look wif yer eyes now an' see. An' doan stop this wagon, either. Jus' keep goin' les we 'tract attention. See all them soldiers? They be watchin' us even now."

I looked. She was right. We were in the middle of town, just having passed Mr. Murchison's tailoring shop and the shop of Mr. Castelo, the shoemaker, and Mr. Wyly's store. Across the street was our jail, which had been a modest affair until the British came. Now a stockade was built in the surrounding lot, with gateposts and guards. And they did cast an eye on us as we rambled on by.

I could not help looking, though. I had not been in town since the last week of May. And now it was not our town anymore. Oh, the few places I knew were still there, but even the familiar landmarks, the church, the Quaker meetinghouse, the saw- and grain mills, seemed deserted and brooding places.

But the jail! You could smell it, evil smells that bloomed in the morning heat. You could hear it, some kind of a low din behind the stockade fence that sounded like the clanging of tin cups, the rumble of wagons, the moanings of men, and the shouts of officers, all at the same time.

I wanted to stop the wagon. Oh, I wanted to stop. I felt a pull in me for this terrible, monstrous place, as if a rope had been thrown from its door across the street and wrapped around my heart. My daddy was in there. Every nerve and sinew in my body seemed to be pulled out of me in the direction of that jail.

"Keep goin'." I heard Miz Melindy whisper urgently. "If'n we stop, we be in trouble."

"Maybe if we stop and ask they will let me see my daddy."

"Foolish girl! Keep goin'!"

"How do we know they won't let me see him? I haven't asked."

She took the reins from me then, and the whip. Cracked it over the mules and they moved faster on down the street, out of town, past the magazine, of which Daddy had once been custodian. The British had erected a large earthworks topped with jagged, pointed fences. It was fortified with ugly cannons, barrels pointed down at us. Sentries stood on the earthworks above, with the Union Jack hanging limply in the hot morning air.

Miz Melindy was guiding the mules. She had taken charge. I pulled myself together. "Let me have the reins. I can do it."

"Then do it. Afore you get us both killed."

Through my tears I guided the mules off the road toward the gentle plateaus and forests of evergreens, the swamps that drained down to the Wateree, the gum trees that bordered them, the cane, the fringes of sycamore and oak, all familiar to me. And for the next hour we did not speak. All that could be heard was the creaking of the wagon, the slapping of the wooden water bucket tied to its side, calls of birds, and the sound of the river in the distance. Our going was slow.

ALONG ABOUT noon we met the woman. We had gone but six miles, half the distance north that would bring us past Uncle Henry's plantation, four miles past Hobkirks Hill. We weren't going to Uncle Henry's. It would be too dangerous. We'd had no word from him in weeks, and for all we knew he could be entertaining some British officers. And though we had a letter of passage from Rawdon, we wanted to attract no unneeded attention.

We were ready for some refreshment, the mules needed rest and water, and I was worried about Miz Melindy, who looked wilted. I chose a spot near a spring, let the mules have their water, and helped Miz Melindy down from the wagon. "We can rest under that sycamore," I said.

We ate and drank. The chicken first, because it would spoil soon. Mama's lemon tea, which was still cold. Above us were some sandy plateaus and a gathering of evergreens.

"I smell corn cooking," I said of a sudden.

Miz Melindy sniffed and nodded. "We gots company." She raised her head in the direction of the evergreens. "Up there."

"I'll go see." I stood up, but she put a hand on my arm.

"Mebbe British."

"I'll get the musket."

"No musket. That letter you gots from the popinjay be your musket. Go up there wif a musket and they know fer sure you trouble."

She was right, as usual. I felt for the parchment in the pocket I wore around my waist and climbed the dune to the top. At first I could see nothing for the stately longleaf pines. Then I caught sight of the woman. She was a bit in the distance, hovering over a small fire built in the sandy soil. Around her huddled four small children. For a moment I watched her as she bent to her task. I soon perceived that she was not only cooking some corn, she was grating some on a rough stone and making a coarse meal of it.

The children all seemed to be under the age of ten. The oldest, a boy, saw me first and pointed. The woman looked up and for a moment, with less than a room's length between us, we just stared. Then she stood up. I could see that her dress and apron were torn and smudged, her hair in disarray. She had lost her cap. Her eyes looked as if she hadn't slept in a fortnight.

"Who are you?" Her voice trembled.

"I mean you no harm. My name is Caroline Whitaker. I'm from Camden."

"Who's with you?"

My first thought was to lie, to say "my trusted aged servant." But something in this woman's face, some truth or sorrow, or both, come together in a way I'd never seen truth and sorrow come together before, made me know that lying now would be blasphemy. This was not the time nor the place for lying. Certainly, the time was past. There had been too much lying, about everything, in my life anyway.

"My grandmother," I said. "We're headed north a bit to fetch my brother, who's been wounded."

"Patriot or king's people?"

"Patriot," I said. And no sooner had the words passed my lips than I minded that I had finally said it. Another truth. No more lying to myself about that, either. Here in the isolated windswept plateaus off the Wateree, I'd said it, with the stately longleaf pines and this bedraggled woman and her four towheaded children as my witnesses. As good a place as any, I figured.

"Patriot," I said again, as if to savor the taste of it on my tongue.

"Were you burned out then, too? By Huck?"

"Who?"

"Captain Christian Huck. And he should burn in hell for having such a first name. For he is anything but. Sent out of Rocky Mount with a force of four hundred. He's laying waste to the countryside. Started with our log meetinghouse. I'm Mrs. Martin, wife of Reverend Martin. Sunday last my husband spirited up his congregation. Spoke of princes trampling people's rights. He dwelt on the butchery of Buford's men at Waxhaws and admonished the congregation to go see the tender mercies of Great Britain in the church at Waxhaws, where the wounded lie without arms or legs. He even cited the law of Moses. So many men left to join Sumter as a result that when Huck and his men came through this morning, they turned us out of our house, drove off our stock, burned the meetinghouse, stripped us of everything. You can still smell the smoke. Our home was about five miles inland. We fled to the orchard and watched them burn the house. Then we made our way here. It's far enough away if they come back and close enough to home if they don't. Can't go back yet, though. Have to wait a spell. We'll spend the night here. But all I have to eat is roasted green corn. I've managed to make some of it into a meal of mush."

"Where is your husband?"

"Gone to join Sumter."

"Why is Huck doing this now?" More to the point, why hadn't we heard of it at home? Why hadn't Rawdon heard of it? Was his intelligence that bad?

"Don't you know?"

I shook my head no.

She pushed some hair off her forehead. "Sumter's forces finally came out of hiding and camped along the Catawba, making their presence known."

"When?"

"Yesterday. On the fourth."

"Why?"

"I suspect they think it's now time. Anniversary of the declaration against the king, yesterday. I heard Huck is out to break the resistance of anyone on the Patriot side. They were talking, at our place, of burning down the ironworks that was turning out weapons for the Patriots. I suspect that's where they went when they left us yesterday."

Her face was burnt from the sun. Crazily, I thought of Mama's admonition to use Georgia Ann's lotion on my face. Perhaps I could offer this woman some. And then I looked at the hungry, drawn faces of the children. Their arms were full of scratch bites.

Lotion for the face? Food was what they needed. Real food, not mush made from dried corn.

"You can't spend the night here," I said.

"We'll manage."

"Why don't you and the little ones come down the dunes and sit with us a spell? We have food. And Miz Melindy, my grandmother, has remedies."

She hesitated. "I wouldn't want to go putting you out."

I stepped forward. "You all come along with me now," I said kindly. "And we'll see how we can help."

Chapter Eight

JULY 5, 1780

I FELT GOOD LEADING them down the sandy dune to where we had set up our noon meal. The act of turning from that place where Mrs. Martin had gathered her small family after being burned out of her own home for being a Patriot was in itself a turning in my life. No more would I deny, to anyone, that Miz Melindy was my grandmother. No more would I shilly-shally over which side I chose to come down on in this war.

I brought them to Miz Melindy. "This is my grand-mother," I said. I saw the slight widening of Mrs. Martin's eyes, but that was all. She made no comment, just sat as Miz Melindy directed. *Poor thing*, I thought. *After what she's just been through, seeing a negra woman as grandmother to a white girl is nothing.*

We fed them. There was cold chicken in great plenty. Miz Melindy brought out the corn dodgers and some apples. They ate. The children were famished. I explained Mrs. Martin's situation to Miz Melindy, who nodded quietly, surprised at nothing herself.

"My grandmother can put some salve on the children's bites," I offered after we finished our repast. "And I have some lotion I can give you for your face."

She agreed. So Miz Melindy took the children to the stream, washed them, and applied her remedies. I dug out Georgia Ann's lotion and showed Mrs. Martin how to apply it to her face.

"You are too kind," she said.

"What will you do now?"

"Go back up there." She indicated to the place in the trees above us. "And try to figure out what to do."

"You can't stay here the night."

"I'll keep the fire going."

"And what of tomorrow?"

"I'll wait here until my husband returns. In a day or so I'll venture back home and see if he's there."

"And if he doesn't return?"

She did not answer, at first, and then she did. "God is good," she said. "He'll be back. He said he would."

I mulled the matter for a moment. Before Cornwallis came, I would have believed it in my heart, too. But there was something in my heart that stood in the way of believing anything much anymore. Kit's body still hung there inside me, twisting in the wind.

"Look," I said, "why don't you come on a ways with us?"

She looked frightened. "Where?"

"Well, I know somebody who could help you, until your husband comes back. Maybe provision you. Give you the loan of a wagon and horse at least. And tell you where there is a house that is safe, where there are Patriots."

"Who is this somebody?"

"My uncle, Henry Rugeley. He lives six miles north. His place is at the fork of Flat Rock and Grannys Quarter Creek. I'm traveling the hidden paths. But I can lead you close to his plantation."

"This is a big plantation?"

"Yes, he's very wealthy. He's my mother's brother."

"If he's so wealthy, why haven't the British done him harm?"

I hesitated for only a moment. "Because he's a Tory, the leading Tory in these parts."

"You want to send me to the house of a Tory for help?" Now her fear became something I could feel, something in the air between us, something real, like smoke from a fire.

"That isn't the way of it," I said.

"What is the way of it then? You see me and my children. Refugees, no place to lay our heads because of the British. And you would send us to the house of a Tory? I hate Tories. I am a reverend's wife, a good Christian woman, but God forgive me, I would kill every Tory with my own hands if I could."

She was shaking. Tears were in her eyes. I moved closer. "Uncle Henry is a man of good parts." I told her then what he had done for the governor and his aides when they were fleeing north. While I was doing the telling she remained silent, white-faced, and during this time Miz Melindy came back from the spring with her children. They saw their mother's distress, and she opened her arms and enfolded them.

"I promise you that my uncle Henry will help you," I finished.

She sat with the children all around her. "Why should I believe you?" she said. "You lied to me once already."

"Lied?" I was stricken.

"Yes. You said this woman is your grandmother. How can she be your grandmother? She's negra, you're white."

"She is my grandmother, I tell no lie," I said. Then I looked at Miz Melindy. "Who else would she be? Why would I say such if it were not true?"

"How do I know? Mayhap you're under the flag of the British, spying. Mayhap you're delivering her to the British. They take all the negras they can get hold of."

Miz Melindy spoke then. "Ask her 'bout her friend," she said, "if'n you think she be wif the popinjay British. Ask her 'bout what they did to her friend."

The woman waited. Quietly, I told her about Kit Gales. The children stared at me out of opaque blue eyes in which I could see that innocence had drowned, but nothing else had surfaced yet to take its place.

"Now," Miz Melindy asked when I finished my tale, "now ask her where her daddy be."

"Where?" Mrs. Martin asked.

"In jail in Camden. Since the day Cornwallis came," I said.

She heaved a great sigh and nodded. "Please forgive me for not trusting you, but I have been through so much these past few days."

"It's all right," I told her.

Not much more was said. We assembled the leftover food and put it away. Nobody spoke, but she handed the children over to me and I set them all in the back of the wagon. "Do you want to ride?" I asked. "It's about six more miles."

She said no, she would walk. And so we proceeded north, staying in the quiet hidden places and not venturing out under the open sky, until Uncle Henry's place came into view.

"There it is," I said. "There's Clermont, Uncle Henry's plantation."

We were hidden in the pine woods by Grannys Quarter Creek. But we had a good view of the place, the large log barn, the neat outbuildings, pastureland, the acres of corn, the orchards of peach and apple trees, the lush foliage half shielding the elegant house.

"Look at that," Mrs. Martin whispered. "It bespeaks him a tolerable good-liver."

"Yes, he is," I agreed. But I was looking for something else: signs of visiting British. I reminded myself that Uncle Henry held office under the king. But I saw no signs of British. "There are no horses about. Which means there are no British on the place," I told her.

"Doesn't he have horses?" Mrs. Martin asked.

"Yes, but he keeps them hidden. He may be a Tory, but he isn't going to leave his horses about for the British soldiers to steal."

We stood looking at the place for a moment or so, thinking our own thoughts. I thought of how often we'd come here for visits, my family and I, how I'd run about in the barnyard with Georgia Ann and Johnny, how Uncle Henry would give Mama cuttings from his garden, how, as I got older, I'd wandered about in his wonderful library inside.

Mrs. Martin got tears in her eyes again, looking. I minded that she was likely thinking of her own place, now in ruins.

"We're behind schedule," I said, "so we'll just go on. If he isn't home, his servants will help you. But they'll need a note from me. Only, I didn't bring pen or paper. I must give you something." I looked around in the wagon, about my person, trying to find something that would identify me to Uncle Henry or his servants if she brought it down to the house.

"I know!" And I grabbed the gloves Mama had given me. They were on the wagon seat. "Just show him these. He gave them to my mother as a gift last Christmas."

She took the soft leather gloves, fondled them in her hands. "I don't know," she said. "I don't know if I should do this."

"You said you believed me. You said you were sorry for not believing me."

"I know. I do believe and trust you. About everything. You've done me a good turn, and I am beholden to you both." She included Miz Melindy in her gaze. "But still, he's a Tory. He may have changed in his outlook since you last saw him."

"He's a Southern gentleman," I said. "They don't

change. He is known for his benevolence and hospitality."

She nodded and sighed and gathered the children around her. Then she smiled at me weakly and led them down the path out of the forest of evergreen.

The last I saw her and the children, they were walking toward Uncle Henry's house. Would she go through with it? Would she walk through the open pastureland and into the barnyard? Or would she, the minute I turned away with the wagon, run back to where they'd come from?

I didn't stay to see the matter through. I climbed back up on the wagon seat and turned the mules' heads and went on with my journey, never once looking back.

Chapter Nine

JULY 5, 1780

WE WENT ON for two more hours. We'd wasted a lot of time with Mrs. Martin and her children, and I couldn't get shut of the nagging doubt that she really hadn't taken them to Uncle Henry, that she'd turned and fled. Well, I couldn't worry the matter. We had our own concerns.

The sun was lower in the horizon across the Wateree River when we stopped. I figured we'd gone about fifteen miles this day. I jumped down from the wagon seat and looked around. To the left of me was the river, with its usual sandy shores, behind it the tangled undergrowth and pines, silent and foreboding. We ourselves were on a sandy path in a thicket of overgrown vines and interlocking trees. I wished I could run down to the river. I wished I could wade right in. The waters ran low and were capped with white in several places. And then I sighted a boulder the size of a small pony on a rise a short distance above us.

"I think I know this place," I told Miz Melindy. "I think I came fishing here with Johnny once. And if I'm right, there should be a little stream a bit yonder." I pointed through the trees. "I'll go see. And I'll take a bucket and fetch some water for the mules."

"Hep me down," she said.

I did so. She took off her straw hat and wiped her face with a kerchief.

"Never mind 'bout me. This time you best take the musket. Doan know but what you might run into civilians. Sometimes they be worse than soldiers."

I led her to the shelter of the boulder, fetched the musket and bucket, and set off. Within several minutes I found the south-running stream. I set down my musket, took off my shoes and hose, and waded in. The bottom was sandy, and the water felt so good on my feet and ankles. I was tempted to take off my petticoat and chemise and slip in. I wagered that in the middle of the stream the water would be up to my waist. But I had Miz Melindy to worry about. And the mules, who were waiting to be unharnessed for the night and fed and watered. So I filled my bucket, put my hose and shoes back on, and started back.

I left the musket. I'd have to come back for more water for us.

Before I even cleared the thicket of vines and trees, I heard voices. I set the bucket down and peered through the trees.

A woman stood over Miz Melindy, holding a musket. I heard Miz Melindy's voice, low and rambling. The woman was looking around. The musket was pointed right at Miz Melindy!

I didn't think. What I should have done was run back for my own musket. But instead I ran down the slope. "Don't! You leave her be!"

Now the musket was pointed at me.

"Stand where you are. Stand fast."

I stood, thinking bleakly that I should never have left my musket. And then I stood thinking, numbly, how it was the second time this day I'd been so confronted by a woman in the wilderness. And in both instances I'd felt the intruder.

"Come on down here, slowly."

I obeyed, walked toward them. Miz Melindy had struggled to her feet and was leaning next to the boulder. She was tired and, of a sudden, looked smaller and older than I'd yet perceived her to be.

The woman with the musket was tall and angular, and the first thing I noticed was that the right side of her face was red and swollen. The second thing was that she was well dressed but plain. Her face was not burnt from the sun. And she appeared to know, very much, where and who she was.

"Who are you?" she demanded.

"Caroline Whitaker from Camden."

"And what cause do you embrace, Caroline Whitaker of Camden? The king or those he tramples beneath his boots?"

"Those he tramples. My father is the leading rebel in Camden. Haven't you ever heard of John Whitaker?"

"Everyone has. By what lunacy does he allow his daughter to go roaming about when the British are laying waste to the countryside?"

"My father is in prison. Put there by Cornwallis."

She took my measure with cold gray eyes. I could see at once that she did not believe me. I went on to explain our mission, how we were on our way to bring my brother home.

"By whose leave?"

I just stared at her.

"No one just roams the countryside these days without someone's leave. Do you have written permission from someone?"

I knew I was trapped then. But there was naught I could do about it. "Rawdon," I said. "Colonel Rawdon, who occupies our house." I drew the letter out of my pocket and gave it to her.

She read it. "It says here your brother is a Loyalist and was in the fighting at Charleston."

"Yes." I could not betray Johnny. Not even to save myself.

She handed the letter back to me. "You're going to fetch home your Loyalist brother, and I should trust you?" She glanced suspiciously at Miz Melindy then. "Is she the best Rawdon could send to accompany you?"

"She knows the art of physick," I said. "My brother is very sick. And she's my grandmother." The last part was said in defiance. Let her think what she would. She wasn't about to believe me no matter what.

She didn't. "Come along with me, both of you."

Miz Melindy started toward the wagon.

"Where?" I demanded.

"To my place. It's about an hour east of here."

"For what?"

She glared at me. "Look, I don't know what kind of claptrap you're giving me. But listen, and listen well. I haven't time to bandy about with you. We were an hour ago visited by Huck and his men. My son and son-in-law were just returned from Sumter's camp and were employed in melting my pewter dishes for the purpose of making musket balls. My good pewter dishes, do you hear me?"

"Yes, ma'am," I said.

"Huck's men were on us before we were aware of it. They seized my son and son-in-law, discovered the musket balls in their pockets, said that they had murderous designs against the king's men. Tied them with ropes and pronounced immediate sentence. They are to be hanged at sunrise on the morning of the twelfth. A group of redcoats took them off. Then Huck himself searched my house and threw our family Bible into the fire because he said it was from such a book that we have become damned rebels. I fetched it from the fire and for my trouble, he struck me with his sword across my face. Well, that was a dear blow, and he shall soon pay for it. Now come along, I say!"

I helped Miz Melindy into the wagon. I put the bucket of water in because the mules needed it. At first I thought to ask to be allowed to go back and fetch my musket, then decided against it. If she let us go, I'd come back and fetch it, I thought.

"Are we your prisoners?" I asked.

"Until tomorrow morning," she said. She walked beside the wagon, leading us along a path I hadn't noticed before. It went through a part of the woods that was less dense and looked frequently traveled.

She never wavered with that musket, either. Kept it on us the whole time.

In an hour we came to her place. It was a lovely small plantation, well kept, and with the fields and orchards in the full growth of the season. But it seemed deserted. The windows of the two-story house were all open, but no activity came from inside.

"Mary!" she called out.

For a moment there was no answer. Then the barn door opened and a girl came dashing out on a sorrel mare. She looked to be about Georgia Ann's age, but that was where any similarity ended. She wore a man's tricorn on her head, and a long red braid hung down her back. Her simple linen petticoat looked as if it had been dyed with tea. It was hiked up as she rode astride. She wore men's boots and a weskit over her chemise. A musket was tied onto the mare. Her face was full of freckles. "Who are they, Mother?" she asked. The horse pranced a bit, yearning to be off, but she controlled it well.

"Don't know. Found 'em down by the river, just as you thought, Mary. Claim to be rebels, but I think they're telling me a pack of lies. I'm holding them until you get a good head start. Likely overnight."

"Where?" Mary asked.

"In the corncrib. You'd best be on your way."

"Will you be all right, Mother? Your face!"

"I'll be all right."

"You'd best put some ice on it." And with that the girl rode off, raising dust in the barnyard. How I envied her, the way she galloped off on that horse. She rode well. How long had it been since I'd been able to ride like that?

The woman looked at us. "My name's McClure," she said. "My husband and his men made a stand at the ironworks of Colonel Hill but were outnumbered. The enemy destroyed the works. I'm sorry, but you'll both have to stay in the corncrib for the night. My daughter is off to carry the news of what's happened here to Sumter's camp. I have a husband and two other sons there." She led us to the corncrib. It was empty except for some old stalks.

I surveyed it dismally. "I know you don't believe my story," I told her, "but my brother lies wounded up north. He's waiting for us to come and fetch him home."

"You were going to stay the night where I found you," she said, "so you'll just spend it here, is all. In the morning you can be on your way. Go on, in with you, both of you."

"I can't expect Miz Melindy to sleep in there," I argued. "She's an old lady. Can't you see how old she is?"

"It's arright, chile," Miz Melindy said. "Come, we'll fetch blankets from the wagon. I could give you somethin' fer that face, Miz McClure."

"No, thank you. I'll be fine."

We fetched blankets, water, a sack of food, and Miz Melindy's pouch with her remedies into the corncrib. Then, while Mrs. McClure still had that musket fixed on us, I fed and watered and unhitched the mules. Then we got into the corncrib.

She locked it securely. "I'll send my servant out with supper," she promised.

"We have supper," I said. I knew it was ungracious. I knew I was being what Mama would call boldly vigorous. But I didn't care. I arranged the blankets over the dried cornstalks, making a sort of bed. I was worried about Miz Melindy.

But I needn't have been. She settled right in. Out of the food basket she took what remained of the corn dodgers. "Chicken spoilt by now," she said. "Best we eat the hardtack."

"I don't want anything."

"Best you eat anyways. You weren't so fool stubborn we coulda had a hot supper."

"Don't want any of her supper. I'd rather starve."

"Eat your pride, maybe," she said.

"You hush!" I warned.

"Woman's only doin' what she's gotta do. Makin' sure her own doan get hung. You should know what that means. Wouldn't you o' done the same to save yer friend?"

She was right, of course, but I didn't care. "Mind your tongue about Kit," I told her. "There was nothing I could do to save him."

"Didn't say there was."

"Well, mind your tongue anyway."

She looked at me out of bleary eyes. "Where's the musket?"

"Back at the spring. I left it there."

"Why for you leave it?"

"Because I was intending to go right back. And because I was carrying a bucket of water for the mules, that's why for."

"If'n you brung it, 'stead of leavin' it there, we wouldn't be in this mess now, smart girl." She took a bit of corn dodger. "Smart girl wif pride. I brung some salt. Want some salt on yer pride?"

"Mind your tongue!"

"You doan tell me to mind my tongue. I say what I please."

"You're a servant," I snapped at her. "And if you don't mind, when we get back home I'll have you punished!"

She slapped me then. It was so fast that I didn't know what happened. She scarce moved but reached out with her old withered hand, like a snake, and slapped my cheek.

I blinked, reeled. My face stung. My mouth fell open.

"I be a servant," she said. "But I be yer grandmother."

The hopelessness of my situation came over me then like a downpour of cold rain. Here I was, in a corncrib on some rebel woman's plantation, a prisoner with a negra woman who was my grandmother, with cold corn dodgers and hardtack to eat, far from home. I wanted my mother. I wanted my daddy, whom I might never see again. I was tired and hurt sore. My hands had blisters from holding the reins without gloves. My arms ached. So did my head. I wanted my own bed, even if it was in that upstairs chamber, with Rawdon and his officers playing cards below. I wanted to be home.

I commenced crying. It was the only thing to do. I cried so that my whole body shook with the effort. Then, of a sudden, I was enveloped in Miz Melindy's arms, bawling my heart out against her thin bosom, while she held me and stroked my tangled hair. "You jus' like yer mama, you know that?"

I sniffed. "Which one?"

"Yer real mama. Head like a rock. Would never listen. It's what brung her to ruin. Wouldn't listen to me no way. Got herself smitten wif yer daddy. I tol' her an' tol' her, he only gonna dally wif you. What will come of it? But she doan listen nohow. You gonna regret it the rest of yer life, I tol' her. To yer dyin' day. And I know she still do."

Through the top of the corncrib I'd been watching the stars as I leaned against Miz Melindy. And then it was as if those stars burst into a million pieces.

I pulled back from her and wiped my nose with the sleeve of my shortgown. "What do you mean, you know she still do?"

She gave no reply.

"She's dead. How can she still regret it? She *is* dead, isn't she?"

The look in her eyes told me before she did. I think she would have sat there all turned in on herself, mouth a grim slash, and never told me. Not even if I beat it out of her. But the look in her eyes had already done it.

"She isn't dead, is she?" I leaned forward. I gripped her shoulders. "You must tell me, Miz Melindy. Please tell me. Where is she?"

She shook her head slowly. "No profit in it, chile."

"Yes! There is profit in it! Tell me! Why isn't she dead? They all said she was! But now I know. I suppose I've always known. Something inside me always knew that what they told me were lies. I just never wanted to face it. But here, now, in this Godforsaken place, I want to face it. I want to know. *Where is my mother?*"

"You cain't tell 'em I tol' you."

"No, I won't."

"You promise now. Or they sell Miz Melindy off. An' then you have nobody to tell you nothin' 'bout yer mama, ever again."

"I promise. Tell me."

So she did. "Sold," she said.

"Sold? Where?"

"Some man come one day. Right before you was brought to the big house to live. Yer daddy sell her to this man."

"Where did he take her?"

"I hears things. But I doan know if'n they be true."

"Tell me."

"The West Indies."

"The West Indies? Why?"

She shrugged. I saw tears in her eyes. Then she put her hands over those eyes and wept. Quietly, she wept. The only way I knew she was crying was by seeing her shoulders shake.

I sat there for a while not knowing what to do. Overhead the stars were just the stars again. From somewhere in the distance a hooty owl called. Then another nightbird. I heard a horse whinny in the barn, saw candles in the house windows. The world was falling back into place, starting to make sense to me.

My daddy had sold my real mother. Of course! That was why Miz Melindy hated him so! He'd sold not only her sister Cate, but my *real* mother, with the slender hands and the pert little nose. Light-skinned. The daughter of Miz Melindy and Old Boney. And there was the reason Old Boney held a grudge against Daddy. There was the thing between them that I could never get a purchase on.

I spoke. My voice was hoarse at first. "Georgia Ann told me that Mama and Daddy arrived at some kind of an understanding when I was brought to live in the house," I said. "Was that it? That I would be brought to live with the family only if my real mother was sold?"

She nodded yes.

"But who made the demand? Was it Mama Sarah?"

"I doan know how they come to it, chile. I doan know."

I leaned back against the corncrib and stared up at the stars again. My real mother still alive. I couldn't absorb it. It would take time. Alive somewhere in the West Indies. Would I ever get used to it? How could I? "I feel betrayed by all of them," I said. "My whole family. Even Johnny."

She took her hands away from her face. She wiped

her face with her apron. "Onliness one who betray you was yer mama," she said.

"Mama Sarah?"

She shook her head. "Yer real mama. By doin' what she done. I gots no love fer yer daddy, but yer mama knew what she was about wif him. She knew the chance she was takin'. After you was wif me for a while, when Johnny an' Georgia Ann made you their playmate an' brung you up to the house, after they saw what a beautiful chile you were, what could yer daddy do? Leave you in the quarters? A white chile? Make you a slave?"

I pondered that, tried to picture it. I couldn't. What would have become of me? Would I have been a servant for Georgia Ann? Johnny? Georgia Ann would have allowed it, but not Johnny. Never Johnny.

Still, if the price for my being part of the family was that my mother was sold off, how could I abide it?

"What do they do in the West Indies?" I asked Miz Melindy. "Slaves. What do they do?"

"Sugar plantations," she said. And when I pushed her that was all she would say, so I knew it was bad. "It's hot, isn't it?" I asked. "Hotter than here in South Carolina."

She did not answer, but her eyes did. I shuddered and was about to say something else when someone came walking across the barnyard with a lantern in hand. A negra servant from the house. She had a tray of food. I could smell it. It was soup.

"I gotta open this door," she said, "and give you

these vittles. But you gotta promise you ain't gonna git away. Or I be in trouble."

"Trouble we gots enough of," Miz Melindy said. "All we wants to do now is sleep."

So the door was opened, the tray handed through. There were wooden spoons and bowls, and Miz Melindy set the whole business down on the floor between us and spooned the soup out of a large tureen into the bowls. The door was latched again, and the servant disappeared.

It was some kind of stew. I don't know what, but never did anything taste so good to me. And after we ate, we set the tray in a corner and made up our makeshift beds. But I could not sleep.

Thoughts swirled in my head. *My mother is alive somewhere, this very moment, perhaps looking up at the same stars.* How could that be? I didn't know how anything could be, lying there. I loved my daddy, but he'd sold her off. How did I feel about him now? Was it wrong to still love him? What about Mama Sarah? Had it been done at her bidding? And if so, how could I go home and face her, live with her again in that house?

But what if Mama hadn't been sold off, if she'd been kept on the place and I in the quarters with her?

I heard Miz Melindy scuffling about. Then I felt a hand on my shoulder. "Put this on yer tongue," she said.

"What is it?"

"A leaf. Hep you sleep. Open yer mouth."

I did so. Felt her set something on my tongue. It was bitter tasting.

"It will melt afore you knows it," she said. "Lie back an' afore you knows it you feel nothin'."

I lay back and waited. All around me were night sounds. Cicadas, frogs from the distance croaking, the hooty owl again, and the rustling of a slight breeze in the trees. I smelled the farm smells, just like home. Tears came to my eyes, and I thought my heart would burst inside me. Home. Would I ever be there again? Did I want to be?

And then, in the next instant, I felt Miz Melindy's nothing.

Chapter Ten

JULY 6, 1780

I SLEPT THE NIGHT, dreamless, and when I woke the sun was shining. For a moment I couldn't place things. Something, something was terribly wrong. What? Oh yes, Kit had been killed by the British. I awoke every morning with that pall over me. But no, there was more. What? Oh yes, my mother was still alive, and a slave in the West Indies.

I sat up. The world was the same. It hadn't tilted, the sun still came up, the birds still sang. I saw Mrs. McClure and her servant doing the chores in the barnyard. A tray of breakfast rested on the ground outside the corncrib. Miz Melindy was already up.

"How cruel," I said. "I'm about starved. And they lock us in and leave the breakfast there?"

"Why don't you try the door?" Mrs. McClure called from where she was flinging food to the chickens.

I did. It was open. I got out and stood up, stretched,

and groaned. My back hurt. The cornstalks made a poor bed.

"There's the well for washing," Mrs. McClure said, still throwing the feed around. "And the necessary is over yonder."

I helped Miz Melindy out and found a place for her under a nearby tree.

"My bones ain't woke yet," she said.

"Do you need to use the necessary?"

"I needs to eat."

She did have an appetite. I fetched the food and it was a fair amount and past middling. It was very good. Eggs all mixed up with bacon and some kind of greens thrown in. Bread and fresh-churned butter. Tea. All the while we ate I watched Mrs. McClure and her servant doing the morning chores. And every time my mind took a new turn, the fact of my still-alive slave mother was there, hanging inside me, getting in the way of things. Replacing Kit's hanging body.

Well, I'd learned to live with that. Somehow I'd just have to learn to live with this, was all. Taste the bitterness of it on my tongue, like Miz Melindy's leaf that finally put me to sleep last night. Get used to it till it became numb, a part of me.

When we were finished, I helped Miz Melindy to the necessary, then went in myself. Afterward, I washed at the well, where there was soap and flannel for drying. I sponged myself good. Then I drew a fresh bucket and gave it to the mules.

I'll just act natural, I thought. *And hitch them up,*

and see what happens. She's gone into the house. Maybe that means we can leave now. But then, just as Miz Melindy was setting her sack of remedies in the wagon, the back door of the house opened and Mrs. McClure came out with a sack in her hand.

I saw that the puffiness had gone down from her face, but it was fast turning blue. I stood to the side of Orphelia's head and she stood across from me, at the side of Jackaroo's. Warily, we regarded each other.

"You look different this morning," she said.

I lifted my chin. "Oh?"

"Older. Last night I thought you but a child. You're too young for the morning's light to be cruel, but you look older than I imagined."

I am, I thought. *A hundred years older.* Then I minded that I must watch this woman. She saw things plain.

For a moment she patted Jackaroo's nose and looked about. "The season of harvest is fast approaching," she said wistfully. "Wives and widows will have to cut and gather in the corn, grain, and flax."

I said nothing.

"And there are a fearful lot of widows around these days. In just the last few weeks we've five newly made. Mrs. Anderson, Mrs. Land, Mrs. Boyd, Mrs. James Barber, and Mrs. Joseph Barber. Joseph was taken in a skirmish and carried to Camden jail, where he died. Likely of starvation."

"I told you that's where my daddy is," I said.

She looked at me. "I'm sorry I had to lock you up.

But I had to give my daughter the chance to reach Sumter's camp so my men will be rescued."

"I wouldn't have stopped her."

"How could I believe you when you lied to me so?"

"Lied? I told you the truth about everything. I even gave you Rawdon's letter that said my brother was a Loyalist."

She glanced at Miz Melindy, who'd gone back to the corncrib to fetch a blanket. "That's not what worried me. A brother is still a brother, even a wounded Loyalist. It's the other lie you told, about her being your grandmother."

"She *is* my grandmother."

She pondered that for a moment, then lifted the sack and put it into the wagon bed. "Well, that may or may not be, but I wouldn't go bandying it about if you expect people to take you at your word."

"Well, it's the truth."

"Sometimes the truth is best not spoken."

"It's been lied about long enough. I'll not lie any longer."

Her mouth twisted in a wry smile. "Not even to keep yourself from a night as prisoner in a corncrib?"

"Not even for that," I said.

She sighed. "If you're telling me the truth, you're a fool for principle. The trick is to know when to stand by it and when to leave it be. Stand by it foolishly and you'll have lean times and no friends. Abandon it foolishly and you'll have great plenty and friends, but you'll hate yourself for life."

"And what did you do when you fetched that Bible from the fire?"

She put her hand to her face. "I haven't decided that yet." She turned away. "I've provisioned you." It was all she would say to me.

I helped Miz Melindy into the wagon, clucked to the mules, and we started off. Once, I turned to see Mrs. McClure watching us, shading her eyes from the morning sun.

"What did she give us?" Miz Melindy asked.

"I didn't look in the sack," I said.

"Seemed a nice-enough person. Doan know why she acted so ornery last night."

"It was the letter from Rawdon," I said, "and I couldn't tell her Johnny is in hiding from the British. I don't want that bandied about, in even the most innocent way."

"Sad," Miz Melindy said.

"What?"

"People all look like each other, all talk the same, all farm the same. Sometimes all fightin' fer the same cause. An' nobody kin trust nobody, no matter what."

I FETCHED my musket, which still lay by the spring, and we continued north, staying a good distance from the river. At first the effort of guiding the mules through the woods took all my attention. And my hands hurt, for they had blisters. We had to stop after about an hour so Miz Melindy could put salve on them and wrap the blisters in lint. We'd lost two hours going to the McClures'.

"Where did you learn to do all this?" I asked as she was wrapping my hands.

"From my mama."

My eyes opened wide. "I never knew you had a mama."

"Everybody do. She knew 'bout curin' an' herbs back home. An' learn more when she come here."

"When did she come here?" I asked. And then, before she could reply, "When did you come here?"

"I didn't come. I was brung."

"You mean by the slavers?"

"That's what I means."

"When?"

" 'Bout forty years ago."

"In seventeen-forty? How old were you?"

" 'Bout twenty. I was brung wif my mama and sister Cate."

"From where?"

"Why you gots to know all this now?"

"I just do. Where did you come from?"

"Angola. Round the mouth o' the Congo River."

"And when you got here, what happened?"

"Come to Charleston. Was bought there by your gran'daddy. Me an' my mama an' Cate. One reason was, we was likely."

"Likely?"

"That's right. Some slaves come offa the ship, they play at bein' unlikely. Mean. Stupid. No-count. Me an' my mama an' sister be likely. An' we make no bones 'bout the fact that we know cures. Yer gran'daddy, he like that. Special' since he say they gots the sickly season here in the summer."

"Where did my granddaddy take you all?"

"To his place on the Cooper River. Rice plantation wif a nice house. That's where I first meet Mr. Bone."

I had never thought of either Miz Melindy or Mr. Bone living anywhere but on our plantation in Camden. But, of course, my daddy hadn't come to Camden until '64. "Did you love Mr. Bone?" I asked.

She had finished securing the lint on my hands. "My, we is curious today, ain't we?"

"Can't you tell me that? Did you love him?"

"I kin tell you that you better git these mules goin' or we never gon' reach Johnny this night."

I started the mules off. I knew better than to push her. So I waited, and soon she commenced to speak again.

"When a woman is brung over on a ship like that, she cain't bear no chile fer a while," she said.

I stared at her. "Why?"

"That journey be so bad it do things to a woman. You wanna die, hope you die. That journey kill everythin' inside a woman that have to do wif makin' a new life. Some cain't have a chile fer three or four years after. So I doan want to do wif no man. Mr. Bone, he was in charge of yer gran'daddy's plantation. He be good to me. I worked the rice fields. My mama was in the plantation house. Cookin'. There be no mens to wed. Only the ones I work wif."

"What was wrong with them?"

"Where I come from in Angola, you doan wed inside

134

the tribe. The tribe all like brothers an' sisters. Bad to wed in the tribe."

"So you mean that all the men you knew had been in your tribe in Angola?"

"No. But bein' so close, they become your tribe. So I doan take up wif no man. Five years go by. I doan take up wif no man. Then I take up wif Mr. Bone."

"Because you had no man to wed outside the tribe?"

She shook her head and sighed. "Jus' 'cause," she said. "An' that ain't no reason. Yer mama get born. Yer gran'daddy know it ain't right I gots a chile an' no husband. So to please him I jumps the broom."

I knew that was an expression negras had for marrying. "Who?"

"Doan matter who. A good man from the plantation. I knows I shouldn't of wed him. Against the rules, but I did it to please yer gran'daddy. Soon my husband die, an' the chile I have wif him die, too. Time goes by. Yer daddy grows up an' weds yer mama. Has Johnny. Miz Sarah, she lose a lotta babies along the way. Then they have Georgia Ann. My mama dies. But she been bringin' me along an' teachin' me to cook. Time goes right by the front door every day, like the Cooper River. Then one day yer daddy buys the place in Camden an' we all move there. My Cecie is growin' up to be a purty woman. I wants her to jump the broom wif a man in Charleston an' stay. But yer daddy, he say no, she gotta come along wif us." Another long sigh. "Cecie an' Cate come along wif us. Yer mama in the family way again an' sickly. An' that be it."

"What about Cephas and Isom? Mr. Bone isn't their father."

She went quiet for so long I thought she had stopped talking. But she hadn't. " 'Bout five years after yer daddy wed, even before he move us to Camden, he decided I need a new husband. So he buys me one."

"My daddy bought you a husband?"

"Tha's what I said."

"And what happened to him?"

She shrugged. "He learns trade in the warehouse in Charleston. When we all move to Camden he asks yer daddy to let him be licensed to trade wif the Cherokees. Yer daddy, bein' in the mercantile business, thinks this is a good idea. But my husband gets a Cherokee chief drunk an' they kill him."

"So you were left with three children and still no husband."

"An' I never wanted no more," she said.

"But how did you make it through with all the sorrow you had?"

She laughed. "You jus' make it, is all. You set yerself to the task. You take a turn an' set yer heart to look in other ways. Lookee there."

"Where?" I looked in the direction in which she pointed. What I saw was a farmhouse. We had, in all my listening to Miz Melindy, come upon a road and the mules had simply directed their course on it.

"Listen." She put a hand on my arm.

I listened. Someone was yelling. All around us the landscape was quiet except for the sounds of birds. Lots of birds around here, some geese and pigeons, too. But when they quieted down in their chatter, I still heard the yell. More like a wail.

I knew by now that such a quiet was deceptive, that the lacy trees, the verdant fields, the dappled sunlight could be hiding some evil. I looked to the farmhouse. Solid, it was, with gables, four of them. Well kept, as were the fields and outbuildings. Neat fences lined the road that led to it. Nothing seemed to be amiss.

"We shouldn't stop," I said to Miz Melindy. I felt the evil all around me. Something hovering, waiting, like a buzzard hidden in the tree branches.

Her hand tightened on my arm. "Somebody in pain."

"The whole world is in pain," I said. "At least this part of it is, anyway. Haven't we found enough of it already?"

"We cain't go on an' leave a body in pain," she insisted. " 'Tain't right. 'Tain't Godly."

"What has God got to do with anything, Miz Melindy?" I snapped. "God isn't here anymore. He knew enough to get out of South Carolina two months ago."

"You go down that road," she directed firmly, "an' we gonna see who be in pain. You go down that road or I take the reins from you. You think I cain't?"

I looked at her.

"You think I cain't git outta this wagon an' stay here with my sack of remedies?" She made a move to get down.

I turned in the direction of the farmhouse road. I handed the reins to her. "Here, take them. I've got to hold my musket." And I reached behind me and grabbed it out from under the canvas.

We passed a pasture with some cattle. Beyond it stretched the cornfields. We crossed a small bridge with a narrow stream and wound up the dusty road. Barns, corncribs, a kitchen garden with beans, squash, turnips, all well kept. An old dog, reddish brown, came out, barked weakly once or twice, then stopped and wagged his tail. Miz Melindy drew up beside the well. The back door of the house stood open. Chickens scratched in the yard. Curtains flapped in open windows. I felt a hundred eyes watching me. I could not shake the fear.

Then the yell again, from inside the house. "Help me, help, please!"

It came from an upstairs window.

"I go wif you," Miz Melindy said. And she reached for her sack of remedies and started to get down. I jumped down and helped her. We started toward the back door. All the while I kept a wary eye on the out-buildings. Fear lay over me like a jacket. I had taken it on late yesterday when Mrs. McClure held that musket on me, and clutched it close last evening when Miz Melindy told me about my mother. I was discovering now that it was not a garment you could get shut of very easily.

We went into the house. We went through the room for dining. Warily we made our way past table and chairs. Numbly my mind took in the pewter plates on a sideboard, the smell of herbs hanging somewhere, a vase of flowers, long runners on polished floors. We went into a center hall where the stairway wound upstairs. Across the hall was a room with books. Somebody lived here, several somebodies. The place was well cared for, a home.

"Hello!" Miz Melindy called out. "Who be up there?"

"Help me! Oh, help me, please! They've tied me here to my bed! Please come, do!"

"Anybody up there with you?" I asked.

"Nobody! I'm forsaken! And the cows have to be milked. Please!"

We started up the stairs. It was slow going because Miz Melindy was not accustomed to stairs. We paused on the landing where there was a window that looked out onto the rich farmland. *What a pretty place*, I thought. But then I minded that no place was pretty anymore. We continued on up and followed the man's voice to a room at the end of a hall.

As he had said, he was tied to the bed. He was not young, but not yet old, either, and he was straining against the ropes that held him.

"Do you have a knife?" he asked.

"In our wagon," I said.

"You'll find a knife in that drawer." He pointed to a desk by the wall.

I ran over, went through two drawers, and found the knife, a hunting knife, sheathed. I drew it out and went to work on the ropes that bound him. They were not thick, but were well knotted. "Who tied you?" I asked.

"My son."

"Your son?" I stopped cutting. "But why?"

"Because I'm a rebel and he's a Tory. He rides with Huck. And he wants to be sure I don't warn Sumter that Huck is attacking."

I had freed one hand and went around the bed to the other side. "What's your name?"

"Winterich," he said. "And who are you two?"

"I'm Caroline Whitaker from Camden, and this lady is my grandmother. Yes, she is. And don't tell me you don't believe me because it's true." I continued cutting.

"Miss Caroline," he said sadly, "I believe anything you tell me right now. You're talking to a man who would swear on the family Bible that his son would never turn on him. But this war has done strange things to people. Where are you headed?"

"North, to fetch my brother home. He was wounded in the war. We started out yesterday." The last shred of rope gave and he was free. He sat up on the edge of the bed, rubbing his wrists. He eyed me warily. I know he had more questions, but he knew better than to ask. "I am beholden to you," he said.

"Are you all right? Can you get up?"

He stood up, reached for a jacket. He was fully dressed, even to his boots.

"Where is the rest of your family?" I asked.

"Sent the wife and girls off to her sister's on the coast just before Charleston fell. They didn't want to go, but I knew what this inland war would be like. I fought the Cherokees. My son and I kept the place with some negras. But I suppose they're gone. You didn't see anybody about on the grounds, did you?"

"No."

"Just as I thought. The British are taking them all. I was so afeared nobody would come and the stock would suffer, or I'd die here. I can't thank you enough. Is there anything I can do for you?"

"Some cold water would be nice for us and our mules," I said.

"Do more than that. Got regular fixings for a meal downstairs. You might like to sit at a table and eat properlike."

"I'd admire to," I told him, "but we've got to reach our destination tonight."

Miz Melindy nodded in agreement.

"Well then, I'll just give you some fixings to take on your way with you."

He gave us ham, bread, cheese, cold milk, even cake. I fetched a basket from the wagon and packed it all in. He walked out the door with us. "Somehow I've got to get out and tell Sumter what Huck is about," he murmured.

"He knows," I told him. "We left a plantation this morning where Huck visited. The woman's daughter left on a fast horse last night to get to Sumter's camp."

"Good, good." He smiled and looked around at his farm, as if to assure himself it was all still there. His dog reached under his hand for patting. He patted its head. "We're so accustomed to minding our own places and not minding each other's business," he said. "And now we've learned that we must not only mind each other's affairs, we must be our brother's keeper in this war, mustn't we?"

I said yes.

"You're a good girl, going to fetch your brother.

Come back and pay a proper visit when the madness is done with, Caroline Whitaker," he said, "and your grandmother with you."

I promised him I would. And then I asked him if he knew anything about Sumter.

"He and his army haven't been idle. I heard they've sent men into North Carolina to procure powder and shot and pack horses. He has smithies busy manufacturing swords and repairing broken rifles all around. He has men constantly in the field with mounted riflemen, encouraging fearful Patriots, collecting recruits, and putting down Loyalists."

"Have you seen any British hereabouts?"

"Except for my son, no." And then he did something strange. He stopped talking. At least his voice stopped working. It had a catch in it at the mention of his son. He gazed off into the distance and tears came into his mild blue eyes. "He's been my heart and soul, that boy. I lived for him. My world is worthless without him."

"He'll be back," I said.

"Back? A son that goes over to the side of the British? Never!"

"My brother is coming home," I said.

Right off I felt Miz Melindy nudging me. But I shook her off.

"But your brother was no Tory."

"Yes, he was. He ran off to fight with them. And my daddy's the leading rebel in Camden. My daddy's in jail right now. It cut into my daddy something fierce when Johnny went off to fight with the British. But now my brother's had a change of heart and he's coming home."

"That so?" The mild blue eyes got a new light in them.

"Yes. It's so."

He put his arms around me when we left. He hugged me and kissed my cheek. "Bless you," he said. "You've given me something to live for."

We ate in the wagon to make up for time. "Why'd you go an' tell him about Johnny switching sides?" Miz Melindy scolded gently. "You could git Johnny in trouble. Git all of us in trouble."

"Because," I said, "he needed to know that more than I needed not to tell it. It restored his afflicted spirit."

"Foolish girl."

"You're just jealous because with your bag of remedies there was nothing you could do for him."

"Didn't need no remedies."

"Yes, he did. His heart was broken. He needed it fixed, and I fixed it for him."

"Oh, you kin fix hearts now?"

"Yes," I said.

"Then you should hang out a sign, Miss Fixer-of-Hearts. Charge two shillings fer every heart fixed."

"I wouldn't charge."

"Oh?"

"I wouldn't charge because it made me feel good to do it. And I haven't felt good in a long time," I said.

"Then maybe now you know how I come through," she said.

"What?"

"What you said afore. How did I come through?

143

Now you know why I never let my sack of remedies outta my sight. Now give me some o' that cake, Miss Heart-Fixer, an' stop hoggin' it all for yerself. An' after you finish doin' that, you kin jus' ask yerself who made you stop the wagon inna first place. Who had to threaten to git out an' walk if'n you didn't stop?"

I gave her the cake. She was an ornery old woman. Never had I met such an ornery woman in all my born days.

Chapter Eleven

JULY 6, 1780

IT WAS LATE afternoon when we came upon that place where the Catawba becomes the Wateree. The place where I knew I would find Johnny. If he was still alive.

We had traveled all day, stopping often to give the mules a rest, to get fresh water from a spring, all day in the heat that had a shimmering and dense quality to it. With the sound of the river always in the distance, it became an unreal quality. So hot and the river so near and we could not venture out from the wooded areas filled with jack pine and red cedar tree branches that slapped against our faces, sumac, twisted vines, paths that seemed to turn in on themselves, sudden gullies that caused Jackaroo and Orphelia to stop short in fear. Then I'd have to get out and urge them to move to a place where the gully was not so deep. Prod them through it, trying to think what Mr. Bone would do. Then I remembered his words.

"She's a fast walker. No draggin' the hindquarters. Jackaroo, now, he'll hold back till she gets tired. Then he'll pick up the slack. Keep on Jackaroo so's he don't make her do all the work."

So I'd keep on Jackaroo, pushing, begging, talking nice to him and being firm. "You're such a handsome fellow, oh yes. Why, if you were a horse Rawdon would be making off with you in a minute. We'd have to hide you like we did Fearnaught. And then you wouldn't be here with me now. Aren't you glad you're not a horse, you darling thing, you?"

And so I urged him on over every gully, while Orphelia did her share of the work without bidding.

Miz Melindy would get out of the wagon, too, of course, at every stop, so as to lighten the load. And that meant helping her down and up again. I was fair worn to pieces before we reached our destination. Besides the gullies, there were the mosquitoes and gnats to plague us; my hands hurt, my body seemed like Quaking pudding for the jolting of the wagon. And then, just when I thought I could not abide it for one more minute, we came to that place where I knew Johnny would be, if he was at all.

A cove not far from the river. A place where a spring celebrated itself by bubbling in a small pond before it trickled down into the river. Fallen trees, great in girth, one with a hollow you could crawl into. Johnny had brought me to this spot once just to show it to me.

"You could hide here forever and nobody on God's whole earth could find you," he'd said, "here where the Catawba becomes the Wateree."

Johnny and Cephas were there. Oh, immortal, sweet God, they were there. Near the tree with the big hollow. Johnny leaned against it, Cephas nursed a small fire, leaning over it, coughing. The cough had a weak, persistent sound. I smelled fish cooking. Grey Goose was tethered nearby. "It's them," I said to Miz Melindy. "They're still alive!"

"Praise be."

I climbed out of the wagon, looked around just to make sure they were alone, even let my eyes scan the sandy earth for signs of multiple horse or boot tracks. There were none.

"Johnny!" I called out softly.

He looked, saw me, started to get up, but did not. Or could not. He waved us forward.

"Johnny, it's been so long. I'm so glad to see you!"

He reached his arms out to me. I had to kneel down to receive his hug. I felt the frailty of it and him, drew back, and looked into his face. His eyes were too bright, fever bright. His face was lean. He did not look hale; he looked sickly.

"Johnny, I thought we'd never get here."

"And I thought nobody would ever come."

"Well, we're here now, me and Miz Melindy. She's brought remedies. Are you all right?"

"Just a little sore, is all. My back is healing slowly. Miz Melindy's remedies are welcome." He scowled, leaned back against that old tree, held my hand in his own. His grip was still firm, strong. His clothing was tattered, of course, the shirt torn, no more stock around his neck, his breeches patched, his hair overgrown, and

147

there was more than a day's worth of beard on his face. He wore moccasins.

Now he smiled. "I'm better than Cephas. Could have made it home but for him. I'll not leave him. That wagon will do the trick nicely. Carry him home."

"What's wrong with him?"

"I think it's malaria. That prison they put us in in Charleston was a foul place. Thank God for guards who can be bribed. And for friendly Catawbas. I came across one old codger who I knew hunted alone out here, and he's the one who gave the note and message to Nepoya. What's happened, Caroline?" he asked. "What's amiss?"

"Amiss?"

"Name of God, why did they send you and Miz Melindy?" He peered over to where Miz Melindy and Cephas were talking while she was taking things out of her remedy sack, setting them on the ground—things in jars, things wrapped in corn husks, tea, herbs, ointments. Cephas was coughing, a dry, raspy cough. He, too, was thinner and his clothing beggared all description.

"The war, Johnny. The war came to us."

"When?"

"The last week in May. Cornwallis came."

"And?" His brown eyes were dark pools of questions. No, not pools, gullies. Gullies I had to maneuver around.

But I couldn't. "He put Daddy in jail in Camden."

A slight drawing in of his breath. But if this was cause for grave concern he did not betray it to me. "And?"

"Then Cornwallis went back to Charleston. Took some of our negras with him. There's lots of men in jail in Camden."

"So I heard."

"Cornwallis hanged my friend Kit Gales."

He sighed. "I'm sorry, Caroline. I know you two grew up together. What else?"

"Then when he left, Rawdon came."

"What do you mean 'came'?"

"He's in our house. Now. Some of his men are camped on our place. Cornwallis was in our house, too, before he left. He's confined me and Georgia Ann and Mama to one room upstairs."

I saw something in him quicken. "Is Mother all right?"

"Yes, she's good, Johnny." I would not tell him that she was cooking now for Rawdon. I would not tell him too much just yet.

"Didn't she tell them I was fighting with the king's men? That she's remained a Tory?"

"It didn't matter, Johnny. They said she made a bad choice in husbands."

"Why are your hands bandaged?"

"They're blistered from the reins. Miz Melindy bound them up."

He looked down at my hands, at the bandages. He chewed his lower lip. His face was still handsome but different. The handsomeness was chiseled down to a fine determination, an anger. Soon, very soon, his face would not be handsome anymore. Soon, very soon, the determined anger would take over. If he did not forgive

149

the things that were done to him. And if he did not forgive himself.

As if reading my mind, he spoke. "I didn't understand, Caroline. The rebels say they fight for freedom. I've been free all my life, here in Carolina, free as a bird. I had a good life, and like so many others I didn't want it changed."

I said nothing.

"I joined the army I thought gave me my rights as an Englishman. And then I found different. If there's more to it than that, Caroline, I don't know the more. I made a mistake and now I want to remedy it. And I've been languishing here helpless, plotting."

"Well, you won't be lying here helpless anymore now that we've come to fetch you home."

"You still didn't answer why Rawdon sent you and Miz Melindy and not someone else to fetch me. A slip of a girl and an old lady."

"It's the way of things, Johnny."

"What way? What aren't you telling me, almost-sister of mine?"

When he said that it melted me, just like butter in the fry pan. But that was all part of Johnny's charm. I was glad to see he still had it.

"Rawdon couldn't spare any of his men. And anyway, it wasn't his idea, it was mine. I offered to come fetch you. It was my idea, after Isom gave me the note."

"Nepoya got it to Isom?"

"Yes."

"You didn't see her, then."

"No. But she sent us a bow and some arrows, because she heard Rawdon was in the house."

He smiled ruefully. "Go on."

"That's it, Johnny. When I got the note I asked Rawdon to let me come fetch you. He didn't want to at first. Said Loyalist militia were of little use to them. Said he couldn't spare a man. Said lots of things. Then I listened and learned that he needed intelligence about Sumter."

"How did you listen if you were confined to your chamber?"

"He let me out. To help Miz Melindy cook for him. Cornwallis took Doreen, and Jade can't cook."

"Mother permitted this? You and Miz Melindy in the kitchen?"

"We had to humor him, Johnny. To keep Daddy alive."

He slumped down a little bit against the tree. "Things have changed. Go on."

"Well, like I said, Rawdon was near daft trying to find out where Sumter was. And so I told him about you."

"What did you tell him about me?"

"How you'd lived with the Catawbas and fought the Cherokees. How you knew the woods and fields and swamps, and how you knew so many men in Sumter's army."

Now he sat up straight. "You told Rawdon I would spy for him?"

"It was the only way I could get him to let me come fetch you, Johnny. Don't be mad."

"Mad? I'm going to go a-helling back and kill the gol-blamed piece of slime when I get home, not spy for him!"

"No, Johnny, you mustn't."

"Why mustn't I?"

"Because then they'll kill Daddy."

He knew he was trapped. His eyes went wary, a little crazy for a minute or two. He picked up a flask beside him, took a long swig of something out of it, and wiped his mouth with his shirtsleeve. "Kill him," he said. "I've been lying here for days calculating how I'm going to kill the lot of them, and now you come along and tell me I have to spy for him. Well, I'm not coming home if that's what I have to do, Caroline."

"You have to come home, Johnny," I said. I felt panic rising inside me. I had not counted on this.

"I don't have to do anything. I'm free, remember? I'm a rebel. A hunted man. They catch me on the way home, they'll kill me. Hang me like they did your friend."

"I have a note from Rawdon," I said. "I have a paper giving us safe passage." I took it out of my pocket and showed it to him.

He waved it away in disgust. He mumbled some profanity under his breath. Then he asked, "How's Fearnaught?" He said the word like a prayer.

Finally there was something good I could tell him. "Rawdon has cast an eye on her, Johnny. Isom took her up to Nepoya's place. She's hidden. I thought that the best thing to do."

He nodded. "Good girl, you've done good. I near

gave my life for Grey Goose. I'll not let them take Fearnaught."

"That's why you have to come home, Johnny," I said.
"Please. Because we need you." I started to cry. "And
you've got to get Cephas home or he'll die. You know
that. You don't want Cephas to die, do you, Johnny?"

He wasn't like most men, weakened by the tears of
a woman. There was little that could weaken Johnny,
and in a way I knew that was in itself a weakness, that
nothing could bring him around if he didn't want to be
brought. He was too principled, Mama had often said,
"if there is such a thing." And she'd sighed saying it.

Well, there was such a thing. I was a little like him
when I'd chosen to stay the night in the corncrib rather
than say Miz Melindy was not my grandmother. Mrs.
McClure had been a little like him when she'd fetched
the family Bible out of the fire and received a blow from
the flat of Huck's sword for her trouble.

"No, I don't want Cephas to die," he said angrily. "I
told you I could have left him here and gone on to join
Sumter. Sent the note home so he could be fetched,
not me. Cephas and I were boys together. We're all tied
up with these negras of ours, Caroline, whether we like
it or not."

"Do tell," I said to him.

It was one of his favorite expressions and one he
used when he wanted to be most sarcastic. "How are
you two getting on?" He glanced at Miz Melindy.

"We do sometimes and sometimes we don't," I said.
"But she's my grandmother. And it wasn't right I was
kept from her, Johnny."

"So something good has come out of all this, then?"

"You could say that."

"Well, now that you two are here there's no reason you can't take Cephas on home. Miz Melindy can treat him, and I can go on to join Sumter."

"That's where you were headed then, to join Sumter."

He nodded. "Couldn't quite make it. Heard he was north of us, hiding out."

"He's come out, Johnny. Sumter and his men have come out of hiding."

He was disbelieving. "They never!"

I nodded vigorously. "On the fourth. And when the British command at Rocky Mount heard of it they sent out a man named Huck. He's laying waste to everything, Johnny. We ran into two women whose plantations he visited. On one he took the women's kin who were home to make musket balls. She said they're to be hanged."

"What was her name?"

"McClure."

"Her husband's a good man. He's been going about with his men, inducing others to join the Patriot cause. I was wishing I'd run into him. Huck out on a rampaging sortie? Name of God. That Huck is somebody to be reckoned with. Was a Philadelphia lawyer. Well, the die is cast then. I can't let you all go on home alone. Not if Huck is roaming about with his devils from hell."

"You don't have to really spy for Rawdon when you get home," I said. "You can just pretend to be doing it, can't you?"

"I'm no good at pretending, no good at such. I'm

a right-on-target person, a no-nonsense, no shilly-shallying, no boot-licking person. If I'm with someone I'm with them. If I'm not, they'll soon know it."

"You're a fool for principle," I said.

He looked at me, anger in his eyes. "Do tell."

"Yes. The trick is to know when to stand by it and when to leave it be. Stand by it foolishly and you'll have lean times and no friends. Abandon it foolishly and you'll have great plenty and friends, but you'll hate your-self for life."

"I always told Mother the wife of that tutor of yours was teaching you seditious things."

"It wasn't her. It was Mrs. McClure said those words to me. After she kept us locked in a corncrib all night so her daughter could make a getaway and warn Sumter that Huck was out ravaging the countryside."

"She locked you in a corncrib?" He was disbelieving. "Didn't you tell her your father is a leading rebel?"

"Yes, but she thought I lied to her about something else."

"What?"

"I told her Miz Melindy is my grandmother. So she didn't believe me. And the next morning was when she told me about how foolish principle sometimes is."

"Why did you tell her such?"

"I couldn't lie about it, Johnny. Not anymore. I felt there was too much lying."

He was silent for a moment. Then he spoke. "Do you think Miz Melindy has something in that bag of hers for my back? It gets to hurting around this time of day."

"Of course, Johnny! Here we are jawing away and you hurting! How could I be so silly?"

I went over to where Miz Melindy was cooking. She had given Cephas some herbal decoction, and he was lying back on a blanket now, his cough quieted. He smiled at me. I smiled back. "Johnny needs some help, too," I told her. "You go attend to him. I'll watch the supper."

Whatever the mixture was that bubbled in a pot over the fire, it smelled delicious. I set myself to stirring it. And after Miz Melindy had ministered to Johnny, I brought him a bowl of it. He ate ravenously.

I sat and ate with him. I could see his mood was improving.

"We'll work it out," he said, "about what face I present to Rawdon. We'll work it out on the way home."

I nodded and smiled at him. I had to unharness the mules yet, feed them, and maybe wash myself in the pool that bubbled so close by, celebrating itself before it trickled in a spring down to the river.

Chapter Twelve

JULY 7, 1780

AFTER BREAKFAST THE next morning, when I went to harness the mules, Johnny came to help; then, seeing how easily I handled them, he stepped back, smiling.

"You've grown up," he said.

I went about my business. "Do tell," I said.

He pulled my hair. "I'm sorry about Kit. I suppose that can make a girl grow mighty fast."

"Yes," I said again. "But it isn't that as much as—" I stopped.

"As what?" His eyes took my measure. As usual, he missed nothing.

What had I intended to say? With a shock I minded that I hadn't thought about Kit much in the past day, that when I turned inside myself, what hung there now, in the way of everything, was the specter of my real mother, the slave.

"There is something else, Johnny," I said.

One eyebrow went up. "There always is."

"Did you know that my real mother is still alive?"

A shadow came across his face.

"Did you know she was sold to the West Indies?"

He was silent for a long minute. "Yes," he said finally.

"Why did you never tell me?"

"There was no profit in it."

"No profit in the truth?"

He shook his head sadly. "Would you have stayed living with us if you knew?"

"Likely not."

"And where would you have gone then? To Miz Melindy? She'd have thrown you out. Who told you this anyway? Georgia Ann? She'll answer to me if she did."

I stared at him. "Georgia Ann knew?"

"Everybody did. I put the fear of God into Georgia Ann. Well, is she the one?"

"No. Miz Melindy told me."

He didn't know what to say to that. He sighed, he rubbed his nose, he took his hat off and ran his hand through his hair, then over his face. "I ought to shave before we get started home," he said, "just in case we get stopped by anybody. I have to look presentable. Do you think Miz Melindy has any hot water left from breakfast?"

Johnny made me crazy sometimes. There just wasn't any other way to put it. One minute he'd be caring and affectionate, next he'd pull away from you, go inside himself, act like you didn't exist. Mama says all men are like that. When they can't abide something they pretend it isn't happening. Still, how could he dismiss out of hand what we'd just spoken of?

"Don't you care that Miz Melindy told me?" I asked.

He turned his tricorn hat around in his hands. " 'Course I care, Caroline. I have an abiding interest in you. You know that."

"Well then?"

"Well then what?"

"You were ready to light into Georgia Ann if she was the one. But now that you hear it's Miz Melindy you act like it doesn't matter."

"It matters, Caroline. But not for the reason you think. It matters because I reckon Miz Melindy thinks you've grown up now, too. I reckon she thinks you're old enough to know. So now you've got to prove to her you are grown up enough to know."

"And what does that mean?"

"Means that you have to stop thinking only of how you feel about it. And get a fix on how she feels. How she's felt all these years. Means you have to start to know that sometimes bad things happen in families. Dolorous things, god-awful things, stupid things that hurt everybody. And it takes time for people to get shut of their feelings about them. And, oh hell and tarnation, Caroline, I'm hard put to understand it all myself. It means our family was almost torn apart by it all, and we can't abide any more tearing apart. Especially not now, when the British are tearing at us. We've got to stick together."

I said nothing. I just patted Orphelia's nose.

He sighed again and looked off into the distance.

"We've got to get home, all of a piece," he said quietly. "That's what I've got to care about first right now. And when we get there, I've got to figure out how to keep from killing this Rawdon person. And find out if Pa is still alive. And when the damn British will get out of our house. I know it's important to you, Caroline, this business about your mother. And it's shameful, yes. But if you're the girl I think you are, you'll stuff your feelings in an old sock someplace until we all get through what all's lying in wait for us ahead. Then you can carry on like a Cherokee at a Quaker meeting if you've still a mind to because I didn't tell you the truth. Or, if it suits your fancy, you can shoot those arrows at me that Nepoya gave you. D'ya hear?"

I heard. His quiet, steady tone brought me back to my senses. "Do you think we'll get back all of a piece?"

He shrugged. "I'm sure as hell a-going to try. Now I've got to shave and put on a clean shirt so I don't look like the rapscallion I am if we come across any British on the way."

"British?" I looked sharp.

"I don't mean to go a-scaring you, Caroline, but there are British patrols about. Day before you came, one passed by right on that sandy path down there by the river."

"Well, I've got the pass from Rawdon if we meet any," I reminded him.

He nodded. "That's right nice," he said, "but Cephas and I didn't have it at the time. Hid in the hollow of that tree like a possum chased by a pack of coon dogs."

I watched him take up his haversack, his musket, pick up a pot of hot water from the fire, and go down the sandy path to the river, set down his shaving things, take off his shirt, and start to wash. From the distance I could see how stiffly he moved as he drew the shirt over his head. He'd not said a word about the whipping the British had given him. It wasn't Johnny's way to complain.

Had they done grievous bad harm to him, then? Without thinking I slipped along down the sandy path, hiding myself in the undergrowth so he couldn't see me. I went far enough until I could see him.

Bent over the water he was, intent on shaving. I could hear the scraping of the razor across his face, the lapping of water at the river's edge, the cry of an eagle far overhead.

And I could see the damage done to his back, the scars from the whip—ugly, purple scars—the flesh scarce healed, and where it was healed, disfiguring.

Oh, Johnny!

"Sometimes bad things happen in families," he'd said. "Dolorous, god-awful, stupid things that hurt everybody. And it takes time for people to get shut of their feelings about them."

He'd spoken with such certainty, such bitterness in his voice. Now I knew. He hadn't been speaking about what my daddy had done with Mama Cecie. Or of her being sold off. All that was far in the past now. He'd been talking of what the British had done to him.

I turned back and walked up the sandy path to our

campsite, my feelings spent. It didn't matter what Johnny had been talking about. He could stand behind his words. I must put store in them.

When he joined us a bit later he went right over to Miz Melindy and helped her lift Cephas into the wagon bed. "I doan need to ride," Cephas protested. "I need to keep watch wif you."

"You will ride while you can," Johnny said firmly. "Rest. Later there will be time aplenty for watching." He was gentle with Cephas, even tender. They had been through much together, yes. When the note had come to us from Nepoya, it had said Johnny was wounded and needed fetching home. I knew now that Johnny could have made it home if he'd wanted. Could have made it to Sumter's camp, too. But he wouldn't leave Cephas. As he had said, we were very tied-in with these negras of ours.

"Have you any cloth for a sling?" he asked Miz Melindy.

She rifled about in her belongings until she came up with some linen.

He ripped it lengthwise down the middle. "Now put my left arm in a sling," he directed.

She cocked her head. "Where it be hurtin'?"

"It isn't. But if we meet the British, the pass from Rawdon says I was wounded. I can't have them know how. Let them think it's my arm."

She fashioned a sling and tied it around his neck. Then he helped her onto the wagon seat. Then he bent down and wrapped Grey Goose's left foreleg in the rest of the cloth. "If the British cross our paths, she's lame," he told me.

"But she doesn't act lame."

"She will. I've taught her how." He grinned at me, and we started off. He did not ride Grey Goose but tethered her to the back of the wagon and walked on ahead of us, his musket in his good hand.

OUR JOURNEY was arduous and slow. And before long I noticed that we were not going back the way we'd come. Johnny knew all the secret paths and byways better than I. It was good to have him leading and soon, what with the morning sun climbing in the sky, the soothing sound of the river in the distance, which we could not always see but could always hear, the calling of the birds in the thickets of trees, the jangling of the mules' harnesses, and the steady rhythm of the water bucket banging against the outside of the wagon, I gave up my vigilance and allowed myself the luxury of mulling over my thoughts.

First I thought about Johnny, about the difference in him. Before he'd gone off to fight, his brown eyes had been laughing, teasing. Or, when sad, harboring nothing worse than a poetic melancholy. Now there was a smoldering fire in those eyes. I suspected it warmed him, that likely it had kept him going when he was in that British prison. But now it served as a warning to others not to trifle with him. Then there was the other thing, the hard edge about him, the faint tinge of dry bitterness that I had been unable to get past, that I knew I would have to get around if I wanted to find the real Johnny again.

But it came to me then. With the war all of us would soon have some barrier, either inside us, as I had mine, or erected as a fence around us, invisible but keeping others at a distance. I supposed that was what war did to people. Still, I worried about Johnny. I worried that he was spoiling for a fight and it would erupt when he saw Rawdon in our house, his men camped all over our grounds. Would I be able to keep him reasonable?

After I had worn those thoughts down like a dog wears down a bone, I thought of something else, outside the whole cloth. I thought of what Mrs. Wyly, the Quaker woman, had said at meeting one day, the words she had stood and given as her own personal sermon, the words that soon went around Camden town and were even printed in the *Charleston Courier* right before Charleston fell.

Dear Friends:

There are three things I very much wonder. First is, that children should be so foolish as to throw up stones, brick-bats, and clubs into fruit trees to knock down the fruit; if they would let it alone, it would fall of itself.

The second is, that men should be so foolish and even wicked as to go to war and kill one another; if they would only let one another alone, they would die of themselves.

And the third and last thing, which I wonder at most of all, is, that young men should be so unwise as to go after the young women; if they would only stay at home, the young women would come after them.

I remembered how Daddy had read those words from the *Charleston Courier* to us one morning at breakfast. "He's got a right smart wife, that Samuel Wyly," Daddy had said. "I thought we Presbyterians had it all figured out, but it seems to me we could learn something from the Quakers. They've got wisdom enough to spread around."

What wisdom did Mrs. Wyly have now, I wondered? With her husband cut to pieces? What wisdom did Daddy have? And what about me? I had nary a bit of it. It seemed to me that I became more of a dimwit with each new day.

Riding along in the wagon I thought of how different all our lives were now. It had been just four days short of two months ago when Mrs. Wyly spoke those words.

It was coming on toward noon when we sighted the British patrol.

WE SIGHTED them before they sighted us, and the first thing Johnny did was hold up his hand for us to halt. Then he walked back to us casually, gave his musket to Cephas, who was already sitting up in the wagon. He bade Cephas to lie back down and covered him over with the canvas. Then he turned to me.

"We give the pass from Rawdon. We play the game. If they get arrogant, I'll go with them. You take the others on home."

"You can't," I protested.

"I'll just be drawing them away from you all. If that happens, Cephas won't let them take me very far, will you, Ceph?"

"Not too far," came the whispered retort from under the canvas.

"They'll not bother you or Miz Melindy. They have little taste for taking women prisoners. But they'll not take me or Cephas back to their hellhole of a prison. And I'll kill them with my bare hands before they get Grey Goose."

Having said such he walked back to the horse and stroked her nose. Then he whispered things in her ear and gentled her. When he walked back to the front of the wagon to continue on, I saw that Grey Goose was walking as if she were lame.

I was delighted by Grey Goose's performance. But my delight soon turned to terror as the British approached. There were four of them. One officer. He wore the same red as Rawdon, had the same haughty look. The others looked scurrilous in visage and appearance.

Johnny took off his tricorn. "Good day, gentlemen," he said.

The officer nodded. "State your business," he said. "By whose leave do you travel about in a vicinity patrolled and occupied by His Majesty's troops?"

"Up until recently I was one of His Majesty's troops," Johnny answered. "Loyalist. I was wounded at Charleston and have been trying to make my way home ever since."

The officer cast an eye to Johnny's arm in the sling. "State your name."

"John Carlisle Whitaker."

"Sir," the officer intoned. "I expect military protocol. Even from Loyalist militia."

"Sir," Johnny said. He said it plain. But it had a hollow ring to it.

"Have you paper to prove what you claim?"

Johnny turned to me, and I stepped forward. "This is my sister Caroline Whitaker. She has a pass written by Colonel Rawdon to come fetch me. He makes his post in Camden."

"I know where Rawdon makes his post," the officer said savagely. At the same time he put his hand out for the paper.

I walked over to his horse. I had to stand on tiptoe to hand it to him. He would not reach down. Then I stepped back near Johnny, well out of the way if anything were to happen.

The officer gave the paper a cursory reading. "What are you doing hereabouts if your home is in Camden and you are up from Charleston? I know how inept the Loyalist militia are, but are you that lost?"

I saw Johnny's jaw tighten. I knew what the sight of that red coat, so inordinately bright in the sandy browns and grays, the muted greens of our surroundings, had done to me. What horror must it have conjured for my brother? I prayed he would contain himself.

He did. And I thanked the Lord for what he had learned, living with the Catawbas, for he kept his face innocent of his feelings.

"I was trying to find Sumter," he said.

The officer raised one quizzical brow. "Sumter?"

"Yes. I'd heard he was in hiding to the north. I'd also heard Rawdon needed intelligence. But I was unable to go on for my injury."

The officer then deigned to raise his eyes and look at me and Miz Melindy, who was hunched over on the seat of the wagon. "Who is this old crone then?"

I was about to open my mouth, but Johnny's look stopped me. "Our family servant. An old negra who knows well the art of physick. Rawdon sent her along to accompany my sister. Without her ministrations, I'd not be standing. My wound was badly infected. She has cures."

"Does she have a cure for rheumatism? What with the damps from the river and swamps, my rheumatism is killing me."

"Miz Melindy?" Johnny asked.

Immediately she reached around in the wagon and drew out her sack. For a while she poked around in it, then came up with a small vial. "Jimsonweed," she said. "Put it in tea, two times every day."

She held the bottle out. I would have fetched it, but again Johnny's look stopped me. A clammy silence settled upon us all. Then the officer nudged his horse over to the wagon and put his hand out for the bottle. He examined the contents, nodded, and moved his horse back to where his men waited.

"Very well, you may proceed on your way," he said.

"Thank you, sir." This time I heard a mocking tone in Johnny's voice and prayed the officer would not hear it, too. But then, of a sudden, he had his mind on other things.

"One moment!" he barked.

I had been about to climb back up on the wagon seat and stopped in my tracks.

"The horse. That's a fine-looking specimen you have there. We're sore in need of horses, as you know if you were at Charleston."

"She's lame," Johnny said. "It's the reason I needed fetching home. Couldn't ride her."

It was like a challenge. The officer's eyes narrowed. He gestured with his head. "How so? Untether her."

Johnny did so. While he did so he stroked her and whispered in her ear as if to quiet her. Then he led her toward the British officer.

The man's face immediately fell on seeing the agonizing limp. "Why don't you shoot her?" he demanded.

"I thought I'd try to get her home," Johnny answered. "We have a servant there who's good with horses. I put great store in his opinion. If he can fix her up, I'll give her to Rawdon. He has some of Tarleton's cavalry at Camden, and I've heard he's desperate for horses. I thought it was worth the effort. Sir."

The officer eyed him maliciously. "You colonials have all the answers, don't you?"

"No sir." Now Johnny's voice was pure ingratiating. "Myself, I don't even have the right questions."

Satisfied with this degree of humility, the man gave up. "We're wasting time. We have a ways to go. Do you know this country, Whitaker?"

"Like the back of my hand, sir."

"Well, where is the Godforsaken ferry I'm looking for?"

"You're crossing the Catawba, sir?" Johnny asked.

The man looked perplexed. "Isn't this the Wateree?"

"Yes sir. But a ways north it becomes the Catawba. If you could tell me where you are headed, I could direct you to the proper ferry."

"There's more than one?"

"Absolutely, sir." Johnny was dead serious. And lying. There was only one ferry, north of us at Fishing Creek. He simply wanted to discover where these men were headed.

"We're going to Williamson's Plantation," came the answer. "To Huck's headquarters."

"Ah, then you'll want the Fishing Creek ferry, sir," Johnny explained patiently. "Just follow the river north a bit. About one mile. There will be a signpost. Cross there and you have only about another five miles inland to reach Williamson's Plantation."

The man nodded and grunted and pushed past us. "Name is Captain James Doughty. Give my compliments to Rawdon," he said. Then I heard him grumbling. "Six more miles in this Godforsaken heat. Let them keep this god-awful country, is what I say. Nothing but gnats and swamps, damps, unbearable heat, sandy soil, gum trees, poison ivy, and uppity inhabitants."

I started to laugh quietly. So did Johnny. Then from under the canvas of the wagon came Cephas's muffled cry. "Git me outta here afore I expires. I cain't stand it one more minute, Mistuh Johnny. I jus' cain't."

Chapter Thirteen

JULY 7, 1780

T HE SKY ALL afternoon was hard blue, the sun beat down, and I feared for Miz Melindy in the heat, but she never complained.

I could see that Johnny was tiring. The going was slow.

"Why don't you ride Grey Goose?" I asked him.

"Don't want to be seen by the British."

"There are no British about."

"We don't know that. They could see us afore we see them. We were lucky last time. How could I say she was lame if they spotted us and me riding her?"

"Then I think we should stop early. It must be near three and Miz Melindy is spent."

"Soon's we find a good spot."

He was absolutely demented about the place we camped. It must be just right. Near enough to a river or stream for water, not out in the open lest we be exposed, yet it must be a place not too overcome by brush, for we must have a fire. "A little on a rise," he said, "so we can sight anyone coming along. No gullies. Gullies are bad. You get trapped in them."

Finally he stopped, looked around, sniffed the air like a hound dog, and took us to a sharp left, away from the river. For a bit we wandered through low sandy inclines, not even respectable enough to be called hills, with lots of stunted pines. Then we came upon some spongy bogs. Clouds of gnats plagued us. Bullfrogs sent out their throaty greeting. It was getting darker, I minded, as I guided the mules behind Johnny. And then I realized that was because, of a sudden, we had come into a forest of sorts. Then I heard it. Gurgling water. A spring.

"Here," Johnny said. "We camp here for the night. Know where we are?"

"No," I said.

"About an hour's ride from Uncle Henry."

"Why can't we stop there for the night?" I thought of Uncle Henry's elegant dining room, of servants laying a supper of cold meat, hot biscuits, relishes, cheese, tea. I thought of soft beds, thought of Uncle Henry's benign face.

"You know better than that. Why didn't you stop on the way?"

"Couldn't be sure British weren't about. And not enough time."

"Exactly. Besides, we don't want to compromise old Uncle Henry now, do we?"

"What does he mean by that?" I asked Miz Melindy

as she and I were cooking supper. Johnny had taken his sling off and was washing Cephas down at the spring. Cephas was having the sweats.

"You wanna know what I think?" she asked. "I think he doan wanna see his uncle 'cause the man be a Tory. An' the British hurt him so, he wanna turn his face from anybody who like 'em."

I looked at her, startled. "Even family?"

"Tha's what I think," she said.

"But then, what about Mama? She's a Tory. And she's family. Will he turn his face from Mama?"

"How you know she still be a Tory?" came the answer. "After days of cookin' fer that popinjay an' waitin' on him an' Georgia Ann at table."

I sank back on my heels by the fire. "Oh, Miz Melindy, what will Johnny say when he finds Mama cooking for Rawdon?"

"You didn't tell him?"

"No."

"Well, you best tell him. Afore we gits home. Or the sight of it might spirit him up to do somethin' grievous awful to the popinjay an' bring the wrath of the rest of 'em down on us all. You contrive to tell him tonight, y'hear?"

"Yes." And then I had another thought. "I'll have to tell him about Georgia Ann being smitten with Rawdon, too, won't I?"

"That would be wise," she allowed.

"But how can I do that? Johnny will never accept it."

"Some things he gonna hafta 'cept," she said.

"He won't, Miz Melindy," I said dismally. "I know Johnny. I can't tell him. I'll have to lie."

"Hope you better at lyin' than you be at stirrin' them greens, girl."

I brought my attention to my task. "I have to lie," I said again. "Yes, that's it. I'll tell him that Georgia Ann is being nice to Rawdon, humoring him, for Daddy's sake."

Miz Melindy made a sound in her throat. Humor, or contempt. Or both.

"And I'll get to Georgia Ann first thing when we get home and tell her she has to lie to Johnny, too."

"What makes you think she gonna do it on your say-so?"

"I'll tell her she must, or Johnny might kill Rawdon on the spot. She'll do it; I know she will. She won't want anything to happen to her darling."

Again Miz Melindy made that sound in her throat. And then I knew it was contempt.

CEPHAS WAS not faring well. He scarce ate supper and his sweats turned to shakes. Miz Melindy prepared a pot of hot water and mixed some of her herbs.

"Doan wanna be no trouble," he said to me as I handed him the cup of blended herbs.

"Cephas, when are you ever trouble? Don't let Johnny hear you talk such folderol. He'll be hurt sore."

He drank the remedy. "Good seein' you agin, Miz Caroline. How's things to home?"

"Not good. Lots of the servants left with Cornwallis." I told him the names. "But Boney is keeping things running, and it looks as if we'll have a harvest. And enough people left to gather in the corn and grain. We're fortunate. On so many smaller places the men are gone and widows are left alone. And I'm afraid that this winter there will be want."

"We'll have to lend a hand," he said. "Do 'em a good turn."

"Yes, I'm sure that can be managed," I said.

Johnny went down to the riverbed and collected some stones, heated them in the fire, wrapped them in a blanket, and put them around Cephas to stop him from shaking. After a while, what with Miz Melindy's herbs and the warmth, Cephas fell asleep.

It was dark and the moon rose. Night birds called, cicadas chirped, bullfrogs spoke to one another in their creaking language. Moths, or whatever they were, fluttered outside the circle of our firelight. Across the fire from me, Johnny sipped his mug of coffee and started talking with Miz Melindy, asking her about the condition of the crops at home. I wandered off to relieve myself of my water in the nearby woods. As I was coming back, I heard Johnny ask Miz Melindy about Cephas.

"Will he be all right?"

"Right as rain once we git him home."

"He's dear to me," Johnny said.

There was another change in him, then. Never before the war would he have come out and said such. And I don't think he would have said it if he knew I'd been listening.

"He stood by me in that prison compound in Charleston. He worked as a manservant in the officers' quarters and made friends with one disgruntled young officer who helped us escape. I couldn't have done without him, Miz Melindy."

"He's a good boy," she said.

"No, you must know. I must tell you. Tell someone. He offered to take my whipping for me. Said it was on his account that I knocked the officer down. I can't forget that."

Their voices dropped lower then, and I couldn't hear what else was being said. I didn't want to, I suppose. I'd heard enough.

"JOHNNY, I need to talk to you."

"You should be sleeping, Caroline."

It was late. The moon was high. Overhead in the night sky, stars sparkled. I saw Orion, the great hunter, with his bow. "Johnny, there's something you should know, before we get home."

He nodded.

I told him about Mama and how she was cooking for Rawdon and waiting on the table, how it was the only way Rawdon would agree to let us come to fetch him.

"I'm liking this less and less, Caroline," he said.

"There's more, Johnny. I want to tell it all before we get home. Georgia Ann has supper every night with Rawdon. He insists on it."

"What do you mean, he insists on it?"

"He doesn't like to dine alone." The lie came easy,

slipping off my tongue. I hoped I was better at lying than at stirring the greens, lots better. "She humors him. To help save Daddy."

"How much"—the words came distinctly and carefully across the firelight—"does she humor him?"

"She charms him. Talks with him. Listens to him. She can't abide doing it, but she told me she decided it would keep peace in the house while he was there. And it is harmless. And might help save Daddy . . ." My voice trailed off. I do not know if he believed me. Johnny was smart, Catawba Indian smart.

"Is there anything else I should know?"

"Yes. One more thing. We haven't told Georgia Ann that you're a rebel now. Mama and I thought the fewer people who know, the better, being that Georgia Ann sups with Rawdon and all."

"You are a dear thing, almost-sister of mine," he said. "Now you'd best get some sleep."

I did so. I lay down next to Miz Melindy. She was snoring. Johnny sat up by the fire, his musket in his hands. What had he meant by that last remark? The thought I had before drifting off was that Johnny was smart enough not to let me know if he did not believe me.

I DOZED and dreamed of home. I saw Mama cooking in the kitchen, Georgia Ann fussing with herself before the mirror in our chamber; I heard Daddy's voice in a distant room, heard his laughter, so I ran through all the rooms downstairs to find him. Rawdon had secured his release from prison! But I went from room to room and there was no Daddy. Only Mama, talking to me in her low, reassuring tones. And the crackling sound of a fire. I was in the kitchen again with Mama. She was telling me Daddy wasn't ever coming home. They were going to ship him south to Charleston. And then to the West Indies. "Just like your real mama, the slave, was shipped out," she was saying. "Oh, it's God's punishment on us for what we did to your mama. Can you forgive us, Caroline?"

Then, before I could answer, she was saying, "But I'll find your daddy. I'll look for him and look for him until I find him." Then there was a hand on my shoulder, and I woke to find Miz Melindy leaning over me with a finger in front of her lips. She gestured to the fire.

There, standing next to Johnny, was a woman. A young woman with a shawl wrapped around her. Her hair hung disheveled around her shoulders. The first thing I noticed about her was that her clothing had once been elegant. She even wore stiff stays. Her lawn apron was besmudged with dirt; the skirt of the Holland gown was tattered and muddy. There was a small tuft of ribbon in her hair, half done. Her shoes had high heels, now worn down.

Hers had been the voice I heard in my dream, not Mama's. It was she who had said, "I'll find him. I'll look for him and look for him until I find him." And she had some sort of accent.

"I'm afraid he's far off by now," Johnny was saying.

"Who is she?" I whispered to Miz Melindy.

"Looks like mebbe that Scotch woman from Glasgow who come round to home lookin' fer Cornwallis."

"Did you see her at home?"

"No. Boney tell me 'bout her. Boney says she was wif Cornwallis in Charleston."

"She looks all ragged and spent."

"Boney say she got malaria fever, is why." She struggled to her feet. I helped her. "You stay here," she told me.

"What are you going to do, Miz Melindy?"

"You hush an' go back to sleep. An' stay here. I'm gon' give her some remedies like I give Cephas."

I lay back down, watching her make her way around the fire to where Johnny and the woman were still engaged in low conversation. The night had chilled, as it sometimes does when you are near the river. I huddled under my blanket. The three of them were talking now in those low conspiratorial tones. I fell asleep again, their voices lulling me.

Chapter Fourteen

July 8, 1780

IN THE MORNING I thought I had dreamed the woman, but she was still there. For a moment I couldn't conclude what was going on. Everybody was eating breakfast, but it was a hurried affair. Johnny was shoving the food into his mouth while he was walking around. Cephas was up and appeared to be middling well. Miz Melindy was spooning some mush into the woman's mouth while she sat against a tree.

"Why didn't you wake me?" I asked petulantly.

They didn't answer. I noticed the mules were already harnessed. "That's my job," I told Johnny. I felt slighted.

"Your job is to eat your breakfast so we can get started," he said.

I hated him when he got that way. "Who is this?" I stared at the woman.

"It's Agnes," he answered.

"Agnes who?"

"Just Agnes, for now. We're taking her with us on to home."

He was still pacing. I followed him away from the others. "If her name is Agnes, she has malarial fever," I told him. "And she isn't just anybody. She's already been to home. She was there before I left, looking for Cornwallis. A soldier chased her. Nobody wanted her around."

"Well, we're taking her there again." He was fixed on it. "Show her to Rawdon. She was Cornwallis's woman. This is how precious bad they treat their women, the British."

The plan had been devised in the night, it seemed, by him and Miz Melindy.

I could figure why Miz Melindy wanted to take Just Agnes home: to treat her malaria. Miz Melindy could not abide to let anyone who was ill out of her sight. It was a matter of pride with her that she make them well again.

And it went without saying why Johnny wanted to take Just Agnes home. To show Georgia Ann.

I didn't care about either of their reasons. Either or both would bring Rawdon's wrath down upon us. But I did not dare speak my mind to Johnny about it. Once he was set in his ways, nobody could stop him about anything.

They put Just Agnes in the wagon bed. Miz Melindy had removed the woman's shoes and hose and bound up her feet, which were swollen and bleeding. She had put some salve on the woman's arms, too. They were scratched with cuts from the underbrush. So was her face. Before we left, Miz Melindy put salve on my hands and wrapped them in fresh lint. Johnny put his sling back on and checked Grey Goose's leg bandage. We all looked like we'd been through a war. Cephas insisted he was well enough to walk, though. And he did.

We were within twelve miles of home. As the wagon jostled along I heard Just Agnes moaning and crying out how she was going to find Cornwallis, how she would keep looking for him until she found him.

Every so often Miz Melindy would make me stop the wagon so she could attend to Just Agnes, to make her sit up and force some tepid tea mixed with herbs down her throat. To bathe her face with more cool water. With each stop, as we got closer and closer to home, I became more agitated. We were wasting so much time on this woman who was only going to make trouble for us. Didn't we have enough trouble as things stood?

At noontime, when the sun was high and the cicadas screamed all around us, we stopped again. We were a couple of miles outside the town of Camden in a grove of trees with a lot of low scrub pine in front of us. It was a good place to stop. We could see down the sandy embankment to the road that ran along the river. But the stately trees gave us shade and, because of the scrub pine, we couldn't be seen.

But this time the stop wasn't for Just Agnes. This time it was to avoid some British cavalry. Johnny covered Just Agnes with the canvas in the wagon, leaving only her head exposed. She was shivering now and shaking grievous bad.

"Heat gonna kill her if'n we doan get home soon," Miz Melindy said.

Good, I thought, *let it kill her. What do we need with her and her malaria?* It was different with Cephas. Miz Melindy had brought him around and would keep him in the quarters with her when we got home. If I knew Johnny, he'd want to bring Just Agnes into the house. Would Rawdon allow her into the house?

I knew the answer to that almost before my mind knew the question. No. And so there would be a set-to then with Johnny and Rawdon over it. Because it was Rawdon's house now, and Johnny would not be able to accept that. Just Agnes would be the fine point that would bring them to a confrontation.

I knew my thoughts were un-Christian, of course. But I felt no guilt whatsoever as we hid behind the scrub pine in the tall trees and watched the British cavalry go by in their green coats, the officers' gorgets reflecting the sunlight, black boots shining, sword hilts gleaming.

I stood next to Johnny. "Likely they're from home," I whispered. "Rawdon sends them out near every day."

"Look like no cavalry horseflesh I've ever seen," he said.

"They're short of horses. I told you. They're making do with what they've stolen from the countryside."

I don't know how long we waited there in the protection of the trees with gnats and flies buzzing around us and Just Agnes's moans filling our ears. But Johnny wouldn't let us proceed for a while.

"There could be more coming," he said.

He was right. In about twenty minutes another unit came by. Cephas stood next to Grey Goose the whole time, so she wouldn't make a sound.

And there was Just Agnes moaning like a stuck pig.

"Hush her up," Johnny whispered.

Miz Melindy was on the wagon seat holding the reins, so I went over to the wagon. Just Agnes was thrashing and mumbling something about her darling Cornwallis. Her face was beaded with sweat. What to do? Miz Melindy turned and made a sign to me, and with the turning the mules jerked forward and started dragging the wagon forward, out of the cover of the trees and scrub pine, down the sandy embankment to the road.

Now we were exposed under the bright blue sky. Immediately Johnny went to steady the animals and back them up the embankment. It was slow, painstaking work, especially with his one arm in the sling, and he and Miz Melindy were well occupied with the task.

Then, just before we got back into the covering of the trees, another group of cavalry appeared from around a clump of trees in the road.

Just Agnes was still crying out.

What had Miz Melindy meant me to do? Never mind, I knew.

I drew the blanket up over Just Agnes's face, then the canvas, so that her moanings became weaker and wouldn't carry on the summer air. I held the canvas down on the wagon sides and walked backward while from up front Johnny prodded Orphelia and Jackaroo with becalming words and Miz Melindy guided the reins. Behind me I sensed Cephas quieting Grey Goose.

It seemed like that group of cavalry took the Lord's whole eternity to go by. We were just inside the shelter of the pine trees now, hoping they wouldn't look our way. We hadn't yet made it to the concealment of the scrub pine. But Johnny stopped, likely not wanting to make any more movement to attract their eye.

But he did make one more movement. With his good hand he cocked his musket.

The sound carried on the summer air, but the green-coated men were joking and laughing amongst themselves as they rode along, their horses' hooves making clouds of dust. I was thankful for that dust. And I stood there, beads of sweat breaking out on my face and neck, dripping down my bodice, and my hands straining to hold tight that canvas over the wagon bed.

In a moment they were gone. Johnny pronounced that was likely the last of them and we continued on. I lowered the canvas and the blanket from Just Agnes's face. She had stopped moaning. She was sleeping peacefully. I hopped up on the wagon seat next to Miz Melindy.

Johnny grinned at us. "That was close," he said. Then he looked back at the wagon. "She's quieted down, I see."

"Yes," I said. "She's sleeping."

We went on. Not through the town of Camden but around it, which took a little longer, a path that would take us the back way into our plantation. First we would have to cross a stream.

"We'll stop and wash up," Johnny said.

When we set foot onto our land Jackaroo and Orphelia knew it, the way animals do. They jogged along, ears all perky, high stepping it. They were home!

I felt my own sense of triumph. I'd done it! I'd accomplished what I'd set out to do. I'd brought my brother and Cephas home!

The stream was a ways from the house and barn, and we stopped beside it to let the mules and Grey Goose drink. Johnny took off his sling, knelt, and dipped his two hands in the water, cupped them, and drank. So did Cephas. And I sensed it was more of a ritual than a thirst quenching they were doing. They had both fished in this stream, swam in it as boys. Now they splashed each other, laughing. I helped Miz Melindy down from the wagon and hugged her.

"We're home," I said.

She made a pleasant sound in her throat. I fetched her some water from the stream in a cup, dipped in a rag, and let her mop her face.

"Never been offa this place since I come here," she said, "an' I never wanna go offa it agin."

I was kneeling at the stream, wiping my face and neck and arms with a cooling rag when, out of the corner of my eye, I saw Miz Melindy bringing some water to Just Agnes in the wagon. *Ought to let her sleep,* I told myself. *Not rouse her now.*

Grey Goose was sipping the water right next to me, and I watched her. Johnny was patting her and whispering in her ear, then he checked the binding on her leg. "Just for a little while longer, girl," he told her. "Just until we can get you past that piece of slime and into the barn. Then we'll stay the night and ride out tomorrow on the pretense of spying for him."

I felt a shock go through me. "Tomorrow?"

"Got to," Johnny said.

"Why so soon?"

"The sooner the better."

He was up to something, I minded. But he would never tell me. Oh well. Likely it was better if he rode out of here tomorrow. The less he was around while Rawdon occupied the place, the better. I felt cheered.

Then, in the next moment came Miz Melindy's cry, shrill and agonizing. We turned.

"What is it?" Johnny called out.

"Daid," she said. And she raised her arms and her face to the heavens. I saw tears streaming down her face. "Daid, Lawd, Lawd, she be daid, Mistuh Johnny! Sure 'nough."

Chapter Fifteen

❦

JULY 8, 1780

I WANTED TO BURY Just Agnes on the spot, but Johnny said no. He said it grimly and with such fierce intent my arguments got washed right away.

"We take her to Rawdon," he said.

Miz Melindy argued, too. "No point, Mistuh Johnny. Doan go draggin' the poor thing round."

"I'm not dragging her. I'm fetching her to where she wanted to go," he said.

The discussion between him and Miz Melindy went on, and while it did I took myself to a nearby clump of trees to throw up. I was sick and trembling when Johnny stood over me and handed me a flask of water.

"It's been a trial for you," he said. "The whole trip."

"No."

"What then? Surely it's not Agnes. You scarce knew her. And you've seen people die before. You said you saw your friend Kit hanged. Did you do this then?"

"Yes. But this is different."

"Why?"

I looked up at him. "I killed her, Johnny."

"Nonsense."

"I killed her." I stood up and told him between sobbing breaths how I'd held the canvas over Just Agnes while the cavalry went by.

He was silent for a moment. "Not long enough a time to have killed her."

"She was moaning before that. She got quiet after."

But he would have none of it. "You didn't kill her. Come along now, we must to home."

He put the sling back on and I tied it around back for him, thinking, *He wears it like a badge of honor now.* We started back to the wagon.

"Anyways," Johnny mumbled, "if you hadn't held the canvas over her, we might all be dead. Name of God, that was Tarleton's cavalry who passed us by. Don't you know what they did at Waxhaws? They give no quarter. They'd as soon have run us through with bayonets as eat breakfast. And I'll hear no more of the matter. Get up on the wagon. We have to look as normal as possible when we drive in."

"WHAT DO you think he's going to do when we get there?" I asked Miz Melindy as the wagon creaked over the dry rutted back road of the plantation.

" 'Pears to me he gonna show Agnes to the popinjay," she said.

"It will cause trouble."

"Mistuh Johnny no stranger to trouble."

"I think he wants to show her to Georgia Ann," I

said. "I know he didn't believe me when I lied to him about Georgia Ann and Rawdon."

"You ain't no good at lyin'," she said. "No better'n you is at stirrin' greens."

I looked at her. "Miz Melindy, what were you directing me to do when you turned around as the cavalry was coming?"

"Cover Agnes wif the canvas," she said. "She was wailin' so."

I looked into her yellow-brown eyes. They did not so much as blink. She held her gaze true. Had Johnny had time to whisper to her what I'd told him about killing Just Agnes? Was she just trying to wash away my guilt?

"I'm so confused, Miz Melindy," I said.

"We's all that, chile. We's all turnin' round an' round, chasin' our tails since the popinjays come."

"No," I said. "I think it has nothing to do with them. I think we're just confused people. Look at me. I didn't speak to you for most of my life. Now we've taken this trip and I don't know what to do when I get home. What do I do, Miz Melindy? I've come to know you. You're my grandmother! Since I've been traveling with you I feel I know you like I know myself. I can't just let you go back to the quarters and not come visit you anymore."

I wanted her to say I could come visit whenever I wished. But she didn't. "This be a diff'rent time," she said. " 'Cause o' the war. War try to wash away the rules. We negras knows that. White folk lets up on the rules a bit on account o' the war. But after, the rules hold.

We knows that, too. Ain't nothin' gonna change 'tween the white folks and negras 'cause o' the war. So you gotta go back to yer life an' I gots to go back to mine."

"Why?"

" 'Cause that's how it be."

"But Miz Melindy," I protested.

"This be a diff'rent time," she said again, "this time we had. Special." She put her hand over mine and smiled. "But it be over now. You gotta go back to the way things was afore."

"But things aren't the way they were before. Look at Johnny. He was a Loyalist, now he's a rebel. Daddy's in prison and Georgia Ann's taken up with a British officer. Uncle Henry is a sworn king's man, but he's helped people who aren't. None of us are the way we were before."

"I tol' you, it's the war. White folks go a bit crazy."

"No," I said dismally, "the war just brought it all to a head. I think none of us know who we really are."

She pondered that for a minute. She nodded her head. "It's the river," she said.

I stared at her. "The river?"

"The river give us all life," she said. "Flows by an' we all part of it. But the river doan know what it be, either. Up north it be the Catawba. Here it be the Wateree. Below us, where it runs itself into the ocean, it be the Santee. It be the river," she said. And she seemed so certain that I didn't dare question her.

The river? When she said things like that I did not feel part of her, did not feel she was part of me. It was the old negra superstitions talking now. And then, before I could untangle my muddled thoughts, I looked up and saw we were coming right through the quarters. Negras were rushing out to greet us. Johnny held up his hand and we all stopped. He went back to where Cephas was leading Grey Goose, took the reins, and whispered in the horse's ear. Immediately, she started to limp badly.

Even the horse will be confused, I thought. *She'll not know whether she's lame or hearty.* And then it came to me. We were really home. Had it been only four days since we left? It seemed like a hundred years!

The negras crowded around Johnny and Cephas, hugged them, made noises of joy. Mr. Bone came out of nowhere, shook Johnny's hand, took him off, and conferred with him.

I helped Miz Melindy down. I fetched her remedy bag from the wagon. It was by Just Agnes's feet. I turned to say something to Miz Melindy, but the negras had already taken her and Cephas in hand and were escorting them to her cabin.

They were taking her away from me. And she wasn't even looking back. Why didn't I run after her? Because I couldn't. I didn't belong. I knew it and they knew it. It had been a special time for us, like she said. And now it was over.

So I just stood there like a fence post with Miz Melindy's remedy bag in my hand while they led Miz Melindy and Cephas into her cabin and the door closed behind them. Scooby, the old rooster, came stalking over to me, head held high. He was going to peck me if I went near Miz Melindy's porch. But I didn't care.

Let him peck. Quietly, I crept over to the porch and left the remedy bag at the door. Scooby stretched his neck straight out and made a beeline for me, his wings spread. "Shoo," I said, "Shoo!" I made as if to kick him. I fluttered my apron at him and ran back to the protection of the wagon.

From inside the cabin came shouts of joy, whooping, sudden silences while Cephas related his tale. I smelled cooking: coosh-coosh. Johnny and Mr. Bone were still conferring. Old Boney was being right serious. Johnny was listening intently and nodding his head. "When?" I heard him ask.

" 'Bout four days ago," Mr. Bone said.

I saw Johnny's shoulders sag, and he muttered a curse word then. "Does my mother know?"

"I think not," I heard Old Boney say. "The private what sits in the kitchen tastin' all the food your mother cooks told me. But I know he didn't tell her."

Johnny nodded, and they came back over to the wagon. *What? What happened four days ago that Mother doesn't know?* Mr. Bone patted Jackaroo and Orphelia. "How'd they handle?" he asked.

"Good," I said.

Johnny led him around to the side of the wagon and lifted the canvas. Mr. Bone stared at Just Agnes. "That's her," he said. "She was here before Caroline left. Creepin' around. Come from Georgetown on the river with the Catawbas. Said she was in Charleston with Cornwallis. The soldiers ran her off. That's her, poor thing." He took out the musket and went over to Grey Goose, took up her reins, and led her to the barn. "I'll keep the leg bound," he told Johnny. "Give her a good rubdown. Have her ready."

I started to unhitch the mules.

"Leave 'em," Mr. Bone said.

"I can do it."

"Know you can. You done good. But you're home now. It's my job. Leave 'em."

I left them and walked up to the house with Johnny. Home now, I shivered and looked around. The place seemed the same, as if I had never left. I looked with longing back to the barn, to Orphelia and Jackaroo waiting patiently while Mr. Bone unharnessed them, to the wagon that had been my only home for four days, the wagon with Just Agnes lying in it, to the quarters and Miz Melindy's cabin, where I couldn't go anymore because what had been between us had been special. And it was over now. And I had to go back to my life. Because that's the way things be.

Johnny put his arm around my shoulder, and we went down the brick walk to the house.

"Johnny, what'll I say to Mama?" I asked him.

"About what?"

"About knowing what happened to my real mama. Do I tell her I know?"

"Do you want to?"

"I don't know," I said.

"Then don't say anything until you do. When the time comes, you'll know what to say."

Two sentries were at the door, of course. New ones. They did not know me, and they came to us alert, aiming their muskets at us. I thought of how Johnny must look to them, in his frontier clothing, his face so lean and brown, his sheathed knife, his bullet pouch, his trusted musket in his hand.

"Halt and state your business." The command was sharp.

Johnny smiled. "My business is to come into my home, to see after my mother and sister. My business is to rest awhile and take some nourishment. My business is with Colonel Rawdon."

I pulled Rawdon's note out of my pocket and handed it to one of them. He read it and bade us wait. He went inside while the other guarded us with his musket. I thought how foolish it was. Johnny could kill him if he chose. He just didn't choose to at the moment.

After a few moments the sentry came out. "The colonel will see you," he said.

We went inside, and I thought as we stepped over the threshold into the back hall how strange it was that we needed permission to enter our own home.

Nobody was in the hall. I looked around at the cool dimness, the curved stairway, the quiet, familiar, solid graciousness. I had forgotten how orderly, how elegant, it was. The tall case clock ticked silently. Someone had arranged flowers in a bowl on a table in the hall. The floorboards gleamed. From a distant room came a man's laughter. *It should be my daddy's,* I thought.

But it was Rawdon's. The old secure feeling that had enveloped me like a cloak upon entering fell away. Again, nothing was the way it had been before.

Johnny turned to me. "Go on upstairs to Mother," he said. "Tell her I'll be up in a while to see her. Go on, clean yourself up. Put on a nice dress for the funeral."

"Funeral?" I gaped at him.

"Yes. We're going to bury Agnes of Glasgow. Tonight. In the churchyard. Go on now, do as I say."

I went.

I STOOD with Mama at the window of our chamber, watching as Johnny led Colonel Rawdon, accompanied by two sentries, down to the barn, where the wagon still sat with Just Agnes's body in it. I saw Johnny flip back the canvas. For a moment the men stood looking down at the body.

"I think it's disgusting." Georgia Ann came up behind us. "Why didn't Johnny just bury her? To what aim, bringing her here like this?"

"He had a point to make," I said.

"What point?"

"She's the discarded mistress of a British officer." I realized then that my sister did not know what British officer. The gossip about the place had not reached her. I'd let Johnny tell her.

"Johnny's being his own stubborn self, you mean," she said languidly, turning away and going back to her dressing table. She was wearing her favorite silk robe. She poured herself some tea from a tray that Jade had brought up for me with some cold meat and bread on it.

"I can't believe Francis even agreed to go and look at her," she said.

I turned from the window. "So it's 'Francis' now.

196

My, things have progressed. Well, in case you've forgotten, Francis has been waiting for Johnny. Our brother is to do some important work for him. He's smart enough to know he should accommodate Johnny's wishes."

She was seated, sipping her tea. I thought how pale she looked, how puffy and languid. She was getting fat, I minded. Her arms were plump. So was her face. But there was something else about her face that I couldn't put a name to.

Filled up, I thought. Not denied. And then the word came to me. *Satisfied.* Contented. Like a cat who'd had too much cream. I know what I looked like. Freckles had broken out across my nose from the sun. My face, arms, and neck were browned. My hands had calluses from the reins.

And Georgia Ann looked more than her seventeen years, too. If I'd just met her I'd venture to say she was in her twenties. But it had nothing to do with age. It had to do with experience.

Why, I thought, *she's been doing more than walking out with Colonel Rawdon. She's been allowing him to play free with her.* Didn't Mama see it?

I looked at Mama. "I must change this dress," she said. "I look a fright. I wouldn't want Johnny to think..." Her voice trailed off and she went to get another dress from the clothespress in the corner.

Think what? I asked myself. *That Rawdon's been working you to death?* Because he had been. I'd seen with a shock that Mama's hands were rough, with some cuts in them, the nails broken. And there were circles under her eyes. No, I didn't want to tell her I knew about my slave mother being sold to the West Indies. Not now. I loved this woman like my real mother. Was that disloyal to Mama Cecie? I didn't know. I only knew I felt a fierce protectiveness for Mama Sarah.

And I could kill Georgia Ann for letting Mama wait on her and Rawdon.

I walked over to the table with the tray on it, took some meat and bread on a plate, poured myself some tea, and went back to sit by the window. "You'd best get dressed," I told my sister, "and be ready for the funeral."

"What? What funeral?"

"Agnes's. Johnny aims to have her buried this day in our churchyard."

"Well, I never! A common doxie!"

"Doxie, is it?" My mouth twisted in a wry smile. "Well, you should know, Georgia Ann."

"Mama, did you hear that? Did you hear what she said? She said I'm a doxie."

"Don't fight, girls. Georgia Ann, your sister just got home after a tiresome journey. Can't you be nice to each other?" Mama had slipped a fresh gown over her shoulders. I could see she didn't care a fig what I called Georgia Ann. Her mind was on Johnny. She patted her hair into place, reached for a fresh apron, and went to the door. "I'm going downstairs to say hello to Johnny."

"He said he'd be up, Mama," I told her.

"Well, I'm going down. I'll send Jade up with some hot water for your bath, Caroline. You'll feel better. Georgia Ann, don't taunt your sister. Find a nice fresh dress for her. We all need to look presentable when we go to the funeral."

"I'm not going," Georgia Ann said. "I see no reason to go to the funeral of a common doxie."

It was the moment I'd been waiting for. The door closed after Mama. I set my cup down and looked at my sister. "You'd best not tell Johnny you've been dallying with Rawdon."

"I'm not dallying with Rawdon."

"Look, Georgia Ann, I don't give a king's shilling if it's so. But I'm telling you right now that Johnny will kill him."

"Johnny's a true Loyalist, have you forgotten?"

"He's still your brother. And you know what he's like when he's mad. Remember last Christmas at the party in Charleston when Charlie Skirving took you out for a midnight drive in his carriage unchaperoned? And came back drunk as a lord?"

She remembered. Her blue eyes went wide. The Skirvings were Loyalists. Mama and Daddy hadn't been at the party. Johnny had called Skirving out for a duel, and when Skirving refused the challenge, Johnny had whipped young Charlie right in the street, and him the son of a prominent physician. "Did you tell Johnny about me and Francis?" she asked.

"I'm nobody's fool, Georgia Ann. I lied for you. I told him you were supping every night with Rawdon, charming him, listening to him. I told him you were doing it to save Daddy."

"And? What did he say to that, then?"

"I'm sure he didn't believe me. In part, it's why he brought Agnes here. To caution you."

"I need no cautioning. Let him believe what he wishes," she said. "What do I care what he believes?"

"You'll care, Georgia Ann. Johnny was very taken with Agnes's plight. It's put him on notice about how the British officers dally with women. He's a Loyalist, yes, and he wants to help Rawdon. And if you want that to happen, and want to save your darling Francis from Johnny's rage, you'll go along with what I told him. Pretend you're granting him your favors to save Daddy."

"What do you care for me?" she asked. "Or for Francis? Why would you want to protect us?"

"I don't want to protect you," I told her. "I want to keep Rawdon and the British from doing any more real harm around here. I want to keep Johnny from ruining himself with Rawdon."

A dreamy, wistful look came into her blue eyes. She got up and wandered to the window. "I'll do anything to protect Francis," she said.

"Good. Then you'd best dress for the funeral."

"I told you, I'm not going to the funeral."

We faced each other across the carpet. And it came to me then. If I was Johnny's almost-sister, Georgia Ann was my not-quite-sister. We could never be sisters, she and I. Why had I always envied her, then? How could I have ever aspired to be like her? To let her make me feel I was less, because we were so different?

"You'll go," I said. "I'm sure Francis will want you there." I said it as if I knew something she should know.

Which I did. I was dying to tell her who Agnes's lover really was. Jade came into the room with my bathwater then. "I'd like some privacy," I told Georgia Ann, and I drew the curtain that had been rigged across the room and left her to her own devices.

Chapter Sixteen

JULY 8, 1780

JOHNNY STOOD IN the middle of our chamber. He was freshly shaven and dressed immaculately in civilian breeches and linen coat, a froth of ruffles and black stock at his neck, ruffles at his wrists, boots polished. He wore a bright white new sling. The only concession to the military was the sword.

"What do you mean, you're not coming to the funeral, Georgia Ann?"

She was seated at the window doing some crewelwork. "I see no reason to. Colonel Rawdon hasn't requested it. I'm going to stay right here and get myself ready for supper."

"I request it," Johnny said.

She concentrated on her crewelwork. "Really, Johnny." She sounded bored.

In three strides Johnny was standing in front of her. In one movement he took the embroidery hoop from her hands and laid her work aside.

"Do you know who Agnes's lover was?"

Georgia Ann examined her fingernails.

"General Charles Earl Lord Cornwallis."

"You lie," Georgia Ann said. But her face paled, saying it.

"Do I? Must you hear it from Rawdon's lips? He recollects her from Charleston. Why don't you wish to come, Georgia Ann? Can you not abide to see how the British use women?"

"I heard tell that Agnes came from Glasgow," my sister said.

Johnny reached out, grasped Georgia Ann by the forearm, and pulled her to her feet. "Get dressed," he said between clenched teeth. "Get dressed, or by heaven you'll be sorry you drew breath this day. I swear it."

She pulled herself free and rubbed her arm. "What care I how the British treat women? I'm no British jade."

"Caroline, fetch a dress," Johnny ordered.

I did so. I went to the clothespress, pulled out a dark blue calico, and handed it to Johnny. He took it and threw it at Georgia Ann's feet.

"Appropriate," he said. "Plain enough. Look here, sister of mine, I know what you're about. You don't fool me. If I had time and things were different, I'd beat the tar out of Rawdon with a buggy whip. Then I'd start on you. But I have more important things on my mind. I can't afford to indulge myself in such luxuries. You've made your choices. There's little more I can do now but show you Agnes. But that I will do. Mother?"

"Put the dress on, Georgia Ann," Mama told her.

Georgia Ann started to weep quietly. She picked up the dress. "And you're so holier-than-thou, I suppose," she shouted as Johnny started for the door. "You and your Catawba woman!"

Johnny stopped at the door, hand on the knob. He turned to look at her. And I'd have died before I earned such a look from him. There was contempt in that look. Cold amusement. Derision. "You're not fit to tie Nepoya's moccasins," he said. Then he went out.

THE AFTERNOON had darkened. Storm clouds loomed on the horizon. A hint of rain was in the air and the leaves of the trees rustled with warning wind. On some of the trees in the churchyard, the leaves turned up and showed their silver undersides.

There were ten of us: Mama, myself, Georgia Ann, Johnny, Miz Melindy, Cephas, Colonel Rawdon, two sentries, and Mr. Bone. There were more, of course, in the background: negras from the quarters. Just outside the cemetery were Orphelia and Jackaroo. They'd pulled the wagon that brought Just Agnes to the churchyard. I knew, of course, that Miz Melindy had washed and anointed Just Agnes's body. Mama had sent a dress down to the quarters for her to be buried in: a white dress.

I also knew that the minute the coffin Old Boney had hammered together in the last couple of hours was lowered into the ground, the negras would start to sing. They always sang at funerals.

I almost dreaded it. The negra spirituals made me

feel forlorn and weepy. And my spirit was so cast down already I didn't think it had much further to go.

I was wrong. There are always depths inside us that we do not know exist until the possibilities are opened to us. I stood numbly while two negras from the quarters held the ropes of Just Agnes's coffin and Johnny said the prayer.

There was no minister. There hadn't been in some time now. All the neighborhood ministers had gone off to join Sumter.

In the distance, heat lightning lit up the horizon. Thunder rumbled. Johnny, prayer book in his one good hand, stood straight and solemn and read the appropriate psalms. Then he closed the prayer book and looked at each of us in turn.

"I knew Agnes but briefly," he said, "but she had the sweetest spirit I have had the privilege to know. She was sickly by the time I came to know her. But through the ravages of that sickness still glowed the winsome Scotch lassie who once lived behind those blue eyes and that loyal heart. Her only fault, far as I could see, was that she was too true-hearted. 'Twas this malady, as much as the malaria, that killed her. It is fitting she should lie here, in a place occupied by the bones of some of our early Scotch settlers. Agnes is at rest now. We who come to bid her farewell are not. We've a ways to go before we can claim any peace on this earth. All I can honestly wish for those here assembled is that we know, in our lifetimes, someone as true and loyal as Agnes of Glasgow."

A mockingbird gave forth then with several versions of song from a nearby tree limb. It was growing darker. The negras in the background lighted the pine-knot torches.

Johnny signaled with his head and the negras holding the ropes lowered Agnes's coffin into the rich brown earth. Then the negras shoveled the dirt on top of it. At once, the others in the background commenced to sing.

The song was lilting and sad. It conjured the heart and soul out of me. I felt myself gathering all up inside to cry. For the song was not only for Just Agnes, I knew that. It was for Kit, who had yet to be buried here. For my daddy, still in jail. For Mrs. Martin and her children, who had lived in the orchard after the British had burned them out. For Mr. Wyly, who had been cut to pieces at Waxhaws. For Mrs. McClure, whose kin had been taken off to be hanged.

It was for Cephas, looking sickly as he stood nearby. For Mama, with her broken fingernails and callused hands, made to bend over a cookfire all day and serve her own daughter at table.

It was for me. I, who had killed Just Agnes.

It was for Mama Cecie, bent under the task of picking sugarcane in the hot sun on some Godforsaken island, destined to work until it killed her. And yes, it was even for Georgia Ann, who had given herself to this reprobate, this haughty Englishman, who stood there, hat in his hands, looking bored to death.

Tears rolled down my face as the negra spiritual picked up in tempo, as the shoveled earth accumulated on Just Agnes's coffin.

Then, of a sudden, I felt someone take my hand. I turned. It was Miz Melindy. She wrapped her frail arm around mine and drew me toward her, toward the warmth and comfort of her body.

She was singing, too. I felt the words rising out of her, felt the vibrations of the song as I leaned against her body. *How can they sing?* I thought. *How can they have such feeling to sing, such hope? And if they can have it, why can't we? Why can't I?*

The singing stopped. Rawdon had been standing well away from the coffin with Georgia Ann. He gave the signal, and the sentries fired their muskets over the grave.

It was finished.

Johnny put his tricorn hat back onto his head. "Thank you all for coming," he said. "Now let's all to home."

I walked along with Miz Melindy, still crying. She had her arm around me. Soft rain started to fall as we wound through the fields, a shabby procession. "I killed her, Miz Melindy," I said.

"You?" She gave a soft chuckle. "Cornwallis done killed her, chile."

I told her how I'd held the blanket and canvas over Just Agnes and smothered her to death.

"She weren't gon' make it," she told me. "I knowed it the minute I treated her."

"Is that true?" I asked.

"Sure 'nough."

I stopped and looked at her, into the yellow-brown eyes. "I've got three people hanging inside me now, Miz

Melindy. My friend Kit, my real mama, and now Agnes of Glasgow."

She nodded slowly, understanding.

"At first it was just Kit. I couldn't get around him the way he was hanging there inside me. A sickness. And then when you told me about my mama, she was there, too. In the way. Stopping me every time I wanted to be glad about something. Or just be at peace with myself. And now there's Agnes of Glasgow. Because I'll always wonder if I killed her, no matter what you and Johnny say."

She was silent for a moment. Then she spoke. "Only three?" she asked.

"What?"

"Three's all you got hangin' there inside?"

I gaped at her. "Should there be more?"

Again she gave that soft chuckle. "Chile, chile, I gots fifty."

"Fifty?"

"Fifty," she said again. "Mebbe more. Time you git to be my age an' see all there be o' this world, you have fifty, too."

"You mean everybody has people hanging inside them?"

"No. Bet that popinjay up to the house ain't got one."

"But it isn't fair!"

"Fair?" She scoffed. "Those peoples you got hangin' inside, they be a comfort to you, too."

"A comfort?"

"Uh-huh. You gits 'customed to havin' 'em round.

You soon put great store in 'em. You come to know they meant somethin' to you. You come to know you kin learn from 'em. Those people you got hangin' inside, they make you diff'rent. Better. You see."

We commenced walking. I was silent for a moment, then I spoke. "But Miz Melindy, how do you live with fifty ghosts hanging inside you?" I asked.

"Kin git a mite crowded sometime," she said, "but lawdy, I'd miss 'em if they wasn't there. Sure 'nough."

I had a thought then. "Do you think Johnny has anybody hanging inside?"

"Uh-huh! You kin see it in his eyes."

"His eyes?"

"You kin always see it in a person's eyes. Shadows. Come from what's hangin' in there, swingin' back an' forth. Shadows," she said again.

Yes, I thought, *she's right. So that's why Johnny's eyes aren't laughing and teasing anymore. He's got people hanging inside him, too.*

Chapter Seventeen

JULY 8, 1780

GEORGIA ANN did not dine with Rawdon that night. Johnny did. So did Mama.

Johnny arranged it. When we got back from the funeral he told Mama to go upstairs and ready herself. She was to put on her most elegant gown.

Georgia Ann stood there pouting. "Rawdon won't like my not being able to dine with him."

"He'll have to like it tonight," Johnny said. "We have business to discuss with him. Now go upstairs with Mother and dress her hair. Soak her hands in some of your lotions." He turned to Mama. "I'll be up to fetch you at seven," he said.

I started down the brick walk to the kitchen, but Johnny grabbed my arm. "No, Caroline. There is to be no more waiting on Rawdon by Whitaker women."

"But I must help Miz Melindy! She's plumb wore out."

"It will be a light supper. I've asked only for a

Salamagundy and hot biscuits. I think Jade and Miz Melindy can manage that. Go upstairs and help your mother get ready."

His voice was quiet but firm. He winked at me and gestured to the house. I knew this was all part of his plan, so I went.

I never saw Mama look so beautiful as she did that night. To give Georgia Ann her due, she washed and dressed Mama's hair and used all her magic lotions to make it shine. Then she worked on her hands and told me exactly what clothing to lay out: the blue satin petticoat, a scarlet under-petticoat, blue satin shoes, blue silk stockings, and stays the color of daffodils in the spring. When Johnny came to fetch Mama and left with her on his arm, she was so beautiful I wanted to cry.

The supper lasted two hours. Jade brought a tray to the room for me and Georgia Ann, but I wasn't hungry. I should have been in the kitchen helping Miz Melindy. The biscuits were cold and not light and fluffy. The Salamagundy had no eggs in it. This wasn't Miz Melindy's way. Something was wrong, I told myself.

I drank my tea and ventured out of the room to sit on the landing in the darkened hall. From there I could hear Johnny's voice, and, on occasion, Mama's. Otherwise the house was quiet. Sentries stood guard outside the door. From outside came the sound of cicadas and the songs birds make when they go to sleep.

I dozed. Then of a sudden Mama was standing over me with a candle in her hand. "Caroline, what are you doing here?"

"Waiting."

"For what?"

"I don't know. I've a sense something's about to happen."

"It's already happened," she said. Her lips trembled as she uttered the words.

"What?" I scrambled to my feet.

"Go on downstairs. Johnny's outside in the garden. He wants to talk with you."

Johnny was in the kitchen garden outside the back door. He took my arm and led me away from the sentries. "What's wrong with Miz Melindy?" I asked him.

"What makes you think anything is wrong?"

"The Salamagundy was poorly. She'd never countenance it."

"You ask too many questions, Caroline. But I'm glad to see you so alert. Miz Melindy is sickly. She collapsed in the kitchen."

I pulled away from him. "I must go to her."

"Not now. She's resting. Tomorrow. Before you leave."

I felt a thrill go through me. Then a sense of doom. "What's happened? Mama, on the stairs, looked dreadful."

"Listen to me now, and listen well." And he bent his head close to mine and walked me through the Cherokee roses on the side of the garden.

"I'm leaving tonight. I'm taking Grey Goose and riding out. If I stay one more day, I'll kill the man."

"Tell me what's happened."

"They've shipped out Pa."

I stopped dead in my tracks. Tears came to my eyes. "When?"

"Four days ago. A march to Charleston with a number of other prisoners. Pa's to be sent on from there to prison in Barbados."

"Johnny, they *can't*. You mustn't let them."

"Nothing I can do about it."

"Nothing?" I pulled free of him. "Talk to Rawdon. Get Daddy back!"

"There is nothing, Caroline! Name of God, don't you think I would if I could?" He spoke through clenched teeth. "Now listen, there is more. We can't think of Pa now. We have to think about here, now, us."

"But does this mean we'll never see him again?"

"When the war is over, Caroline. And it will be over soon, I promise. Now will you keep a still tongue in your head for two minutes and hear what I have to say?"

I nodded yes, but I could scarce separate the words when he told them to me. They came at me all jumbled. He had to keep repeating them.

"I'm on a mission tonight. Rawdon thinks it's for him. But it's to help Sumter. If it works, Rawdon will be livid. And there will be repercussions, so you must leave before he finds out. Tomorrow, late in the afternoon. You take Mother and go to Uncle Henry's."

"Are you daft, Johnny? Rawdon won't allow it."

"It's arranged. Tonight at supper. Rawdon's low on vittles. You know how he likes his table dressed up with the finest provisions. I've told him that if he sends a wagon tomorrow to Uncle Henry's he could be well supplied. I recounted how we stopped there on the way home, and Uncle Henry is asking after his sister. I said Uncle Henry heard rumors that his sister is being treated like a lowly scullery maid and made to wait on the table. That Uncle Henry has been good to the British, is a loyal subject of the king, and is a man to be reckoned with. He asked what he could do to remedy the situation. I advised him that Uncle Henry would feel reassured if his sister could pay him a visit so he could put the rumors at rest. And her daughter should accompany her. I told him Uncle Henry is right fond of you. Then, when you get there, Mother is to take ill and not be able to be moved. You will insist on staying to tend her. The wagon and the food can come here."

"What are you planning that's so bad, Johnny?"

"You know I can't tell you that, Caroline. But when Rawdon finds out, he may take a notion to destroy the house. I've told Mother, and she's ready for it. Now I'm telling you."

"The British destroyed Mrs. Martin's house," I said dully. "She's the wife of the reverend. She was living in the orchard with her children."

"They've taken a fancy to doing such," Johnny said. "Tarleton has been known to dine in a rebel woman's house, then dig up her graveyard to look for valuables. In one case I heard of, he herded all the animals into the barn and burned it while they screamed inside."

"What about our animals, then?" I thought about Orphelia and Jackaroo.

"I've already warned Mr. Bone. He'll get them to the backcountry tomorrow."

"And the negras?"

He smiled at me. "Why do you think Miz Melindy took sick? She's pretending to have malarial fever. Rawdon is terrified of it. Did you see how far away he stood from Agnes's coffin?"

I felt a flood of relief. Miz Melindy wasn't really sickly. Only pretending! "I had noticed," I said. "I thought he was just being his usual haughty self."

"If he thinks the fever is in the quarters, he won't ship the negras out if he destroys the place. She's got to keep pretending, or he'll ship them all to the West Indies."

"When did you think all this out, Johnny?"

"Never mind. Everybody has a part to play."

"What about Georgia Ann?"

"There are some things in life we can't fix, Caroline. Biggest lesson we have to learn is to walk away from them. Georgia Ann is Rawdon's doxie. I thank you for trying to spare my feelings on the matter. But now hear me well. Everything depends on you. You must look after Mother."

"Yes, Johnny."

"Think about getting some things together to take with you, you and Mother. Things you'll need for a time."

"For how long a time?"

"I don't know the answer to that. He may burn the house, the barns, everything. Uncle Henry will look after you and Mother. Now listen to me, Caroline. Before the war came, Pa sent his account books, land titles, bonds, and notes to safekeeping with Mr. Hillegas in

Philadelphia. Mother knows this. So does Mr. Bone. Both know how to contact Hillegas if necessary."

The finality of it all made my head swim. The whole world tilted in front of my eyes. Everything I held dear was in danger of sliding off. I had all I could do to hold on myself.

I grabbed on to Johnny's arm. "When will you be back?"

"Not for a while. After I do what I have to do with Sumter, I want to join Marion."

"Who?"

"Francis Marion. Heads up a backcountry partisan militia. Mounted. They do scouting and reconnaissance to secure information about the enemy's movements. They harass communications. A tough little group. They make their home in the swamps. If I succeed, I'll be a hunted man. And I'd be honored if Marion'll have me."

It was all sliding off, everything. I closed my eyes and leaned against Johnny for a moment. I knew that when I opened them there would be nothing left.

"Suppose something goes wrong, Johnny? What will I do?"

He drew back so he could look at me straight on. "Well now, almost-sister of mine, seems to me you've done right good so far. Getting Rawdon to let you come fetch us. Making your own decisions along the way."

"I'm scared, Johnny. I don't want to make any more decisions. How do I know if they'll be the right ones?"

"How did you know when it was only you and Miz Melindy in that wagon?"

"I didn't. I just did what was in me to do."

"That's all any of us can do, Caroline. What's in us to do. What's in our heart and our innards. And what's in there didn't get to be by chance. It's what Mother and Pa raised us to be. You'd be surprised at what's inside you that you don't know is there yet."

I looked up at him in uncertainty. "Would I be?"

"Sure 'nough, as Miz Melindy would say. She knew what was in there. Why do you think she told you what happened to your ma? Because she knew you were old enough to take it."

"I don't know, Johnny. I don't know if I'm old enough to take it. I still can't abide the thought of it."

"That's out of the whole cloth. There's lots we can't abide the thought of. But we still take it. Work it into our lives. All the anger, the fear, even the bitterness. Learn from it. Use it next time around. I want to tell you before I go, almost-sister of mine, you've done that already."

"I have?"

"You did what I said, and I'm proud of you."

"What did I do?"

"You stuffed your feelings about your real mother into an old sock someplace and tended to the business at hand. It's the first step in growing up, Caroline, putting your own feelings aside and tending to the business at hand."

"I still hurt for my slave mama, Johnny."

"You should. You should never stop hurting for her. Never stop thinking of her. We all should. But not now, not until we tend to the business at hand. If our private hurts keep us from doing that, they've hurt others, too. Can't let that happen, Caroline, can we?"

"Oh, Johnny!" I hugged him tight for a moment.

His return hug near crushed me. "You'll make the right decisions," he said. "Just look inside you when the time comes. And if push comes to shove and you need help before you leave, go to Private Brandon."

"Who?"

"The friend you made in the kitchen. He came to me in secret. He has an ax to grind with the British. Said he'd help if you needed him. Just keep it quiet as possible, so you don't get him in trouble." He smiled down at me. "Some of these disaffected British are our best allies. Now, I'll get word to Nepoya. You'll hear from me from time to time. Take care of Mother."

In the next moment he was gone. I was alone in the garden. Now I had four people hanging inside me. Johnny was there now, too.

I HEARD Johnny ride out that night. I was in the kitchen because I was getting a pot of tea to take up to Mama. Her spirit was cast down on account of the news about Daddy being shipped out. And because Johnny was leaving.

As I came out of the kitchen to go up the brick walk with a tray in my hands, I heard hoofbeats, steady, disappearing into the night. It had started to rain again, a fine, misty rain. When I looked in the direction of the barn I couldn't see anything, but I heard Grey Goose's hoofbeats receding. It was the only sound on the place. I felt it echo in my heart.

Chapter Eighteen

JULY 9, 1780

THE NEXT MORNING, at first light, I was in the kitchen. Not to help Jade but to fetch our own breakfast. We'd need nourishment, me and Mama, for all we had to do this day. And, of course, I supposed I should bring breakfast for Georgia Ann, too, or she'd starve to death.

The first thing I noticed, even through the fog that lay on the place, was the disreputable condition of the kitchen garden. I hadn't paid mind yesterday. But now I was thinking of food. And I saw that the garden beggared all description. The turnips, cabbages, lettuce, onions, beans, even the herbs, were near gone.

Johnny had said Rawdon was short on provisions. I had not realized he was this short. In the time I'd been gone, the British must have ravaged the place.

And if I had any hopes they hadn't, Jade met me in the kitchen and soon set me straight. "No aigs," she said. "The soldiers done killed the last of the layin' hens.

Wrung their necks and cooked 'em over their fires. Not much milk an' butter left in the springhouse, either. Or hams. When you bring back the provisions?"

"Tomorrow."

"Well, you best git a cow from yer uncle. They butchered the last cow, too."

"How could they do that?" I asked. "How could they be so stupid? Don't they know anything about farming?"

"They kin do most anythin' they wants, I s'pose." She opened the flour and sugar bins. "Most near gone. Cornmeal, too."

"What are you cooking?"

"Fryin' some fish for the popinjay. Threw in some greens. Seems they ain't got all the fish from the stream yet, but they soon will. Heard them out in the woods yistaday, shootin' wild turkeys. Mr. Bone say ain't gonna be nothin' left in the woods soon, neither."

I made up a meager breakfast for us and put it on a tray: grits, bread, and butter. "Are there any preserves left?" I asked Jade.

She laughed. "No. Last jar went yistaday. No more relishes, sauces, or chutneys, either. Lard almost gone. Mr. Bone, he say we be arright, though. He say if'n they doan burn the fields we have a fall crop. He took the fodder fer the animals and hid it someplace." She lowered her voice. "He took some hogs inta the swamps, too."

I nodded. "He's a good man, Mr. Bone."

"You shoulda seen old Scooby yistaday. Some popinjay officer tried to catch him. Old Scooby give him a run fer his money."

I smiled and left with my tray.

Mama and I ate in silence in our room. Georgia Ann still slept, wrapped in the bedclothes, her gorgeous hair strewn about her on the pillow.

"Did you tell her we're visiting Uncle Henry today, Mama?" I asked.

"I did. She has no desire to accompany us. I think she fears his knowing of her liaison with Rawdon."

Just then came the sound of horses galloping. I ran to the window. "Soldiers," I said. "And they look as if they've done some hard riding."

"Likely from Charleston," Mama noted. "Last evening at supper Rawdon said he was expecting a contingent from Charleston."

I looked at her. "How could you abide sitting at table with him, Mama? After what he did to Daddy?"

Her eyes, turned to me, were brim full of tears. But there was strength in them, too. "I did it for Johnny. It was important for him that I be there and uphold my dignity. And Johnny says Daddy will be home. After the war. Johnny says other rebel leaders have been sent to Barbados. Some are even raising money for the rebel cause there. Your father will be in good company."

Johnny, I thought. *She hangs so much on his every word.* I was happy for that. But I wished I could believe everything that Johnny had said could come true. I'd feel a lot better about things.

Around midmorning, after she had eaten and dressed, Georgia Ann went down to see Rawdon. After a while she came back up. "Caroline, Colonel Rawdon wants to see you. You are to present yourself to him in the dining room immediately."

"I suppose he wants to see if we're ready to leave," I told Mama.

Georgia Ann gave me her peculiar little superior smile and tossed her head. "Don't count on it, Caroline," she said in a singsongy voice.

Something inside me dropped. "What mean you by that?"

Her nose was so far up in the air that if she were outside, bees would have built a nest in it. "You think Rawdon is stupid? How do you think he got so far in rank? By being stupid?"

From where she sat on the bed darning some hose, Mama looked up. "Georgia Ann, what are you about?"

"You embarrass me," she said, "the both of you. You both knew about Johnny, didn't you?"

I could scarce find my voice. "Knew what?"

"That he was imprisoned and whipped in Charleston for striking a superior officer. That he ran away."

For the second time in less than a day I felt the world tilting on me. The room seemed to swim in front of my eyes. "What nonsense are you talking, Georgia Ann?" I said angrily.

"Nonsense?" She went to her dressing table and preened in front of the mirror. "The lieutenant who just arrived from Charleston doesn't think it's nonsense. He was at Johnny's court-martial there. He's asking for that prize horse Johnny refused to give over in Charleston. The one that caused all the trouble. Couldn't think of the name. I helped him. Grey Goose. I told him Johnny had her here and has ridden off with her."

I was across the room and at her quicker than a duck on a June bug. I managed to grab a fistful of her precious curls before Mama pulled me off.

"Girls, girls, this will never do." She had to physically separate us. "Never have I seen such shameful behavior. Have we lost all sense of being a family?"

Georgia Ann's cheek was red because I'd slapped her, too. She was weeping. "Family? We haven't been a family since Daddy left!"

"Georgia Ann!" Mama made as if to embrace her. "Is that why you are so smitten with this man? Because you miss your daddy so?"

"Well, what do you expect, Mama?" Georgia Ann embraced the excuse as if it were a bouquet of flowers handed to her and pressed it to her bosom. "Daddy's the one who held this family together. We're nothing without him."

"Daddy spoiled you rotten, you mean. And now that he's gone you're looking for another man to spoil you rotten," I told her.

She acted as if I hadn't spoken. "Daddy should have renewed his allegiance to the king by signing the loyalty oath when it was offered him. To safeguard his family. It was the sensible thing to do. He should have taken British protection. Many have. But no, he had to raise his head in defiance and leave his family to suffer the consequences. I miss Daddy, yes, and I loved him. But he's gone. Rawdon has been my one solace, Mama, my one comfort." She was begging for understanding. But Mama turned away.

"Rawdon and his kind sent Daddy to prison, you fool!" I told her.

"Francis didn't. He never would have," my sister retorted. "He told me so."

"Then why didn't he let him out?" Mama asked.

"He couldn't! He tried, but it was outside his power. Truly, he tried, Mama."

Mama was distraught, torn. She made a move to Georgia Ann, then the thought of Daddy made her cry and she had to turn away.

"Must you upset Mama so? How do you think she feels, with her husband shipped off, not knowing if she'll see him again?" I lashed out at my sister. "And what do you mean telling them about Grey Goose? Johnny was whipped in Charleston because he wouldn't hand her over! Do you think he wants to hand her over now?"

"I told you, the man who just arrived, Lieutenant Cantee, knew about her from Charleston. They need horses for Tarleton's cavalry."

"Georgia Ann," I said coldly, "you may have given them your affections and your loyalty. But don't give our horses. You know how much those horses mean to Johnny. And this place."

Her face went white. She moved away. "You'd best go downstairs, Caroline," she said to me. "Rawdon isn't pleasant when he's left waiting."

"I'll go with you," Mama offered.

"No," I said. "I'll go. You stay here, Mama. Finish

packing. The sooner we leave for Uncle Henry's the better."

Georgia Ann gave a snicker as I left the room. I tried not to think what that meant. But I was ready to wager Daddy's pastureland by the creek that we wouldn't be going to Uncle Henry's that afternoon.

"YOUR SERVANT, sir." I curtsied as I entered the dining room.

He did not acknowledge my greeting. He was having breakfast with the young lieutenant, who stood as I entered the room. Rawdon did not stand. He scarce looked up.

"Are you aware," he asked, "your brother was court-martialed and whipped in Charleston for attacking a British officer?"

I drew in my breath. I looked at the lieutenant, but he avoided my eyes. In back of my mind I think I'd feared since the note came from Nepoya that someone would arrive from Charleston who could tell Rawdon about Johnny. Now it had happened.

"Can't you speak, girl?"

"No sir," I answered. "I mean, yes sir, I can speak. But no sir, I haven't heard anything like that about Johnny. He was wounded. You saw he was wearing a sling."

"I saw the sling," he said, "not the wound." He looked at me then but kept his face straight, with no feelings showing.

Somehow I managed to recover myself and meet his cold gaze. "Are you sure it's Johnny you speak of?" I asked. "He is loyal to his king. His loyalty has caused all kinds of trouble between him and my daddy."

"The intelligence was brought to me by Lieutenant Cantee here."

The lieutenant acknowledged it with a nod of his head. "I was at your brother's court-martial," he said. "It was established at the time that he was from Camden, that his father was the leading rebel here."

Rawdon set down his cup, pushed his chair back from the table, crossed his legs in the spotlessly white tight breeches, regarded his polished boots, and jiggled one foot. "Well? What say you to this charge, Miss Whitaker?"

"I say my brother is loyal to his king. Right now he is risking his life on a spying mission for you."

The lieutenant stared at him. "How can that be?"

Rawdon did not like his decisions questioned. "It can be," he said tersely, "because I had no intelligence from Charleston about him. It can be, because he presented himself to me as a loyal subject. It can be, because he was the obvious choice, knowing the countryside and having grown up with some of Sumter's men. And it can be"—now, warming to his subject, he stood up and commenced to pace—"because I have here his mother and sisters. And he knows that if he turns his coat and betrays my confidence, they will suffer. That is how it can be, lieutenant."

"I don't mean to question your decisions, sir."

"He may just come back with the information I require," Rawdon mused. "It has been my experience that these backwoods militia types go whichever way the wind blows. At any rate, we will wait and see." He stopped pacing and looked at me.

"Miss Whitaker, have you ever seen our prison in town?"

"Yes sir. I rode the wagon past it on our way to fetch Johnny."

"Where?"

"In the center of town, where the Public Square used to be."

"That was the large stockade. There are four other redoubts at the four corners of the village. And a fifth fortification on the Salisbury road. You rode past one of five garrisons we have for the policing of the interior of this colony. The others, namely Georgetown, Winns-boro, Ninety-Six, and Agusta, make a semicircle, with Charleston as the center. Here in Camden I am in charge of this prison, Miss Whitaker, and we do not hesitate to punish traitors with the greatest rigor. Lord Cornwallis himself has issued an order that every mili-tiaman who has borne arms with us and afterwards joined the enemy shall be immediately hanged."

My mouth went dry. I felt myself trembling and had all I could do to keep from retorting: "I believe you. After all, did you not send my father on a one-hundred-and-thirty-mile march in this dreadful heat? To be put on a prison ship?"

But I could not permit myself the luxury of anger.

"So we shall wait and see," he added, "if your brother returns. He should be back in three or four days. On this prize horse, which he claimed was lame. And you and your mother shall wait and see, also."

"But, sir, we must go and get the provisions at Uncle Henry's."

"The provisions can wait," he said. "You are to go back to your room and stay there."

My mind whirled with retorts, arguments, reasons. But I could give voice to none. And then the lieutenant gave the conversation a new turn. "So her brother rode off on Grey Goose, then, sir?" He certainly was fixed on that horse.

Rawdon clasped his hands behind his back, and rocked on his heels, pleased to be given more ammunition to come at me with. "Yes. But there is another piece of horseflesh, even more valuable, somewhere on this plantation. Fearnaught." He smiled at the lieutenant. "You should see this one! Come to think of it"— and he turned to me, scowling—"I haven't seen Fearnaught lately, Miss Whitaker. Do you know her whereabouts? I'd like to show her to the lieutenant."

A new depth of fear was being mined inside me. "I don't know, sir. She's turned up missing."

"Missing, is it?"

"Yes. Since before Miz Melindy and I fetched Johnny home. I noticed that she was missing the first morning I went to the kitchen to help Miz Melindy with the cooking, sir."

"Why didn't you report the matter to me?"

I made myself look as innocent as possible. "I thought naught of it, sir. Your men constantly take things. I thought they might have made off with her. Why, they've slaughtered the last of our milch cows and hogs. The larder and springhouse are empty. The kitchen garden is ravaged."

His eyes narrowed. "Your brother's best blooded mare and you thought naught of it?"

"I didn't want to plague you," I amended.

"You thought little of plaguing me the night you refused to play 'God Save the King.'"

"That was vexing my sister, sir. I explained my feelings to you."

He stared at me, straight into my soul. "If you are lying to me about Fearnaught, it will not go well for you or your mother, or this place, Miss Whitaker," he said. "You may retire now to your room. Today we will conduct a thorough search of this place and the surrounding area for that horse. We need it for our cavalry. They ride nags pilfered from nearby plantations. Cantee, you are to head up the search. I want all the regiments questioned. The Twenty-third and Thirty-third Volunteers of Ireland, the legion of cavalry, the detachment of artillery, and Brown's and Hamilton's corps of provincials."

"Yes sir." The lieutenant made ready to leave.

"And, Cantee, send some of your men to the quarters. Bring the negras out for questioning. Don't get too close. There's malarial fever there. Put the fear of God into them. Question the overseer. He's a slippery character. If that horse is anywhere on this place or near it, I want it brought to me by sundown!"

The lieutenant saluted and left the room. Rawdon smiled at me again. "You are dismissed," he said. "Send your lovely sister to me. She will tell us who on the place should be questioned about the horse."

His smile was cold, so very cold. I left. I had planned on going down to the quarters to see Miz Melindy before we left for Uncle Henry's. But then, we were not going to Uncle Henry's. We were prisoners. I didn't know why, but I had a terrible foreboding that I would never see Miz Melindy again.

Chapter Nineteen

JULY 9, 1780

W HEN GEORGIA ANN came back upstairs from her conference with Rawdon, she started packing.

"Where are you going?" Mama asked.

"I'm leaving."

"Leaving? Where? Are you going to Uncle Henry's? Is Rawdon sending you instead of us?" I heard the panic in Mama's voice.

Georgia Ann laughed. "Why would I want to go there? I want to get away from these backwoods. Charleston. I'm going to Charleston, Mama. Rawdon is sending me."

"For what?"

"To see my friends. To go to dances, to plays."

"In wartime?" Mama was aghast. "While your father is likely on a prison ship by now?"

"Yes, in wartime, Mama. I'm going to assemblies,

pantomimes, balls, teas. I'm going to Vaux Hall to attend concerts."

"Does this mean Rawdon is leaving?" Mama asked.

"No, he isn't leaving. But he wants to get me away, to have me in decent company. He wants me to have some new gowns made, to go where my hair can be dressed and I can keep up with the fashions."

"And he wants you in a safe place," I put in.

Georgia Ann smiled at me. "That, too."

"You see, Mama," I told her, "it isn't safe here anymore. If Johnny doesn't come back in a day or so, Rawdon will likely burn this place. And he wants Georgia Ann away from all harm."

"Is that true, Georgia Ann? Would he do this? How could he be so cruel?" Mama asked.

"It's Johnny who's doing it to us, Mama. Johnny who escaped from Charleston after attacking an officer, then came here and pretended to be loyal. I told you Francis was not stupid. But again, he's only following orders. Cornwallis has ordered such punishments if Loyalists betray him."

"And you would take up with such a man, then?" Mama persisted. "If he burned your home?"

Georgia Ann stood up from where she'd been kneeling on the floor packing dresses, shoes, hose, fans, stays, and all the other things that went into making her a nymph into the baskets and trunks she was taking with her. "I love Francis, Mama. I speak plain. Johnny has put him in this position where he must carry out his orders. It is not easy being in command, Mama. But Francis was born to it, and I love him."

"Dear God in heaven!" Mama murmured. Then, after a moment, she recovered herself. "And what of us? Care you naught for us, Georgia Ann?"

"He isn't going to harm you, Mama. He'll let you go to Uncle Henry's when he is ready."

"When he's ready to burn the house, you mean," I said bitterly.

My sister smiled at us. "It all depends on your beloved Johnny now, doesn't it, Mama? Your favorite."

"Georgia Ann, how can you say that? Your father and I loved you both equally."

"Oh, Mama, I say it because it's true. Johnny was always your favorite. Well now, see what your favorite is going to do for you." She reached for a small silver bell, opened the door, and rang for Jade to come and get her things.

When Jade came with a sentry to fetch the trunks, my sister made as if to embrace Mama. "Give my love to Uncle Henry," she said.

Mama turned from her with a suppressed sob.

Georgia Ann just shrugged and looked at me. "Watch yourself. Don't get too saucy with Rawdon. Know your limits."

"What did you tell him of Fearnaught?" I asked.

She smiled. "What I told him may save your hides, Caroline. He wants that horse, and he wants it badly. If he gets it he may soften toward you. He may refrain from burning this place, if push comes to shove. If not..." She shrugged and walked out.

In a matter of minutes I heard the clatter of a horse

233

and carriage outside and went to look out the window. Georgia Ann was going to Charleston in Mama's good carriage, the one that was edged with gilt and had Mama's family crest on it. A soldier was on the front seat, holding the reins. Rawdon stood assisting Georgia Ann in. He had just finished embracing her.

Then the carriage drove off and an eerie sort of silence settled over the place in the white afternoon haze. I sat by the window. Mama took off her petticoat and lay in her chemise on the bed. The room was hot. Every so often a scant breeze managed to waft in the windows. I saw a batch of crows swoop out of a cornfield in the distance, all of a body, all thinking and going in one direction. Like my thoughts. Then, of a sudden, they changed their course and went in another direction. And my thoughts did, too.

WE HADN'T had a noon meal and I was about starved. Where was everybody? I heard no sound from below stairs, saw no movement from the direction of the barn. Had everyone gone off? Could I, perhaps, sneak down and out to the kitchen and fetch us some tea?

I got up, crossed the room, opened the door, and stepped out into the hall, but there was no one about. Even Rawdon had gone out.

And then I heard a sound. But it came from inside the room. It sounded like something hitting the side window by the garden where the Cherokee roses grew. I rushed in and looked out the window.

"Miss Caroline?" It was Private Brandon.

For a moment I was confused, seeing his British

uniform, then I recollected Johnny's parting words to me. "If you need help, go to Private Brandon. He has an ax to grind with the British."

"Yes," I said softly.

"How are you and your mum faring?"

I turned to look at Mama. She was sleeping. Good. "We're all right. Where is everyone?"

"Searching for the horse. Listen, I dasn't dally. But know that I'm on your side. Soon's I can, I'm getting out of here. This garden is on the other side of the house from the dining room where Rawdon makes his headquarters. And away from the sentries. You and your mum had best plan to flee, Miss Caroline. I heard the scuttlebutt. If your brother doesn't come back in three days, Rawdon's going to burn the place. Do you have a place to go?"

"Yes. My uncle Henry's. Twelve miles north of here."

"Would he be loath to take in a deserter and hide him for a bit?"

"My uncle Henry is a Tory, but he's a fair man. You wouldn't be the first he helped, though he might disagree with your politics if you desert."

"You wouldn't happen to have any civilian men's clothing about, would you?"

I thought quickly. "Yes. In my brother Johnny's room. I can fetch some for you."

"Not now. I've got to go. I'll be by tonight. 'Bout eleven. Throw a bundle of it down here before then. It'll land in the rosebushes. We can talk again then about getting you and your mum out of here."

"God bless you, Brandon," I said.

In the next instant he was gone.

SOMEWHAT CHEERED, I went back to my chair by the window and took up a book. At least I had half a plan anyway. You had to plan. Johnny did it all the time. A plan. Then I jumped up. *I ought to fetch the clothing for Brandon now, before anyone comes back into the house.* So I sneaked down the hall to Johnny's room, where I rummaged about and came up with a pair of his old breeches, a shirt, a tricorn hat, shoes, and hose. These I wrapped in a bundle, using the shirtsleeves to tie the whole package up with, and hid them under the bed back in our chamber.

Just then I heard the tall case clock downstairs chime four. And then another sound. The front door opened and someone came running up the stairs. The door to the room burst open.

"Miz Caroline, oh, Miz Caroline, you gotta come 'long wid me." Jade looked as if she were being pursued by Tarleton's legion.

"Where have I got to come?"

"They gon' whip Isom."

"Who?"

"That popinjay what lives here. They done found out he 'sponsible fer the horse. They done found out he know where the horse be. They gon' whip him till he tells. Oh, Miz Caroline, come, please."

Chapter Twenty

JULY 9, 1780

I RAN WITH JADE all the way down to the quarters, where I found a circle of people. On the outer rim of the circle were our negras, all of them, even Miz Melindy, who was being supported on either side by Cephas and a young woman. *She shouldn't be out here sick as she is,* I thought crazily. And then I remembered that she wasn't sick. She was pretending.

Oh, I was so confused. I didn't know what was true and what wasn't true anymore.

"Miz Caroline," I heard some of the negras say. "Miz Caroline's here. She do sumptin'." The murmur of my name went through the crowd.

I pushed my way to the inner circle.

There they had Isom strung up with a rope around his wrists. His feet were just off the ground.

For one terrible, dizzying moment I was on that sandy dune on the Hills of Santee again, watching as my friend Kit was strung up on that tree. For a second,

I thought I would faint. I felt the nausea rising in my throat, but I willed it down.

Colonel Rawdon stood inside the circle with two of his sentries, muskets at the ready. Rawdon was in full dress uniform with a riding crop in his hand. Lieutenant Cantee was there, too. So was Mr. Bone. He held a long rawhide whip in his hand. He did not look happy.

"No!" I ran up to them. "Stop!"

Rawdon smiled and gave me a little half bow. "Your servant, Miss Caroline," he mocked.

"What are you doing?" I demanded.

"That seems obvious."

"You can't whip Isom. He's done nothing to harm you."

"He knows where the horse is, Miss Caroline. We were told that he was left responsible for her well-being when your brother left for war."

Georgia Ann! I felt the anger seethe through me. With it came a weakness that spread through my arms and legs so I felt that I, too, would have to be held up and supported like Miz Melindy. I looked across the circle at her. She met my eyes, pleading.

Pleading for Isom. Her son. My uncle, if you will. Funny, I'd never thought of him that way, but seeing him hanging there so helpless I felt a surge of fondness for him. He'd always been so nice to me when I ran to the quarters as a child to play with him and Cephas and Johnny. He was the one who'd always begged Johnny and his mother to let me stay.

Well, they weren't going to whip him! They weren't!

How dare they! I couldn't bear the thought of it. I would do something to stop it, anything. I stood in front of Rawdon, full of resolve.

"You have our house," I said. It took all I was worth to keep the tremor out of my voice. "You have kept us prisoner. Your men have taken our livestock, raided our larder, ruined our kitchen garden! You've sent my daddy off on a prison ship. My brother is on a spying mission for you! You've even taken my sister. What more do you want of us?"

At this he laughed. "The taking of your sister wasn't difficult. She was ready for the plucking."

I wanted to smash him in the face. I had all I could do to keep my hands at my side. I clenched my fists.

He was amused, enjoying this. He slid his eyes around to all who were watching, mindful that he was center stage. He commenced to pace, preening, clasping his hands behind his back. "The brother on the spying mission is up for conjecture," he said. "The outcome of that is still to be determined. Meanwhile, whether he returns or not, what I want is the horse. I want the blooded mare. Your brother will not spirit two good horses away from me."

"I told you, she's missing. Likely one of your own men absconded with her."

He flicked his riding crop against his boot. "I think not," he said, still with that note of amusement in his voice. "I think this negra knows where she is. I think he has sent her into hiding. If you wish to spare him, convince him to tell me her whereabouts."

Silence. Again I sought out Miz Melindy's eyes across the circle. She would not meet my gaze. She looked to the ground.

"Nobody knows where," I said.

"Very well, if you insist." And he raised his riding crop in a signal to Mr. Bone. "Do your business," he said.

"Ain't never whupped a negra on this place," Mr. Bone said. "No call to. Anyways, Mr. Whitaker ain't never allowed it."

"Well, Mr. Whitaker isn't here now, is he?" Colonel Rawdon returned. "I am here. And I give the command to commence with the whipping!"

No one moved or spoke for what seemed like an eternity. Cicadas screamed their summer song. The heat bore down. The scene was not real. I was dreaming, I decided. I'd fallen asleep in the chair by the window in our chamber and was dreaming.

Then Mr. Bone flung the whip down at Colonel Rawdon's feet. "Whip him yourself," he said. And before Rawdon could reply, Mr. Bone strode off in the direction of the barn.

Everyone looked now at Colonel Rawdon. And then I saw something I thought I'd never see. He started to shake. His face twitched, his hands shook. "Sergeant," he called out, "take up the whip!"

The negras all gave up a groan in a body. Some started weeping.

The sergeant set down his musket, took off his regimental coat, and laid it aside. Then he took off his weskit and laid it aside as well. Then he removed the black stock from around his neck, rolled up his sleeves, picked up the whip, and stepped back to assess the distance between himself and the hanging Isom.

I noted with a sinking heart how burly the sergeant was. I shuddered. He grinned and flicked the whip back and forth in the air a few times so it sang. Once again the negras groaned. "Please, Jesus!" one yelled out.

"Stop that caterwauling!" Rawdon snapped.

They fell silent.

Rawdon crossed his arms in front of him and smiled smugly at me. He had stopped shaking.

I felt the panic rising inside me. It came up through my chest and into my throat, sour tasting. I wanted to run off into the underbrush and retch it up. But I could not. I must do something. I felt everyone's eyes on me.

It was up to me now. I was the one who had to decide. If they whipped Isom they'd kill him. Two hundred, Private Brandon had told me. "I was to get two hundred, so I ran." And what about Johnny? What about the look in his eyes, the murder in his heart?

What was I to do? Let them have Fearnaught? The best blooded mare in the Parish of St. Mark's? She meant the world to Johnny.

"All any of us can do is what's in us to do, Caroline," he'd said. "What's in us to do. What's in our heart and our innards. You'll know what to do when the time comes."

The burly sergeant was drawing back his arm again, this time for the whip to find its mark.

I went a little crazy then. "No!" I screamed. "No more! I'll not have any more people hanging inside me!"

I ran toward the sergeant and knocked the whip from his hand. The unexpectedness of my assault took him unawares. Then I ran over to Rawdon. "No more!" I yelled. "It ends here! Now! With me! I know where the horse is. I'll tell you!"

"Stop!" Rawdon ordered. For the sergeant had picked up the whip and was ready to strike. Now he scowled and lowered the whip, obviously disappointed.

"Doan do it, Miz Caroline," Isom said. His voice was weak, strained. "Doan do it. Dat horse, she be everythin'. All we gots left round here. Doan do it!"

He was right, of course. If they burned the place, Fearnaught was worth money, lots of it. Years of work, of breeding, had gone into her. But I brushed the thought aside, like a gnat in front of my face.

"We've got each other, Isom," I said. But I said it to Rawdon's face. "And we've got our honor. Which is more than they have." I met Rawdon's eyes, saying that. "Cut him down," I demanded. "Now."

"Tell me where the horse is."

"You must promise not to harm the Catawba woman who is keeping her."

"I want no trouble with the Catawbas," Rawdon said.

"No, Miz Caroline," Isom begged.

But I told him. God help me, I told him. I gave him Fearnaught. I gave him Johnny's prize, the most beautiful blooded mare in all of St. Mark's Parish. So they cut Isom down then, and all the negras ran to embrace him, to lead him away.

All but Miz Melindy and Cephas. She stood like an

old gnarled, withered tree, leaning on her son's arm. Across yards of dusty hard ground I looked at her. And she smiled at me. I shall never forget that smile. It was full of satisfaction, of happiness, and yet at the same time it said so many other things. "You see," it said, "you gotta go back to your life an' I gotta go back to mine. But we still part o' each other. 'Cause that's how it be."

I was crying. I couldn't help it, seeing that blissful smile on her face. How could she accept things? How could she be happy?

I made a move to go to her, then stopped. Rawdon was watching me with the eyes of a hawk. "I see," he said languidly, "that when the chips are down your true nature asserts itself, Miss Caroline."

I rubbed my eyes with my hand. "What?"

He flicked the riding crop against his boot. "Your true nature. You're half negra, after all, remember? Blood will out. You protected your own."

I glared up at him.

He gestured toward Miz Melindy with his riding crop. "Why don't you go to her? She wants to embrace you. You just saved her son. Go on, you have my permission."

I wanted to. I felt pulled to Miz Melindy. If Orphelia and Jackaroo were dragging me toward her I couldn't have felt the pull more. But I couldn't do it. If I did, Rawdon would know she didn't really have malarial fever. And if he knew that, he could well ship Miz Melindy and the others out. To be sold to plantations in the West Indies.

"She's sickly," I said. "Can't you see?" And I spoke sharply to Cephas. "Take her back to her cabin! Before she spreads the fever. She shouldn't have been out here in the first place!"

Then I turned and ran to the house so they couldn't see the tears streaming down my face.

Chapter Twenty-One

JULY 9–12, 1780

MAMA SAID I did the right thing. But all evening I could not console myself. I had given over Fearnaught, the one possession we had managed to keep from them.

Fearnaught. I had promised myself I would never hand her over. I had promised her.

She was more than a horse. Everybody on the place knew that. She and Grey Goose were symbols of Johnny's and Daddy's years of hard work. She was my reason for turning rebel. She was my fundamental right as I had reasoned it out to be. Besides, Johnny had near died but hadn't given over Grey Goose. But I had handed over Fearnaught.

Back in our chamber I cried in Mama's arms. "You did the right thing," she said.

I told her what Rawdon had said to me. "He said blood will out. He said I protected one of my own. Is it true, Mama? That I did it because I'm part negra?"

"You did it because you are a good person," she said.

"But I'm part negra, Mama. And because of that I've given them the best thoroughbred mare in the whole parish! And what will Johnny say when he finds out?"

"He will say you did the right thing," she promised.

But I couldn't be sure. Night came, the sweetest night I recollect in a long time, with the smell of Cherokee roses and freshly cut wheat wafting in the windows. Jade brought us a tray of supper, but I could not eat. I had a headache from crying. I was tired and my spirit was sore afflicted. My head was spinning. I did not want to make any more decisions if this is what it left you feeling like. I ate something only to keep Mama happy, then she made me lie down on the bed in my chemise. She bathed my face and neck and arms with cool water and gave me a headache powder. But I could not sleep. I lay there in a stupor, a feeling of anguish inside me as I'd never known. All I could see in front of my face was Fearnaught—her large, liquid, trusting eyes, her beautiful form, her delicate hooves. What would they do with her? Take her into battle?

I must have dozed off, because of a sudden I woke to see a pattern of lights dancing on the ceiling near the windows that overlooked the back of the house. Mama lay sleeping beside me. I got up and went to the window. A cluster of men were in the yard, holding pine-knot torches. In the middle of them were Rawdon and Lieutenant Cantee. The lieutenant was holding the bridle of a horse. Fearnaught!

He was hard put to hold her, though. She was restless, frightened. Her delicate hooves danced, she tossed her neck. I could see fear in her eyes.

"Hold her, you fool!" I heard Rawdon say. The words floated up in the summer night. I felt again as if I were in a dream. Then one cold, piercing thought brought me to.

They did not know how to handle Fearnaught. They might harm her.

Quickly I reached for my petticoat, pulled it over my head, tied the drawstring around my waist, slipped into my shoes, and pattered quietly downstairs, through the hall, and out onto the back verandah.

Fearnaught was still trying to break free of the lieutenant's grip on her bridle. And he was holding tightly, going round and round in circles with her. I ran through the kitchen garden and into the yard.

"You're frightening her!" I said.

"Go back inside," Rawdon ordered.

But I did not. I went forward, to Fearnaught, talking to her all the while. "There's a girl, good girl, darling girl. No need to be frightened. Caroline's here."

My voice gentled her. She held still, but the large liquid brown eyes still housed fear.

"Get back with those pine-knot torches," I hissed.

Rawdon nodded and his soldiers stepped back.

I continued talking. "Do you recollect the last time I rode you? On the High Hills of Santee? We'll ride there soon again someday, my girl. But you must be good now. And mind your manners. Johnny would want you to. You don't want to dishonor Johnny now, do you, girl?"

She gave me a deep-throated whinny. I patted her soft nose, stroked her head. She bent her head to me. "If you put her in her stall in the barn, she'll quiet down," I told Rawdon. "She knows that place."

"She won't go with any of my men," he allowed.

"She go wif me." It was Isom. He came up out of the darkness. "I take her to her stall in de barn."

"Very well," Rawdon agreed. "But Lieutenant Cantee is to go along with you."

Isom shrugged and took the bridle.

"Wait a moment, Isom," I said.

He waited. And again I put my arms around Fearnaught's neck. I whispered in her ear things only she could hear. "We'll find you," I promised. "Be good until then. Be brave. We'll find you, girl, and bring you home again. I promise."

She went with Isom and the lieutenant to the barn. I watched them go. A horse for Isom, I thought. A horse for a negra. Because I was half negra. And blood will out. Was it a fair exchange? Was a house for a bottle of King's Honey Water a fair exchange?

I looked over a rim of trees to where a giant full moon was rising. No, I thought. A horse for a human being. Because I was a human being. Oh, what did it matter anyway? Fearnaught was gone from us. I looked at Rawdon and he at me.

"If you harm her or if she's killed, my brother, Johnny, will find you and kill you," I told him coldly. I was not afraid of him now. "I can promise you that."

Then I ran back to the house, bawling my heart out.

THREE DAYS later I was sitting again in the big old chair by the window while the night birds called, the moon rose, round and full, and the summer insects chirped their crazy song. This was the day Johnny was to return, or Rawdon would burn the house. I'd gone about my business all day, trying to keep busy, fetching meals for myself and Mama from the kitchen, looking for signs of Johnny every time I went outside. But the plantation was still under the mid-July heat. Scarce a thing moved. And there seemed to be no action amongst Rawdon and his soldiers, either. I saw no preparations for burning the place. Below stairs I heard Rawdon's voice on occasion, but otherwise there was silence. I tried to read. I positioned myself by the window so I could see Johnny if he rode in. I half wanted him to come back, and half didn't. Somehow I knew that he was not going to come.

In spite of myself, I dozed by the window. I dreamed of Fearnaught. I heard her hoofbeats racing, saw her mane flying in front of me as we skimmed across the sand dunes on the High Hills of Santee. Then I was rudely awakened.

For a moment I was stunned, not knowing where I was or what was happening. Mama was still sleeping on the bed. Now I heard noises, two of them. A long, impassioned cry from below stairs, as if someone down there were having a bad dream. And the sound of something soft thrown against one of the windows. The one that overlooked the Cherokee rose garden.

I shook myself awake and went to kneel at the window.

"Miss Caroline?" A whisper filled with urgency. Private Brandon.

"Yes. I'm here."

"You and your mum best get up and dressed."

"Why? What's wrong?" I was sufficiently accustomed to the darkness now to see he was wearing the civilian clothing I had left in a bundle in the roses. "What's happened?"

"Messenger rode in half an hour ago. From up north. Huck and his men were attacked at Williamson's Plantation this morning. Huck was killed. His force lost thirty-five men. Fifty wounded. Twenty-nine prisoners taken. Of Tarleton's dragoons, only twelve out of thirty-five escaped."

Again the yell from below stairs. Then something crashed. "What's that?" I asked.

"Rawdon. He's livid, Miss Caroline. Mr. Bone told me all about it, and when I came by the dining room windows just now I listened and learned more. Seems your brother, Johnny, was responsible. He found Sumter and told him where Huck was. And he rescued two rebels they had held who were supposed to be hanged when the sun came up this day."

This day. I struggled to sort it out. "What is the date, Private Brandon?"

"The twelfth."

"That would be the McClure kin then. They were taken by the British and held to be hanged this morning. Are they sure it was Johnny?"

"Rawdon is. He's downstairs throwing things around. I saw a chair go across the room. Books all over the floor. He's gathering up his papers. I heard him give orders. At dawn the house is to be burned. You and your mum best come with me now."

I stared at him, dumbfounded. *What? Go with him now?* I looked back into the darkened room, to Mama's form sleeping on the bed. "Now? Surely he wouldn't burn the house with us in it?"

"Now, Miss Caroline. I promised your brother I'd look after you. Where's your mum?"

"Sleeping."

"I'm up now." And Mama came to kneel down beside me. "I heard it all," she said. And she hugged me.

"Mama, we've got to leave," I said gently. "There isn't any other way. He may allow us out in the morning. But then again, he may not."

"Do whatever you think is best, Caroline," she said to me. "I trust you completely."

The words gave me strength. "Private," I whispered loudly, "how can you get us down?"

He looked about, desperately. "A rope. I can fetch a rope. And throw it up. If you can tie it around something so it can hold."

"The bedpost," I said.

"Yes," he said. "I'll be back in a while with a rope. Gather some things. They're so busy plotting he won't

hear us here on this side of the house." Then he disappeared into the night. I heard him running through
the garden.

I looked at Mama. She had her hands over her
heart. "Do you think you could shimmy down on a rope,
Mama?" I asked.

She nodded. There were tears in her eyes. "We must
take a bundle of clothing," she said. "Hurry."

So we packed then, if that word applied to what we
were doing. But first, for just a minute or two, we stood
in the middle of the chamber that had been our prison
since the first of June and looked around in bewilder-
ment.

I saw tears spill over from Mama's eyes. And my
heart went out to her. How do you take years of mem-
ories in a single bundle? What do you take? What do
you leave behind?

She went to a drawer and took out a pair of hose.
Then to another drawer where she kept her jewelry. She
took out some pearls and put them inside the hose.
Then some brooches and ear bobs. "It isn't vanity," she
said. "We may need to pawn these for money." Then
from another drawer she drew out a bundle wrapped
carefully in satin and tied with a ribbon. She smiled at
me. "The childbed linen," she said. "For you, now."

I felt a wrench in my heart.

She had a small likeness of Daddy that had been
painted in Charleston. It was in a pewter frame. She
tied her pocket around her waist and put it in there.
Then she put on her petticoat, apron, and cap, gathered
another petticoat and chemise, an extra pair of shoes,

and tied it all in a bundle. Watching her, I did the same.

In what seemed like moments, Private Brandon was below the window again. "Ho!" he called up in a loud whisper.

I looked out. He was throwing up a rope. Twice he threw it. Twice I tried to catch it and missed. On the third attempt I caught it, pulled it into the room, and with Mama's help tied it securely around the bedpost.

While all this was transpiring, things below had not quieted down. Every so often I heard a new yell from Rawdon. Heard something else crash. I minded how he must be shaking, how his face must be twitching, his hands trembling. And it gave me impetus to get away.

"You go first, Mama," I told her.

Gingerly, she climbed out the window, holding the rope.

"Steady, don't be fearful, ma'am," Brandon whispered from below.

My heart was in my mouth, watching Mama. I heard her grunts as she painfully made her way down the rope. How that must hurt her hands! It seemed to take forever. Then finally I heard a deep sigh as her feet touched the ground.

"Now you, miss," Brandon said.

The rope dangled before me. Could I do as well as Mama? What were we about, sneaking out of our own home like thieves in the night? If he burned the house, would it spread to the fields? The barn? No matter. Brandon said Mr. Bone had already gotten the negras and the animals to safety. And I knew Rawdon wouldn't let anything happen to Fearnaught. I felt a pang of remorse. I wouldn't be able to see Miz Melindy, Cephas, and Isom for a while. But it was a comfort to know that Rawdon wouldn't pursue them, that they wouldn't be sold to the West Indies. This was the way it be now, as Miz Melindy would say. And as Johnny would say, first I had to tend to the matters at hand.

"Down with you now, miss," Brandon begged.

Still, I was filled with anger that we had to flee our own home. I could feel it coursing through my veins. No more, I'd told Rawdon when I'd stood before him in the quarters and demanded that Isom be cut free. It stops with me.

Well, it would then. "One minute," I said. And I went back into the darkened room to feel around under the bed where I'd hidden the bow and arrows Nepoya had given me. It seemed like years ago now. I found them tied in a bundle, grasped them, and ran back to the window.

"Hold on to them," I told Brandon. "I'm coming down."

"ARE YOU sure you want to do this, Caroline?" Mama asked me.

"I've never been more sure of anything in my life." I turned to Private Brandon, who stood next to us in a clump of trees a bit away from the house, on the side where our chamber was.

"The fire will start in our chamber," I told them. "He won't notice it for a while. By that time we can be on our way to Uncle Henry's. But it'll spread to the barn."

I turned to Private Brandon. "You promise me that Mr. Bone got the animals out of the barn?"

"All but Fearnaught," he said apologetically. "First thing Rawdon did when he got the message about what happened to Huck was send to the barn for the horse. Told Mr. Bone he's giving him to Tarleton because so many of his dragoons were killed. Rawdon's afraid of Tarleton. He's been using his dragoons as couriers all along, ruining the horses and getting Tarleton's legion cut to pieces. He'll use Fearnaught to make up for things. He'll have to."

Fearnaught with Tarleton, the butcher. Fearnaught with Bloody Ban. I felt sick over it. But I couldn't think on it. "Strike those flints now, private. I see you have a musket."

He grinned. "Mr. Bone gave it to me." He had uneven teeth, his face was thin, his nose too big, but I thought him the most wonderful man in the world at that moment.

He knew what to do. He knelt and made a small fire, then asked me for cloth.

Cloth! I'd forgotten. I took off my apron and ripped some strips off it. Quickly he wrapped them on the end of an arrow and lowered them into the small fire. "Ever shot an arrow before?" he asked.

Now it was my turn to grin. "Johnny taught me. I wanted to learn and be like Nepoya."

"Who?"

"Never mind. I'll tell you about her later."

Shortly, the deed was done. The cloth at the end of

the arrow burned handsomely. Thank God there was no wind. I stood, feet firmly planted on the ground as Johnny had taught me to do, set my arrow in the bow, drew back, and aimed for the open window of our chamber.

I released the arrow. It made a pleasant whistling sound as it traveled through the darkness. Its journey was so graceful, a fireball in the night meant to destroy our home.

We stood transfixed. I held my breath.

The arrow went through the open window and disappeared.

"We'll have to wait a bit to make sure it found a mark," I whispered.

"It should find the bed hangings," Mama said.

She was right. Within a few minutes we saw flames in the room, small at first, then climbing, climbing up the bed hangings. Soon there was a bright glow and it was spreading quickly.

I heard a sob from Mama. I looked at her. "Are you all right?" I asked.

"We'd best go," she said.

And so Mama and I ran through the night with the British private while our home burned behind us. We didn't wait to hear the crackling flames or the cries of Rawdon and his officers when they discovered the fire and ran from the house, snatching up important papers as they fled. But I couldn't help wondering, *Won't he be angry that he couldn't start the fire himself?* By the time we reached the creek and turned, we could see bright flames licking out of the upstairs windows, lighting up the night.

On and on we ran, stopping only occasionally to catch our breath. Thank God for the full moon. I could see all the back paths like it was day. We followed the Wateree. When we got to that place where Miz Melindy and I had met Mrs. Martin and her children that day, I stopped and confronted Mama and Private Brandon.

"I don't think we should go to Uncle Henry's," I said.

"Why?" Mama asked.

"I don't know, Mama. It's just a feeling I have in me. Johnny told me that when I had to make a decision I should do what was in my heart and in my innards. And it's in my heart and my innards right now not to go to Uncle Henry's. Rawdon may take a notion to look for us there."

Mama looked disappointed, but she didn't argue. "Where then?" she asked.

"I know a place. The name is McClure. Her husband and kin are with Sumter. It's her son and son-in-law that Johnny rescued from hanging this day. She'll take us in, Mama, I know it."

The sun would be up, I knew, high and hot before we reached the McClures'. But we'd get there. We'd stay hidden once daylight came. I had it all figured. Rawdon would think we'd been careless with a candle. He'd have the charred remains of the upstairs searched for our bodies.

I felt cheated. I wished I had had the gratification of having him know we set the fire on purpose. But then

I felt glad knowing that when he didn't find our bodies he'd send to Uncle Henry's for us and not find us there. And when he found we'd eluded him, his face would be twitching and his hands would be trembling. I had the satisfaction of that, anyway.

Epilogue

FALL 1790

I NEVER SAW Miz Melindy again. She had fooled
me. She had fooled us all. She really did have malarial fever, and I should have known by the way
she looked that day when they were going to whip Isom.
I should have known she was ailing. She must have
acquired it while treating Just Agnes. Or maybe from
Cephas.

She died while she and the other negras were hiding
in the woods. After the fire, after Rawdon moved his
headquarters to town, they brought her back to our
place and buried her. Mr. Bone set the negras to re-
building their cabins and harvesting what he could of
the crops.

Mama and I stayed away near a year, living with the
McClures. Mrs. McClure took us in. Yes, she knew how
Johnny had rescued her son, Josiah, and her son-in-law.
She made us to home. We helped her run the place
until her husband and menfolk came home from the

war. We sent for Mr. Bone, and he brought our negras and they helped bring in her crops, too, and in the spring, helped with the planting.

Rawdon finally left Camden on the ninth of May, in the year of our Lord seventeen hundred and eighty-one.

He left because he ran out of provisions. His supplies were cut off, thanks to Francis Marion, who earned himself the name of Swamp Fox. General Nathanael Greene was head of the American army by then, and Greene and Marion, Sumter, Daniel Morgan, and Light Horse Harry Lee were too much for Rawdon, though he'd won a victory at Hobkirks Hill, just north of Camden, that April.

When he left, Rawdon burned the town. Everything. The prison, homes, possessions of the inhabitants. He set fire to my daddy's mill and warehouse, his brewery. He even burned part of his own baggage and stores.

It's a good thing I heeded the feeling in my heart and my innards the night we set fire to our house and ran. It's a good thing we didn't go to Uncle Henry's. The British made a post out of his place shortly afterward. They used his heavy log barn as a fortification. Then, the following December, Lieutenant Colonel William Washington, who is a second cousin of George Washington, came through with his Continental cavalry. Washington mounted a big pine log on some cart wheels and put it in full view of Uncle Henry's barn. The British surrendered.

Uncle Henry lost favor with Cornwallis after that. After the war ended, Uncle Henry still curried favor with his neighbors, though, because he had never failed to open his house to someone in trouble, whether Patriot or Loyalist. But five months after the war ended, his estate was confiscated by the Patriot legislature and he was forever banished from South Carolina. This gives Mama no end of sadness. Uncle Henry went to the British West Indies. I asked him to look for my mama while he was there. He said he would.

When the British shipped Daddy out of Charleston on that prison ship, they sent him to British Honduras, then on to Bermuda. There he continued working for the American cause. He mortgaged a lot of his land and holdings to Bermuda merchants to raise money to supply the Americans. Up to nine thousand pounds. And he suffered many financial losses at home, too, what with the damage Rawdon did to his properties.

The war ended in October of 1781. As it turned out, it was more than a matter of the men making their speeches, riding off in a flourish, dividing up the spoils, and getting their pretty uniforms all soiled and torn, as I'd thought before I came to understand that it was a matter of fundamental rights. I also learned it was a matter for the women, too. So many of the women hereabouts suffered because of it. Saw their houses burned, their livestock slaughtered, their servants taken. So many of them made decisions, all alone, to stand up to the popinjays. They brought in the crops and ran their places, doing backbreaking labor until their men came home. So many had men who never did come home.

Daddy didn't come home again until January 1782. Before that, of course, he'd been in touch with Johnny, giving directions about having the house rebuilt. After

Rawdon left Camden, Johnny managed a trip home. He got in touch with Mr. Hillegas in Philadelphia and, following Daddy's instructions, secured money from Daddy's holdings to have the house constructed just as it used to be. Mr. Bone supervised.

Of course, Daddy is most proud of Johnny and what he did in the war. As for Johnny, well, I would like to be able to say he wed Nepoya, but he didn't. He came home and helped Daddy get things going again. All the mills are flourishing. So are the distillery and tobacco warehouse.

Nepoya was the love of his youth, when he was free to ride into the mountains and spend days with the Catawbas. "I didn't understand, Caroline," he had said to me once. "I was free all my life, free as a bird. Suddenly I have to join an army and fight for it?"

But he understood quick enough. And soon better than us all. But when we were all free, after Johnny had fought for it, he wasn't free to wed Nepoya. As the only son, he had to marry properlike and could not live in the mountains with a Catawba woman. He wed Harriet Dubose, daughter of Captain Isaac Dubose, with whom he fought under Marion.

I don't know what happened to Nepoya. After the war ended we never saw nor heard from her again. I know that once, before he wed, Johnny went into the hills to seek her out. I don't know if he found her. He never said.

I still have her bow and some of the arrows.

This is the way things be, Miz Melindy would say. I am beginning to understand. Johnny is doing Mama and

Daddy proud. He and Harriet have twin boys. One named Francis. After Francis Marion, Johnny is quick to tell people, not Francis Rawdon. The other is John, after Daddy. Johnny took part in the Convention in Charleston in '88 to ratify the Constitution. And this spring he took part in our own state Constitutional Convention.

But every once in a while, when he thinks no one is watching, I see Johnny looking wistfully toward the mountains as if he lost something up there and wishes he could find it again. And I wonder if Nepoya is hanging inside him, like so many people are still hanging inside me.

As for Colonel Rawdon, he took sick the summer before the British surrendered to the Americans at Yorktown, Virginia. Likely it was malarial fever. He went back to England.

Georgia Ann was not with him, of course. We never heard from Georgia Ann again. Whether Rawdon abandoned her or she him, we do not know. There were rumors that when the war ended she took up with another British officer and went back to England with him. But they were just rumors. Johnny went to Charleston when he first returned from the war, looking for her. Daddy used all his influence to find her, too. But we never did. And even though she vexed me so, she is still my sister, and I hate to think that she is wandering around somewhere, daft and abandoned and maybe ailing, looking for Rawdon, like Just Agnes looking for Cornwallis.

War takes a terrible toll on people, on families. And

if war doesn't, then just ordinary life does. It changes them forever. I guess this is just the way things be.

Oh yes, Johnny still breeds horses.

What of Fearnaught? We got her back. After the British surrendered to the Americans at Yorktown, the British officers were permitted to keep their swords and their horses.

Tarleton kept Fearnaught. After the surrender there were a lot of celebrations. American officers gave dinners in their marquees. They entertained the French officers. Some even gave dinner parties for British officers.

But no invitations came for Banastre Tarleton. He presented himself to Colonel John Laurens, who hails from South Carolina. He asked Laurens why he was being overlooked. Was it an accident? Laurens said no. "No accident at all. It is intentional, I can assure you, and meant as a reproof for certain cruelties practiced by the troops under your command in the campaigns of the Carolinas."

Tarleton took umbrage and rode off on Fearnaught. As he was going down a road at Yorktown, a negra man on foot came up to him. The negra was carrying no weapon, only a club cut from a sweet gum sapling tree.

The negra bade Tarleton good evening and said, "This is my horse. Dismount."

Tarleton said no. Then the negra raised his club. Tarleton jumped off and gave over Fearnaught.

The negra was Isom. You see, he and Cephas went

off and joined the army in time for Yorktown. They helped dig the earthwork fortifications before the siege. They did it with no promise of freedom. They just did it.

Isom rode Fearnaught home.

After the war Johnny freed both Isom and Cephas. They call it manumission, and it isn't often done in South Carolina, especially the way Johnny did it. You see, Cephas and Isom wanted to stay: Cephas because he was so close to Johnny, and Isom because he wanted to continue training horses. So Johnny drew up a paper that said: "They shall be permitted to reside in the house they now live in, have use of the garden, and be supplied with provisions. And, on the first day of July, every year, each shall be given the sum of one hundred dollars in good and lawful money."

After Rawdon left Camden, we exhumed my friend Kit and buried him in our churchyard. My friend Sam was on that march with Daddy to Charleston. We never heard from him again.

Me? I am wed. I wed Josiah McClure, one of the young men Johnny saved from hanging. He wooed me awhile, I can tell you, and I kept putting him off. I didn't want it said that I was marrying him because he escaped the noose, because everybody knew how I felt, seeing Kit hanged. But he was so persuasive, so insistent, that he won. We live on the McClure place now. And the woman who kept me in the corncrib overnight, the woman who tried to tell me when to stand by principle and when to leave it be, is my mother-in-law. I love her very much. Her husband died, and the place belongs to me and Josiah now. She lives with us.

And very often of a morning when I go out to the yard, I look at that corncrib and remember the night I spent there with Miz Melindy, when she told me my real mama wasn't dead but sold off to the West Indies.

I've never gotten past that. Mama Cecie still hangs inside me, sometimes making shadows in my eyes. Like Johnny said, I don't think I ever should get past it. But I try not to let my private pain hurt others, too. Because then it never ends.

I've talked with Mama Sarah about how my real mama was sold off. I've talked to Daddy, too. I've told them I don't know if I can ever forgive them for that. To make amends they have agreed to send Uncle Henry money to make inquiries about her. I know Uncle Henry may never find her. The West Indies has many plantations. And she may already be dead. But at least they have done this and it does help me.

So that's the way things be.

Every once in a while, Johnny lets me ride Fearnaught. She's won many races for Johnny, and her colts have run in his fields. She has done well for him. And though she is past her prime, she still can run. I take her down by the river, I take her into the pastureland. I love riding her. Of course, I'm a married woman now. And I'm a mother. I have three of my own: little Johnny, Sarah, and baby Cecie. Mama says I am a fruitful vine. And yes, she gave me the childbed linen. If I ever get in the increasing way again and it's a girl, I'm going to name her Melindy. So, you see, I have a position to uphold. I can't go racing around like a harridan in front of people.

But when we get off by ourselves, me and Fearnaught, every once in a while I race her. Just like I promised her that day Rawdon took her from us. I take her and we race on the High Hills of Santee.

Author's Note

TAKING ON A book about the American Revolution in the South was a whole new venture for me, because the war in the South was different from the war in the North.

To put it correctly, this is a novel about "the campaigns in the Carolinas." In the annals of American history, *that* in itself has a flavor all its own.

War always disrupts the social order of things. It brings tumult on the home front. And how the people on the home front survive and keep the cornerstone of civilization, as they have known it, alive has always been of abiding interest to me. The Revolution in the South had several unique aspects that made the task most difficult and that must be taken into consideration.

More than in any other area of the country, the Revolution in the South was a civil war and, as I see it, a precursor of the one that would follow eighty-one years later, if only because it had the earmarks of violence that were not found in the fighting in the North.

In the campaigns of the Carolinas, Americans fought Americans in "skirmishes" of an extremely violent nature. Or, as Caroline's mother says in the book: "There are desperate men on both sides settling old scores and family feuds in the guise of attachment to either the Crown or independence. There is widespread looting, burning out."

Indeed, throughout the campaigns of the Carolinas, both Loyalist and Patriot militias burned each other's towns, ravaged homesites, and killed prisoners. Terror reigned. A wealthy plantation owner who had many slaves and was a declared Loyalist was likely to soon find his property destroyed by Patriots. "They have seized my lands, negroes and the usual stock of a Carolina plantation," wrote Thomas McKnight, a wealthy North Carolina plantation owner. "And to hurt me still more, they took my house negroes into the back country and sold them there."

Another peculiarity in this area was the switching of sides of the citizens. Johnny, Caroline's brother in the novel, is a perfect example. Both Loyalists and Patriots switched sides, depending on how the tide of war affected them. Many, like Johnny, started out as Loyalists and became Patriots when they witnessed the "tender mercies" of the British. Many Patriots were cowed by the British takeover, especially when both Savannah and Charleston had fallen and the Americans were left for a while without any fighting force. Quite a few Patriots signed the oath of allegiance to the king. Then there were those like Caroline's father, who, though fictional, had many counterparts in reality. William Moultrie, who headed up his gallant band of Patriots in the palmetto log fort in Charleston harbor in 1776, where the Americans repulsed the British Fleet in that attempt to take Charleston, was one of these loyal Patriots. When Charleston was taken in the spring of 1780, Moultrie became a British prisoner. His old friend Charles Greville Montagu, a Loyalist, wrote offering him command of a Loyalist regiment if he would come over to the British. Not only that, all of Moultrie's family estates would be restored to him after the war. Moultrie refused, calling it a "dishonorable proposal."

There is another matter to consider in viewing the Carolinas during the American Revolution. The backcountry settlements differed from the seaboard plantations. The backcountry did not have rice to bring the residents wealth. These people lived by harvesting lumber, stock, and wheat, and by trading with friendly Indians. Moreover, since they had to work hard to survive, they had little or no time for upper-class intellectual gatherings to discuss politics. Also, they still needed the support of Great Britain for protection, because the wealthier slave-owning aristocrats near the coast had a tradition of dominating the affairs of the whole colony.

Then there was the issue of slavery.

South Carolina's plantation owners were the wealthiest in the country. But the British saw the slaves as a weapon they could use against the Patriots. During the course of the war, thousands of African Americans escaped from their owners. And the British were responsible. They promised freedom to those who fled. And the slaves fled in droves. Not all gained that freedom, of course. Many were sold into slavery again, to the plantations of the West Indies.

History tells us that during this time the rules that governed slavery were somewhat relaxed. What with the thousands of slaves who were pressed into service by the military and public authorities, the rules must have at least been stretched. Some of those slaves had never before been off the plantation. And those left at home now found their duties increased. Some who served with the military, as laborers or foragers, received freedom as a reward. Others did not. And once the war was over, slavery continued the same as before.

But the word *freedom* had been bandied about in this war. It became a household word, not only in the backcountry log cabin or the plantation house but in the slave quarters as well. And once spoken, it was not forgotten.

As all writers know, the South in general has a flavor all its own that we find irresistible. Lush beauty and inherent danger coexist in the landscape. The heat promotes its own rhythms for both the indolent plantation dwellers and the hardscrabble backcountry settlers. The distance between farms or plantations made those dwellings entities unto themselves. A plantation was the world in microcosm, and things went on there that the outside world need never know about. The temptation for novelists to write of this landscape is incredible. But we must always be mindful of this peculiar mix as well as the difference in food, dress, manner of worship, pleasures, practices of work, and family life when we decide to write a book with a Southern setting. Our text must reflect these influences.

Not being a Southerner, of course, I leave myself open to criticism, taking on such a culture. But I am not African American yet have written about Phillis Wheatley and Harriet Hemings. I am not Native American yet have written about the Indian heritage. Women writers have taken on the personae of male protagonists; men have written from the hearts of women.

This is a novel, which in itself is a leap of faith in that it is an attempt to create a world out of nothing. And because it is a historical novel, I now undertake to separate fact from fiction.

As in all my novels, historical fact was vigilantly pursued. The Whitaker family is loosely based on the Kershaw family of Camden, South Carolina, in the time of the American Revolution. Historically, Joseph Kershaw is known as the "father" of Camden. The county of Kershaw is named after him. He had a renowned flour mill in Camden as well as a saw- and grist mill, indigo works, a tobacco warehouse, a brewery, and a distillery. He was a man to be reckoned with, one of wealth and influence who, with the onset of the capture of Camden, was made a prisoner of the British, thrown into jail, and eventually sent to British Honduras. Afterward, he was sent to Bermuda, where he mortgaged his own estates to the tune of nine thousand pounds to help supply the American army. He was released after the war and returned to Camden, but he took heavy losses to personal property in the war, as did many other Patriots.

His wife and children are of my own creation.

Henry Rugeley was the area's leading Loyalist, and the incident in which he befriended the fleeing Patriot governor John Rutledge and his aides and took them into his home, then warned them of the approach of Banastre Tarleton and his cavalry, is taken from history.

The Catawba Indians not only were friendly to the Americans throughout the Revolutionary War, but in the Cherokee War they chose to turn down all offers of friendship from the violent Cherokees and sided with the colonists. That Johnny had a Catawba lady friend, that he had extended visits to their camps and learned their lifestyle, is not far-fetched.

General Charles Earl Cornwallis did arrive in Camden at the time and in the manner that I have written. The two boys who "attacked" them at their arrival did exist. I gave them personalities. One was hanged on the spot and the other put in prison.

Lord Francis Rawdon is true to character, having occupied the Kershaw home (which I have as the Whitaker home) after Cornwallis's departure. There is nothing in this occupation that is a departure from the way the British behaved when they occupied any plantation in the South, although again, everything that happens is of my own creation.

Everything about Banastre Tarleton is true. He and his mounted cavalry emerged as the terrorists of the

South, which is why, as I have written in my epilogue, he was not invited to any of the dinner parties given by the Americans for the British officers after the surrender at Yorktown in 1781. As I have written, Tarleton asked Colonel John Laurens from South Carolina why he was overlooked. Was it an accident? "No accident at all," Laurens said. "It is intentional, I can assure you, and meant as a reproof for certain cruelties practiced by the troops under your command in the campaigns of the Carolinas."

There was, you see, in those days, a certain code of honor in war. And Tarleton had violated it with the massacre of prisoners, which displayed a vengeance above and beyond what even victory required. It is said of him that war not only brought out but highlighted his ghoulish tendencies.

As for the horse he rode off on after Laurens so castigated him, it was a captured horse taken from a Southern plantation. And history tells us that while he was riding off, he was accosted by a plantation overseer, who came to Yorktown searching for the animal and demanded Tarleton dismount and give over the horse. Tarleton refused, the overseer raised his stick, and Tarleton jumped off. The horse was returned to its rightful owner.

The schedule of Thomas Sumter's rebel army, the way they hid out, gained strength, organized and trained, then came out of the woods on the Fourth of July to function as the only working fighting force the Americans had at the time, is all true.

The cruelty the British showed toward the Quaker Sam Wyly is also true.

Just Agnes, or Agnes of Glasgow, as she is known in Camden, is truly a legend thereabouts. There is a battered headstone in the old Presbyterian churchyard that marks her grave. But the legend has several versions, one of which is that she set sail from Scotland to follow a brave young soldier who had set sail for America to fight with the British army. Another is that she was the jade of General Cornwallis himself and wandered about trying to find him once he abandoned her, coming to the house he had occupied in Camden, where she expired from malarial fever and was buried in the churchyard. Whatever the truth of this legend, I feel I have not strayed far from it in my portrayal of Agnes.

As for the roles played by Mrs. McClure and Mrs. Martin, one has only to peruse the three volumes of *The Women of the American Revolution* by Elizabeth F. Ellet to know that all during the campaigns of the Carolinas Patriot women stood firm, holding their homes and families together while their men were away fighting, taken prisoner, or killed. They stood alone, independent and brave, and faced down the British who often occupied their houses. They fought the war on their own terms and prevailed.

What of Miz Melindy? She is of my own creation, but I have done enough reading to know that she could have existed and likely did exist on many plantations, the black grandmother of a child who dwelt in the plantation house. She is a composite.

What if, I thought, that mostly white child must one day confront her black grandmother? What if the rules governing their society are suddenly turned upside down? What if, for some reason, they are forced to take a journey together, to come to know each other?

And therein is the germ of a historical novel.

ANN RINALDI

24 JULY 1997

Bibliography

Ball, Edward. *Slaves in the Family.* New York: Farrar, Straus and Giroux, 1998.

Boles, John B. *Black Southerners, 1619–1869.* Lexington, Ky.: The University Press of Kentucky, 1984.

Ellet, Elizabeth F. *The Women of the American Revolution,* Volumes I and III. New York: Haskell House Publishers, Ltd., 1850, reprinted 1969.

Flood, Charles Bracelen. *Rise, and Fight Again, Perilous Times Along the Road to Independence.* New York: Dodd, Mead & Company, 1976.

Fraser, Walter J. Fr. *Patriots, Pistols and Petticoats, "Poor Sinful Charles Town" During the American Revolution.* Columbia, S.C.: The Charleston County Bicentennial Commission, 1945; The University of South Carolina Press, 1993.

Hibbert, Christopher. *Redcoats and Rebels, The American Revolution Through British Eyes.* New York: Avon Books, 1990.

Kennedy, Robert M., and Thomas J. Kirkland. *Historic Camden, Part One, Colonial and Revolutionary.* Columbia, S.C.: The State Company, 1905; Reprinted, the Kershaw County Historical Society, 1963–1973.

Leland, Jack. *62 Famous Houses of Charleston, South Carolina.* Charleston, S.C.: the *News and Courier* and the *Evening Post,* 1970.

Lumpkin, Henry. *From Savannah to Yorktown, The American Revolution in the South.* New York: Paragon House Publishers, 1981.

Moore, Christopher. *The Loyalists, Revolution, Exile, Settlement.* Toronto, Ontario: McClelland & Stewart Inc., 1994.

Pancake, John S. *This Destructive War, The British Campaign in the Carolinas, 1780–1782.* Alabama: The University of Alabama Press, 1985.

Rogers, George C., Jr., and C. James Taylor. *A South Carolina Chronology, 1497–1992.* Columbia, S.C.: The University of South Carolina Press, 1973.

Spruill, Julia Cherry. *Women's Life & Work in the Southern Colonies.* New York: W. W. Norton & Company, 1972.

Treacy, M. F. *Prelude to Yorktown, The Southern Campaign of Nathanael Greene, 1780–1781.* Chapel

Hill, N.C.: The University of North Carolina Press, 1963.

Weigley, Russell F. *The Partisan War, The American Revolution in South Carolina*. Columbia, S.C.: The University of South Carolina Press, 1970.

GREAT
EPISODES

Other titles now available:

by Sherry Garland
INDIO

by Kristiana Gregory
EARTHQUAKE AT DAWN
JENNY OF THE TETONS
THE LEGEND OF JIMMY SPOON

by Len Hilts
QUANAH PARKER

by Dorothea Jensen
THE RIDDLE OF PENNCROFT FARM

by Jackie French Koller
THE PRIMROSE WAY

by Carolyn Meyer
WHERE THE BROKEN HEART STILL BEATS

by Seymour Reit
BEHIND REBEL LINES
The Incredible Story of Emma Edmonds, Civil War Spy

GUNS FOR GENERAL WASHINGTON

*Look for exciting new titles to come in the
Great Episodes series of historical fiction.*